DISNEY

FAIRY GODMOTHER

AN ENCHANTERS TALE

DISNEY

FAIRY GODMOTHER

AN *ENCHANTERS TALE*

JEN CALONITA

Disney • HYPERION

LOS ANGELES • NEW YORK

First Edition, September 2024
10 9 8 7 6 5 4 3 2 1
FAC-004510-24171
Printed in the United States of America

This book is set in Garamond/Monotype
Designed by Marci Senders
Interior illustrations by Dinara Mirtalipova

Library of Congress Control Number: 2024933847
ISBN 978-1-3680-8958-6
Reinforced binding
Visit www.DisneyBooks.com

SUSTAINABLE FORESTRY INITIATIVE

Certified Sourcing

www.forests.org
SFI-01681

Logo Applies to Text Stock Only

For Brittany Rubiano, my own fairy godmother
—JC

PROLOGUE

WELL, SHE'D DONE ONE THING RIGHT. BLUE, IT WAS CLEAR, WAS THE GIRL'S color.

To call the gown blue, however, was doing it a disservice. The color was more a cross between azure and cyan. Brighter than a clear summer day, the tone was practically luminescent, the exact shade of the girl's eyes, which, Renée thought, getting misty, were the same shade as her mother's. In fact, it was Ella's mother's gown she'd transformed that night. Was she watching this all from somewhere in the universe?

Renée hoped so.

The dress was the pièce de résistance on which she could hang her cape when she recounted the story to Lune and Nelley later. Then again, those glass slippers were sure to draw attention. And, since they were the one accoutrement *summoned* by magic instead of transformed by it, they would not disappear like the rest. Though she might leave that bit out in her retelling.

There were a few other things Renée planned on keeping to herself. Perhaps she wouldn't mention the rodents. No need to recount *every* detail. The important thing, she thought as the girl admired her glass slippers, was that she'd pulled the whole thing together in record time.

Time.

There was something about time she was supposed to remember, wasn't there?

Oh!

Renée rushed to Ella's side, pushing back the sleeves of her oversized cape (which was more indigo than blue. Certainly not azure). "Now, now, now, just a minute. You *must* understand this, my dear." She tapped the wand in her palm for emphasis. "On the stroke of twelve, the spell will be broken, and everything will be as it was before."

Ella nodded. "Oh, I understand. But it's more than I ever hoped for."

Renée felt a rush of warmth for the girl. She truly was her mother's child. There was so much she wanted to tell her about her old friend. About her mother's relationship to her father. The way they'd both looked upon their only daughter the night she was born and how—

A slight breeze rippled through the trees like a whisper.

Her arms burst into goose bumps. She could sense him watching, reminding her to be mindful of . . . of . . . the time!

"I . . . Goodness me. It's getting late. Hurry, dear." She practically pushed Ella up and into the carriage.

The girl took in the curled filigree and the smooth, grooved upholstery, eyes wide. A carriage made from a pumpkin . . . Renée knew her forward thinking about gourds would come in handy.

"Now off you go," she said as the door closed. It began to bump along down the road, headed to the castle where the child's new path awaited her. "You're on your way!"

Ella stuck her head out of the carriage window and waved. Renée did the same, gesturing with her wand until the girl was out of sight.

The night air stilled—a glimmer of fairy dust blowing across the road the only sign she'd even been at this sad little château at all. She sighed. *Time* again. She was running out of it. But there was no need to spy on the human ball. Lune foresaw how this all could end if things went as planned.

Stalling, Renée looked down at the intricate carvings on her new wand, at the inscription written in small cursive handwriting.

For R—a fairy godmother through and through.

A lump formed in her throat. "You can come out," she called shakily into the darkness. "I know you're there."

He appeared much like she had, first as dust that lit up the night sky like fireflies, then merged as one luminescent beam. A shimmer of a man's silhouette revealed itself and he was standing before her, his gold eyes blazing, the mischievous smile on his lips telling her everything she needed to know. He crossed his arms and the moonlight reflected off the sheen of his green double-breasted tailcoat; the one with the gold buttons. In the human world, he looked decades younger than her; she found herself gathering her blue cloak around her.

"Mice, Dubois? Really?"

"Of course, you'd harp on the mice!" she choked out in her gravelly voice.

3

"I thought the move was inspired considering the circumstances. What was I supposed to do, use slugs?"

He started to laugh, causing the animals nearby to pause, sensing the supernatural in their midst. She couldn't help but start to chuckle through her tears. It was just like him to try to get a rise out of her.

"A stroke of genius," he conceded, taking her arm, before using his free hand to wand open a portal in a nearby oak tree. "Your work here is finished. Time to head back now. Don't you think?"

"You're always rushing me," Renée grumbled. Yet she couldn't help but glance down at her silver necklace, the new number glowing like a warning. She took the small bottle out of her robe and quickly drank the bright blue liquid inside.

Where the trunk once stood, there was now a swirling cyclone of light. The fairy realm lay beyond. Even after all this time, it felt like a dream.

He placed his wand in his breast pocket. "Well done tonight. Truly."

Renée stepped toward the light. Everyone was waiting for her.

She paused.

"Dubois?" he questioned.

Renée took one last look at the realm in all its beautiful messiness, its tangle of emotions, its urgency. In that moment, she knew. There was one last thing to be done.

One last miracle to make.

ONE
Thirty Years Earlier . . .

RENÉE DUBOIS WAS KNEELING, THE HEM OF HER DRESS CAKED WITH MUD, her fingernails almost black. To some young women of her age, this would be a travesty, but Renée paid the mess no mind. She had more important matters to contend with.

She bit her lower lip and stared at the silk slipper, two small children watching closely by her side. Carefully, she used a small hoe to lift the wild-flowers out of the dirt, then replanted them in the shoe, pressing soil all around—a makeshift flowerpot. After nestling shells and small trinkets inside, she sat back. "There!" she said, blowing a wayward curl from her face. "The finest fairy gift ever designed in the kingdom of Aurelais."

The children, who also happened to be covered with mud, cheered.

"It's perfect!" her cousin Celine gushed. She'd just turned ten and suddenly found everything in nature romantic and beautiful. "I knew the white flowers would look best."

"I still think we should have used *your* slipper," grumbled her brother, Raymond, attempting to take the yellow shoe. This was the nature of a seven-year-old who saw little affection unless he was in Renée's care. "Yours no longer fit. Renée's do. Now she has to walk home barefoot!"

"I prefer it that way," Renée reminded him.

Celine placed her hands on her small hips. "Raymond, you know perfectly well that Maman would have my head if I wasn't wearing shoes!"

"What if Renée catches a cold?" Raymond argued.

"What if *I* do?" Celine shot back.

Renée could sense an argument starting the way her uncle could predict a storm rolling in. And she knew just what to do to defuse the situation.

She started to hum.

The children looked at her with interest.

"What do we say to a whisper? A whisper?" Renée sang. *"What do we say to a whisper on the wind?"*

Both children smiled, then repeated the ditty they now knew by heart.

"Wisp! Wisp! Shush! Shush! Listen, hush. Wisp-shush-whisper!" the three of them sang.

Renée stood and grabbed both their hands. *"Wisp! Wisp! Shush! Shush!"* she repeated, spinning them round. Sure, she was only wearing one slipper at this point, but she didn't care what she looked like. Or how ridiculous her little songs were. She loved seeing their faces light up whenever they crooned one together.

"Let's hush now and wisp-wisp-shush-shush-whisper. Listen." Renée stopped

short and kicked her other slipper off, too. The children followed suit. One of Raymond's black velvet shoes landed on the muddy river's edge. *Oops.*

"Raymond, you may put the gift by the tree since I picked the flowers," Celine decided, which Renée knew was as close to an apology Raymond was getting.

"No, that's all right," Raymond said. "I'll choose the next one."

They both side-eyed Renée, who smiled as she retrieved Raymond's slipper from the water's edge and attempted to dry it on the bottom of her skirt. "Let's make another present." She handed Raymond his shoe and reached down to retrieve her lone yellow one. "What good is one slipper anyway?"

"Can I pick the flowers this time?" Raymond asked.

"Yes, but don't go too close to the river," Renée reminded him.

"I'll watch him! Let me just place my fairy gift first," Celine said. Her ringlets of brown curls swayed as she carefully put the yellow slipper against the tree, nestling it in between two thick roots above ground that resembled snakes.

Raymond grabbed a fistful of berries. "My gift should have these. Renée made them."

"She didn't make them, silly, she planted the berry bush." Celine paused. "I think."

"I picked the berries," Renée reminded them gently. "But I did plant peas and peppers."

Raymond perked up. "Can we bring the fairies some of those next time?"

"If they're ready, yes," Renée promised, proud of her little garden's bounty. Her father had taught her to farm at an early age, and she still enjoyed the process. Working with dirt and coaxing produce to grow felt more tangibly rewarding than most things in life. There in her little patch of soil, she could plant a seed, tend to it, and watch it become something beautiful.

Where else was such magic possible?

Celine motioned to the piece of pink ribbon tied to the tiny thimble from Renée's sewing basket filled with milk. "I think the fée folk will love these."

"You know what I always say—a fairy can never have too many presents." Renée headed over to the tree to see what else the children had left. She had to admit: The yellow slippers were quite fine. Using a leftover piece of leather, she'd reinforced the toe area and the heel, and added scraps of white ribbon on each to form a bow. She'd had this pair for a mere two weeks, and now that they were filled with the blossoms and assorted rocks, as well as a lone feather, they were fulfilling a far grander purpose than protecting her feet.

The fée, fée folk, fairies—whatever one wanted to call them—weren't picky. But once you'd chosen to leave them a gift, Renée told her cousins, you'd best keep leaving them. Renée had read they were easily insulted. Also fun-loving, mischievous, sometimes destructive, sneaky, and prone to thievery. (Whenever Raymond lost a sock or Celine misplaced a pencil, they were almost certain the fée had swiped the items, and Renée had to agree. Where else could they have gone?)

The three of them tended to keep these theories to themselves, only sharing them with Anne in the kitchen, who packed them extra treats to leave the fée on their adventures. Uncle Gaspian also entertained the children's interest in fairy tales, reading to the three of them by the fire in the salon on the rare occasion he wasn't traveling.

Aunt Olivia, on the other hand, couldn't be bothered with what she called nonsense. ("Renée, please stop filling the children's heads with such drivel!

Teach them something useful, like arithmetic," Aunt Olivia would say.)

In addition to being the children's older cousin, Renée had been tasked by her aunt with being the children's governess. It was Renée's job to guide their studies, to see to it they bathed and minded their manners. This was how Renée earned her keep. Celine had been a newborn when Renée arrived with only the clothes on her back. Uncle Gaspian had taken her in, much to her aunt's chagrin.

That is, until she realized Renée was an excellent governess. Her aunt, who suffered from headaches and could be found in her chambers with the drapes drawn most days, needed quiet, and children were rarely quiet. When Raymond arrived three years later, Renée found she was spending all her free time minding them. Not that she would have had it any other way. The children were the best part of her aunt and uncle's manor.

Their home, on the surface, was lovely. Statelier than her own parents', though those memories were hazy and somber, like the occasional morning fog on the hillside. Her room, like the entire residence, was furnished with chairs and settees in richly colored fabrics and drapes from Bordeaux, and furniture made of exotic woods with intricate gilding. None of these things were meant for small children to sit on, touch, or rip tassels off. That was why, winter, spring, summer, fall, Renée held most of their studies outside. And their favorite spot happened to be the one that was most frowned upon—the river.

Secluded among a grove of oak trees, the water that ran along the river-bank had just the right amount of sunlight dancing through the leaves. The rocks were large and plentiful, perfect for sunning oneself or playing hide-and-seek. The grass felt so lush, Renée often wished she could forgo a blanket and lie nestled in the blades, staring up at the curtained sky. Summer's heat had faded and the leaves were starting to turn a kaleidoscope of autumnal colors. Renée stared at each one in wonder. She knew it sounded foolish, but when she was outside with the air on her face, her hair freed from its bun, she felt both invigorated and at peace. She relished the sound of the river rushing beside her, the musty scent of dead leaves mingling with freshly grown grass after a day's early rain. She couldn't put her finger on it, but it was almost as if she felt more alive in nature than she ever did in her aunt and uncle's stuffy home.

"Do you think the fairies will like our slippers?" Celine asked.

"If they don't, they're ungrateful," Raymond said.

Celine gave him a look that reminded Renée of her aunt. "You'll make the fairies angry. They could be watching us right now and they'll think you're a rotten boy not worth visiting."

Raymond looked up at Renée worriedly. "They won't think that, will they?"

"Of course not," Renée said just as Celine retorted, "Yes, they will."

The two began to argue and Renée started to hum again. Soon the children were singing *"Whisp! Whisp! Shush! Shush!"* as she was leading them gently back to their blanket.

"What did I tell you?" Renée reminded them. "Fairies like soft voices. Calm spaces. We mustn't shout."

"Sorry, Renée," they muttered.

"It's all right. Maybe we take a break from our gift giving and do our reading lesson?" The children groaned. "While I read, you two can have some brioche."

"Can we have the macarons Papa brought back from Paris?" Raymond asked. Whenever Uncle Gaspian returned from his travels, it was always with pencils and a sheet of foolscap for Celine, a new treat for Raymond, or fine fabrics for Aunt Olivia. For Renée however, much as Aunt Olivia insisted she have sensible clothing for a young lady on the cusp of adulthood (her words, not Renée's), Uncle Gaspian always brought books. And exactly the kind Aunt Olivia didn't like—tales steeped in magic. Renée especially adored the ones involving fairy godmothers.

Renée kept these tomes to herself, usually hiding them under her mattress. But she'd brought her uncle's latest offering along today for their picnic, a beautifully bound book titled *Fairies among Us*.

"We ate all the macarons, Raymond," Celine reminded him. She looked at Renée hopefully. "But perhaps Anne gave us some cheese to go with the bread?"

Renée grinned. "I don't know. Maybe if we close our eyes and wish."

The children closed their eyes and chanted the words Renée always said to them when they played in the forest. "I wish. I wish. I wish."

Renée pulled out a linen napkin and unfolded it to reveal the brioche and a small wedge of fromage. She gasped. "Look at that!" The children tried to take the food, and Renée held the napkin out of reach. "At least rinse your hands off first. Carefully!" she added as they ran to the water's edge. "After that rain, the current is stronger."

They did as they were told (Renée was thankful they were good listeners when it came to snacks) and returned, ready to eat. Renée read to them, the only other sound that of Raymond chewing a tad too loudly for Celine's liking. Renée paused and purposefully took a loud bite and the cheese crumbled over the front of her dress. Raymond laughed and Celine's frown faded, their giggles drowning out the sound of the water and even the birds. Renée was never beneath putting a leaf under her nose to make a mustache, dancing in the river (when it wasn't moving this fast), or singing loud off-key. Anything to keep the two of them laughing. It was her favorite sound in the world.

"Renée, do you think the fairies would like the rest?" Celine asked.

"You already bit it! No one wants half a roll," Raymond said.

Celine's face turned stormy again and Renée quickly intervened. "Let's leave it and see if it's here when we come back tomorrow." She put her hand out and took the remnants of brioche from Celine, placing it in the slipper.

"The fairies will want as many treats as they can get tomorrow, won't they? Since it's the new moon?"

"The harvest moon," Renée reminded her. It was something she'd just read to them that afternoon, a fée ritual she hadn't heard of before. Yes, dancing by the light of the full moon was common—fairies often appeared at night, so most fairy tales said. But tonight would be special. The harvest moon occurred on the autumnal equinox, an ever-moving date. Some years the lunar cycle had it falling in September, other years in October. This particular year it was to be on September 22, which felt particularly fortuitous as it had been her maman's birthday. While her aunt never spoke of the date, when her uncle was home, they shared a cake in Maman's honor. "The full moon can sometimes last two or three days with the autumn equinox," Renée said as much to herself as them. "Which means the fairies will be doing a great deal of dancing."

Celine sighed. "I wish we could watch."

"*Watch*, but not join. You can't step in their fairy circle," Raymond reminded her. "If you do, you'll dance till you drop dead of exhaustion."

"Excellent use of *exhaustion*, Raymond. I see you've been practicing your vocabulary words."

"I know not to step in a fairy circle," Celine muttered.

Renée squinted, imagining the enchanted ball, wishing the three of them could witness such a thing. "Do you think the fairies dance like this?" She spun around the oak tree, jumping and leaping goofily. A new nonsense song poured out of her. *"Shilly, shilly, shilly-shoe! This slip-slip-slippery fée dance I do!"*

Raymond doubled over, holding his stomach. "*Shilly-shoe* is not a word!"

"Maybe not, but I like how it sounds," Renée said, leaping in the air. "Shilly-shoe!"

"You're a shilly-shoe!" Celine declared, her smile returning. "And the fée would fly, not dance on the ground. You look silly!"

"Very silly," Raymond agreed. "But not as silly as me." He pretended to swim like a fish.

Celine fell in the mud. She brushed herself off and got up, twirling beautifully, her feet moving in a familiar waltz Aunt Olivia was always begging Renée to practice.

"Watch me, Renée!" Celine said.

"And me!" Raymond said, cutting in front of his sister.

Renée grabbed each of their hands. "Let's dance together," she suggested, the three of them spinning 'round and 'round till they finally collapsed in a heap, the children piling on top of her, their clothing now grass-stained as well as muddy. They stared up at the sky.

"Renée?"

"Mmm-hmm?" Renée's eyes were on some passing clouds, as fluffy as Anne's marzipan.

"Do you think the fairies will come here to celebrate the harvest moon because we left them so many treats?" Celine asked.

"And slippers. Don't forget the slippers," Raymond added.

"I hope so." *I wish. I wish. I wish.*

Celine hesitated for a moment. "Do you think it will be the fée who saved you?"

"Maybe." Renée felt a familiar tightness in her chest. And instantly she was brought back to that fateful moment.

The fire was ten years ago, on a day much like this one when the wind was warm, the air was still, and the earth smelled damp. The memory felt like a dream mixed with a nightmare, depending on the exact moment that pierced her subconscious. Waking up to all that smoke. Shouting for Maman and Papa. Wandering from her bed, discovering the house engulfed in flames, panicking as she tried to scream and choking on the thick air instead. She couldn't get to the door, her cries growing desperate as the heat became almost unbearable. And then she saw it—a small, bright light.

In the fire, it easily could have been mistaken for a flame, but this ball, no bigger than the palm of her hand, jumped and moved as if it were flying. Renée had blinked hard, thinking she saw wings. *Don't be afraid, child,* she thought she heard as the small light led her to the window. Her bedroom was on the upper level, but she heard whispers that crackled like the flames. There was no time to think. No time to worry that this thing, whatever it was, was coaxing her to further danger. *Don't be afraid, child*, the beacon said again as she looked back in desperation for her parents. The entire room was engulfed now. She had no choice. It was die by flames or die by fall. She chose to leap, feeling the wind rush past her as she started to descend, certain she was moments from the end. But the bright light followed her, a glowing cloud of dust surrounding her like a cloud, breaking through the smoke and cushioning Renée's fall.

She floated down and away from the flames as if she were on a cloud, landing a few yards away on the hilltop. *Don't be afraid, child*, the light said again, growing stronger and brighter. Renée quickly realized this thing was not a flame or a beacon. It was a fairy.

The creature moved so fast, it was hard to focus on its appearance. Renée wondered again if she was dreaming. (Of course, the visceral reality of the burning château behind her suggested otherwise.) Renée noted the fairy's cream dress, her gossamer wings. She wore no shoes but did have a small crown of wildflowers perched on her head. It was her eyes, though, Renée couldn't stop staring at. Looking as if they were lit from within, they peered at Renée with sorrow.

Renée started trembling. "My parents?" She looked back at the roaring flames.

The fée faltered. "No, child."

Renée's sob didn't sound like her own. It came from a place deep inside.

"It will be all right," the fairy said.

Renée's body felt like it was engulfed by the fire as she fought all the emotions inside her rising to the surface. Her parents were gone. Seeing the château igniting the night so bright, she suspected it could be seen all the way in Bordeaux, she wasn't sure how she'd survived even with the fée's guidance. Now she was an orphan. Why had she been spared, and her parents had not? It wasn't fair. If this being had powers, couldn't she have saved them all?

The miniature woman reached out a tiny hand and laid it on her cheek. Her touch was as cool as dewdrops. "You're going to be all right, child," she amended, sounding mortal now and very sad. A mortal with wings.

The creature flitted by her ear, lifting a strand of Renée's hair, and whispering, "You're not alone."

In the distance, Renée heard horses racing up the path to the château. She heard a voice shout, "There's a girl on the ground!"

And then the fairy was flying above her, her light growing brighter before she disappeared from sight.

"Do you, Renée?" Celine asked now, tugging on her cousin's arm, pulling her from the memory. "Do you think the fairy that saved you will be here?"

She'd recounted the story to her uncle once when she was still quite small. She had been lying in her new room in his house, the wind howling outside her window, and she'd been frightened. Aunt Olivia never came when she cried, but Uncle Gaspian would if he was home. That night, she told him her secret—how the fairies had saved her. How one told her not to be afraid. That she'd never be alone. He had cupped her cheeks and smiled sadly.

"That fairy is right," he'd said, "but, my dear child, let's keep this secret safe. The world isn't always so kind to magic."

And so, she'd kept the memory to herself for a long time. But once she became the children's governess, she couldn't help but share the secret with them as well. Children, she'd decided, were more than willing to believe in things that couldn't easily be explained. She never wanted her cousins to lose the sense of wonder that she believed lingered in the world if one took the time to sit still, and breathe. "I would hope so. Can you think of a prettier spot in all of Aurelais to celebrate?" Renée said with a smile.

"I want to meet your fairy," Raymond decided. "I'm coming back later."

"We aren't allowed outside at night without Maman or Papa," Celine scolded. "You can't go."

He stuck his tongue out at her.

"I mean it, Raymond! Tell him, Renée."

"Your sister is correct. You can't go outside alone. Truthfully, your maman would not be thrilled to know we were here by the river now either." Aunt Olivia had been so upset at how the children had ruined their clothes last week, she'd all but forbid them from venturing farther than the manor's garden. But how could they stay cooped up on such a fine day? Even Rose, Aunt Olivia's favorite servant, hadn't stopped them from leaving that morning. (Though Renée knew the woman wanted them all out of her hair so she could clean.)

"Told you, Raymond!" Now it was Celine's turn to stick out her tongue.

"Okay, you two," Renée scolded. "You'll turn into frogs if you keep on with that!" She stuck her own tongue out and said, "Ribbit," making them dissolve in giggles.

She, however, on the bridge between child and adult, would not be missed if she snuck away, certainly not by her aunt. She hadn't seen Aunt Olivia leave her room in days. The only interactions she'd had with Aunt Olivia lately were hearing her bark orders to the staff or yell at Raymond to be quiet. What her uncle saw in Aunt Olivia, Renée would never understand.

She looked down at the fairy book Uncle Gaspian had given her. The harvest moon. Her maman's birthday. She could think of nowhere she'd rather be tonight than here among the trees. Maybe, just maybe, the fairies would be waiting for her.

Raymond took her hand. "I'll come with you. Please? I want to see the fée, Renée."

"So do I!" Celine said. "If you're coming back, can I come, too?"

"Please? We can play hide-and-seek." Raymond tried again, jumping up. "BOO!"

She laughed. "Boo yourself!" She hugged him tight. "Your papa is returning. Don't you think he'd be sad if you weren't there to greet him?"

"Yes," they both said sullenly.

"I tell you what—if I do find a fairy here tonight, I will find a way to bring you both back tomorrow so we can all dance with the fée together, just not in their fairy ring."

Celine looked up at her. "Promise?"

Renée pulled her close to her side. "I promise."

"Me too?" Raymond asked, batting his lashes.

"Yes, you too!" Renée glanced up at the fading daylight and swore. "Now we should really get back to the—"

"Renée! Celine! Raymond!"

Renée froze. That wasn't Anne's voice calling them from the hill. It was her aunt's.

She had lost track of time. The sun cast shadows along the riverbank.

"Renée! Celine! Raymond!"

"Gather your things. Quickly," Renée whispered, standing the children up and grabbing the blanket and treats. "We'll walk upstream and then head up to the house so she doesn't see us."

But she'd barely collected the children's slippers when she saw her aunt appear a few yards away and march toward them.

TWO

Renée couldn't recall a single time she'd seen her aunt walk outside the château's grounds. Aunt Olivia was not a big fan of nature. Or dirt. Or the sun. Maybe that's why her skin was so ghostly pale. And why she had so many headaches. She never got any fresh air. Now the woman's normally neat hair frizzed as if she had been awakened abruptly. She was also unusually dressed in a hooded overcoat.

"Maman! You're out of bed!" Raymond said happily.

"Hello, madame," Renée said, using the address Aunt Olivia preferred. "We were just taking a quick respite."

Her aunt's brow creased. "I thought I gave you specific instructions not to take the children far from the manor."

"I'm sorry, madame. We seemed to be getting underfoot this afternoon," Renée said as Celine tried to hide behind her. "We didn't go hiking—per your instructions—but I thought a quick walk might be nice." *Please don't say we've been here for hours, Raymond*, she thought.

Her aunt pursed her lips. "Without shoes?"

Celine crammed her pink slippers onto her feet. "We were only playing, Maman," she said, wiping her dirty hands on a dress that was already soiled beyond recognition. She knew better than to mention the fairy gifts.

Aunt Olivia stepped closer. "Renée, you are their elder. You should be modeling proper behavior."

I'm also their cousin, she thought. *Children need fun.* "I'm sorry, madame. I can assure you the children completed both their reading and their arithmetic. We even held a music lesson." She gave the children a look and Celine jumped in.

"Yes, Maman," Celine said. "You should have heard our new song."

Aunt Olivia ignored her daughter and pointed at the offerings by the trees. "What is all this rubbish you've left on the ground?"

Renée quickly tried to block her view before her aunt saw her discarded yellow slippers that now were sprouting flowers. "We were feeding . . . uh . . . rabbits."

Her aunt pursed her lips. "With ribbon?"

"No, no, no. Of course not!" Renée said as the children's cheeks reddened. "The ribbon is for . . . decorating their . . . fur." She cocked her head to one side and danced around to prevent her aunt seeing the fairy display by the tree. "I've always thought rabbits would make excellent pets. Raccoons, too, to be fair. Or maybe a lovely peacock."

"Ooh! Can we get a peacock, Maman?" Celine begged.

"How preposterous, Celine. Really, Renée. I thought you engaged the

21

children in thoughtful discussions when you were in charge. I told you—I want them to read more poetry. To study art." She picked up a fairy book Renée had failed to hide, and frowned.

Renée yanked the book away without thinking and saw her aunt's horrified expression. "I wasn't reading to them about . . ." She couldn't bring herself to say the word aloud. "We read poetry today and had a science lesson," she added, thinking fast. "In fact, we were just talking about the equinox."

"Yes! And the harvest moon. It's when the fée are coming, Maman, and I want to come back to see them tonight," Raymond said.

Renée winced. From the distance somewhere, she heard a bird chirp. The river gurgled.

"There is no such thing as fairies," Aunt Olivia said, each word enunciated as if they were practicing German. "I see you continue to disobey me, Renée."

"But . . ." Celine started to say.

"Celine! Please. Maman is getting a headache again and it's been made worse by learning the rest of the staff had no idea of your whereabouts. If it wasn't for Rose, I never would have thought to look by the river."

Rose. Renée sighed. "I am sorry, madame," she said again helplessly.

Aunt Olivia looked the children up and down with disapproval. "Papa is returning today and you two look like wild beasts."

"Roar! I'm a lion!" Raymond said with glee.

Renée coughed and Celine shook her head at her brother ever so slightly. Realizing his mistake, Raymond's smile slipped from his face.

Nearby, something snapped a branch in the woods. Renée's hair stood up. She got the distinct impression they were being watched.

22

"I'll get them cleaned up, madame," Renée said, taking Raymond's hand and leading him away before some creature could tear out of the woods and make things worse. She swung his hand by her side and gave him a reassuring smile.

"You've done enough," her aunt said, her tone slipping into more of a bite. "This is the last time I am going to say this: You are never to return to the river and engage in silly fairy talk. The fée are not real! Do you understand me?"

Renée's heart started to thump. She didn't like the word *never*. "But, madame—"

"My word is final, Renée," Aunt Olivia snapped. "No more outdoor jaunts. You're to complete your tutelage in the château from now on."

"No! No! You can't make us stay inside! You can't!" Raymond started to cry. "What about the fairies?"

"Raymond, that is enough!" Aunt Olivia shouted. "You are too old for this behavior."

"But, Maman, fairies are real!" Celine stomped her feet now, too, seeming younger than her brother. "There's nothing wrong with believing in magic!"

"What's wrong is Renée putting me in this wicked position," Aunt Olivia said sharply. Renée hung her head. "I have told her plenty of times that the forest is no place for children. From now on you shall do your studies at a real table and learn real things."

"But, Maman—" Celine started.

"Go see Rose, Celine. Now. Take Raymond. I need to speak with Renée alone."

The children looked at Renée for confirmation. "Go on. I'll be up soon." She tried to keep her tone light.

Raymond dropped Renée's hand and took Celine's. He was still sniffling as they took off through the trees back to the house. Renée felt their absence immediately.

"Let us speak privately." Aunt Olivia offered Renée her arm.

"Yes, madame."

Her aunt paused. "Where are your shoes?"

Renée bit the inside of her cheek. "They fell in the river. I shall make a new pair."

Her aunt tsked. "This is the second time this month! You're lucky we have scraps of fabric around."

"Yes, madame."

"While you're at it, I need a new pair as well. Green this time. And a pink pair, too. You can make Celine new ones as well."

"Yes, madame," she said a third time. If this was all her aunt wanted, then she could breathe easy. She enjoyed the work, especially when the kids helped. Raymond could sew better than she could.

They walked in silence for a few minutes, her aunt muttering about bugs and dead leaves while Renée waited for her to continue to scold her. Aunt Olivia, however, was too busy wheezing, the walk clearly taking a lot out of her. Renée couldn't recall the last time they'd been alone together.

As little time as her aunt spent with her own children, she spent even less with Renée. It wasn't that Renée minded being ignored. On the contrary. When her aunt paid her too much mind, she got a barrage of criticisms. *"Stop slouching! You're chewing loudly. Ladies walk, they do not scurry. That note was off-key. Could you do something about your hair? It looks like a bird's nest. . . ."*

True to form, Aunt Olivia continued her tirade now. "I don't know what's gotten into you. It's as if you *like* that the children prefer your company over their own maman. Is that what you want, Renée Dubois?"

Dubois. Her aunt's not-so-subtle reminder that Renée was not a Damery like her cousins. Aunt Olivia's cool gray eyes took her in with interest and Renée felt her shoulders sink.

"We didn't mean to upset you."

"It's too late for that, but I do not want you disobeying me again. It is time *everyone* focused more on serious endeavors. Is that understood?"

"Yes, madame."

Aunt Olivia patted her arm. "Now, let's hurry back," she said tersely. "You should bathe. We have guests to receive in the salon this evening."

"You mean Uncle Gaspian?"

"He is not a guest, Renée," her aunt said. "No, we are hosting Monsieur Valliery. I've decided you should play the piano when he and his son arrive. You said you were singing with the children. Do you have any new pieces prepared?"

"Err . . ." Renée doubted her lyrics about the whispering wind was what her aunt had in mind.

"No matter." She patted Renée's arm again. "I may have to lend you something from my closet. I have a few dresses from our last trip to the city that deserve to be seen once more. Hopefully they fit. We want to make a good first impression."

Aunt Olivia was offering her clothes to wear? And her sudden interest in Renée's music . . . It was almost as if— Oh, now she saw it. Her days as the children's governess were numbered. Her heart sunk. "Aunt Olivia, are these guests here to see . . . anyone in particular?"

"Renée, dear, your parents left you with no dowry to speak of. You are growing too old to be the children's governess. *Clearly.* It's time for you to marry. And our only hope is a match with someone like Sebastian Valliery."

Renée felt her knees go weak. Sebastian Valliery was a widowed fabric trader her uncle worked with. He was at least fifteen years older than Renée, sweated profusely no matter how hot or cold the weather, and had the horrible habit of repeating "Of course" in reply to everything. His thirteen-year-old son teased Celine and Raymond relentlessly whenever he joined his father to talk business with Uncle Gaspian. She couldn't imagine tying her life to the Vallierys. If she looked as miserable as Aunt Olivia did when Uncle Gaspian came home from traveling, it didn't seem appealing.

But what was the alternative? Becoming a spinster and living with her aunt and uncle her whole life? She couldn't see Aunt Olivia tolerating that either.

"Are you listening, Renée?"

"No. Yes! I mean, I am listening, madame."

Her aunt grimaced. "You always have your head in the clouds. It's a wonder you've managed to tutor the children at all."

Renée heard a commotion and looked up. A carriage was parked near the house. The children jumped in front of it as a man with light brown hair emerged. He was dressed finely in a single-breasted tailcoat, breeches, and shiny black boots.

"Papa! Papa!" the children cried, going running.

Uncle Gaspian. Despite her better instinct, Renée let go of Aunt Olivia's arm and took off running toward him, a rush of affection for her uncle taking over.

"Renée Dubois!" Aunt Olivia cried.

But Renée ignored her, trying to shake off the conversation of the last several minutes.

"My darling Renée!" Uncle Gaspian chuckled. "You're as wretched looking as these two. What have you three been up to?"

"Renée took us to make fairy slippers," Raymond sang like a bird. "The harvest moon is tonight, and they're having a ball, Papa. I want to see them."

Renée paled, hoping her aunt hadn't heard.

"Oh, I see," Uncle Gaspian replied. "And leaving the fairies' presents required you to get dirty, did it? What is a fairy slipper?"

"Renée used her old slippers as flowerpots," Celine told him. "And they could hold all the other fée presents."

Renée smiled weakly.

"Presents?" Uncle Gaspian continued.

"Yes! Anything tiny," Raymond went on. "Fée are quite small."

"Tiny?" Uncle Gaspian put his hands on his hips. "Why the fairy I met on my travels was this tall." He held his hand high in the air. "Maybe taller!"

Renée loved when her uncle played along. It made her wonder sometimes—did he truly believe like she did? Did he ever see magic when he was out there in the world? What she wouldn't give to be seated in the carriage beside him, getting to see the French countryside and what lay beyond it. Maybe then she'd truly find magic.

"You saw a fairy, Papa? A real fairy?" Celine asked.

"Did it have wings?" Raymond demanded. He turned to call over his shoulder. "See, Maman? They're real! Tell her, Papa!"

Uncle Gaspian started to respond. "Well, I—"

"Gaspian," Aunt Olivia said, wheezing as she approached. "Don't encourage them."

"No, Maman. I won't stop believing in magic!" Raymond yelled.

"Raymond." Her uncle's voice was stern. "Do not speak to your mother in that tone."

Aunt Olivia held her heart, looking pale. Gaspian took one look at his wife and let go of the children, helping Olivia into the house. "My dear, are you all right?" He looked at Renée. "Would you help the children?"

"Yes, Uncle," Renée said. "Come along, you two."

Raymond pulled on Renée's dress. "Don't let her keep us inside forever. Please, Renée."

She patted his back. "We will talk about it later. Go hurry along and take your bath."

Rose appeared and grabbed Raymond by his ear. "Let's go, you! And don't count on a bath for yourself," she growled at Renée. A small black mole Renée couldn't stop staring at bounced on Rose's right cheek as she spat her words. "Doubt there'll be any warm water left."

"When is there ever?" Renée said with a sigh, her voice too soft to hear as she followed Rose up the stairs to get changed and prepare for the evening. She was so tired already, she could not imagine making polite conversation.

Thankfully, Anne's supper was running late. Uncle Gaspian wanted to freshen up himself and the children took a while to get ready. With no sign of Aunt Olivia, Renée dressed herself, finding the plainest beige dress she owned and pulling her curly hair into the least-appealing chignon she could think of. Anything to deter Sebastian Valliery from finding favor with her. She stared out the window at the darkening sky, waiting for the harvest moon to rise. How would she get away if she had to entertain a caller all evening?

"Psst . . ."

Anne stood in the doorway, her apron covered in what looked like berries, a dusting of flour covering her arms and a splotch on her right cheek. She was older than most of the other servants and her pale blue eyes were kind. "Want me to poison your suitor? I have the ingredients to do it, I'm sure."

"Anne!" Renée tried not to laugh.

"Monsieur Valliery is such a bore. I don't know what Lady Damery is thinking."

"She's thinking of ways to keep from having to feed another mouth," Renée said, knowing she'd have to say extra prayers for saying something so wicked. She was blessed to have her aunt and uncle, she reminded herself. She was thankful for Celine and Raymond, her greatest joys.

"Well, your aunt and uncle are sitting in the salon until dinner is ready, so avoid going downstairs as long as you can. You might also want to steer clear of Rose."

"I always do. Where are Celine and Raymond now?"

"In the nursery." Anne's eyes were bright by candlelight. "I may have given them a treat to keep them quiet till supper is finished." She held out a small napkin. "Here's one for you, too."

Renée hugged the woman, who always smelled like cinnamon and sugar. "Thank you, Anne." She popped the cookie in her mouth and hurried down the hall to the children's room and, while overturned with toys, found it empty. She snuck down the back staircase, each step she took slow and nimble like a cat, trying to avoid making the floor squeak. She heard her aunt's and uncle's voices.

"It's the sensible option, Gaspian. It's time the girl leaves our charge. We've done it long enough, and he will care for her."

The cookie in Renée's mouth turned sour.

"Valliery? I don't know, Olivia. Renée has too much fire in her for that man."

"Fire? You mean disruption. Honestly, Gaspian, I don't know why you indulge her in talk of nonsense! Why, this afternoon, I found the three of them by the river again."

Her uncle laughed. "She is a bit unconventional, but you can't deny the children are thriving. There's nothing wrong with letting them have a bit of fun, is there?"

Well said, Renée thought. She wanted to move closer to hear them but the steps would creak. Solution: Step out of her slippers. When she was barefoot, she felt light as air.

"She's been our burden for far too long and you know it. It's time the girl grows up and looks after her own household. I'm tired of her disobeying me. And this is a fine offer for someone without a dowry."

"So there's already an offer for her hand?" Uncle Gaspian asked.

Renée felt her heart rate speed up. She could see her future and it wasn't pleasant. A man's wife and a mother to a family already in motion. She'd practically raised Celine and Raymond herself and had been happy to do so, but she was not ready to be a mother. And certainly not to that cruel boy. The thought of having to bear future offspring made her feel ill. This is not what she wanted out of her life. She wasn't sure what she wanted, but she knew it wasn't a life of stuffy manors and little freedom.

"Yes. Don't you see? With business being slow, this is the perfect solution for the girl, for all of us."

For the girl. For a Dubois. For someone who was not their daughter. Renée felt a lump rise in her throat. Aunt Olivia would get her way. She usually did and, in this case, who was Renée to fight her? She had no other family to speak of, and she couldn't be Uncle Gaspian's burden forever.

"Fairy Godmother," Renée whispered, thinking of the creature who had saved her all those years ago, wondering what counsel she would give. "What do I do?"

But it wasn't a fairy godmother who appeared, it was Celine running toward her. The girl's face was fraught, and she seemed on the verge of tears as she raced up the squeaky steps.

"Celine!" Renée grabbed the child by the shoulders. "What is it?"

"He was so upset about what Maman said, he wouldn't listen," Celine cried. "I'm not even sure he has a lantern. All he has is your book! The one you read to us by the river. I know he's going to get hurt! Or eaten. Rose said children out after dark get eaten by hideous beasts. We have to find him."

Renée felt a sense of panic rising inside. "Celine. Where is Raymond?"

Celine's eyes were as round as the harvest moon now rising outside their window. "He's gone to find the fairies."

THREE

WHILE RENÉE DIDN'T CONSIDER HERSELF A PESSIMISTIC PERSON, IT WAS HARD not to think of the dangers that could befall a seven-year-old wandering in the woods in the dark. Her cousin getting attacked by wolves, bitten by a wild dog, lost and falling in a ravine. Every one of those incidents ended the same way: Raymond lost to the night.

She herself had found Raymond trying to catch a fish with his hands too close to the water's edge. Or there was the time he'd tossed random objects in the hearth to see how they would burn. And—on one occasion she, Anne, and Celine promised never to speak of—he had climbed out his window onto the château's roof to admire the view.

She felt her heart flutter unusually fast at the thought of Raymond's heartbreak over his mother's hasty declaration. She tried to steady her breathing and focus on a series of memories to calm her: Raymond playing hide-and-seek in the meadow. Raymond sitting on a rug in the children's room with his toy soldiers. Raymond laughing so hard at one of her jokes, he snorted milk out of his nose. Raymond was her world. She refused to lose him.

Renée cut off Celine's crying. "Don't worry. I'm going to find him."

"I'll come with you," Celine said.

Rose appeared around the corner, hands on hips. "Renée Dubois! Why are you upsetting this child?" She looked down at Renée's bare feet in horror. "We have guests arriving and you do not look presentable. Your aunt will not be pleased about this."

"About what?" Aunt Olivia asked, coming around the corner with Uncle Gaspian. She took one look at Renée's and Celine's faces and paled. "What is wrong?"

"Raymond was angry at Maman and ran away to find the fairies!" Celine blurted before Renée could stop her.

"What?" Uncle Gaspian said. "Where did he go? Did you see him leave?"

Aunt Olivia's and Renée's eyes connected across the room and Renée knew then, no matter what the outcome, Aunt Olivia would never forgive her for this. Chances were, Renée would never forgive herself either. But first she had to find him. Renée launched into action, shoving past Rose.

"Where are you going?" Aunt Olivia demanded. "You cannot leave this house at this hour! Renée? Renée?"

"Renée, wait!" her uncle called after her.

Renée didn't look back. She ran out the back kitchen door, grabbing a lantern from the porch. She could hear them calling her name as she hurried down the dark path, the flame bouncing as she ran. Adrenaline seemed to carry her as she moved faster, destination unknown.

Renée's eyes darted back and forth as she tried to adjust to the suffocating night. She reached the hill, which meant the river wasn't far. The voices in the distance muffled as she hit the tree line, the only clear sounds now that of the night around her. A breeze rippled through the trees, making her jump, but she kept going, pushing past branches and thick leaves to find her way to the water. Her lungs were burning, her mouth dry, her feet stinging. She could feel them getting nicked and bruised as she descended through the woods.

Even with all the tree cover, Renée's eyesight slowly improved thanks to the harvest moon, big and bright against a smattering of clouds behind it. When she looked up, she noticed the clouds streaked across in an unusual pattern. The moon lent its flame to them, and to her, guiding her onward.

Raymond, hang on, she thought as she stumbled, gashing her bare feet against a vine. She shouted out but kept going. Finally, she reached the river's edge.

"Raymond!" she cried, holding her lantern up. "Raymond, where are you? It's Renée!"

The only reply was the sounds of the rushing water, churning like her stomach.

"Raymond!" she tried again, stepping in. She recoiled in shock at the frigid temperature and could feel its current try to pull her in immediately. *Did Raymond fall in?* she thought. The water was pitch-black and ominous, moving faster than it had that afternoon. She tried to squelch her panic.

"He's all right. He has to be," she whispered to herself, stumbling backward out of the water. "You just must think like he would." She held her lantern up again, her teeth starting to chatter. "Raymond, where have you gone?" She looked up at the harvest moon, hoping for answers.

Something rustled behind her, and she turned fast wondering if her uncle or the others had caught up. She saw nothing except dead leaves blowing past her. Her imagination was getting the best of her.

Which way? she mused, refocusing. It suddenly occurred to her that he might be too frightened to show himself. "Come out, come out wherever you are, Raymond! You won't be in trouble!" Her feet crunched on a pile of leaves as she carefully traversed the side of the river. "I want to find the fairies with you! That's why I've come. I—!" Renée cried out, tripping over something hard. The lantern tumbled from her hands, and she quickly grabbed it before it could go out, or worse—break and set fire to the woods.

Her eyes landed on something that made her heart thud.

Fairies among Us was lying open on the ground, its pages rustling in the wind. Next to it was an extinguished lantern, tipped on its side.

She felt tension pulling at the back of her neck.

No, no, no.

Renée spun around, searching for a small boy. She pushed images of him battered or broken out of her mind and started to run along the shoreline now, waving her lantern.

"RAYMOND! Raymond!" she shouted, not caring if she woke beast or wild dog. "Raymond, please! Answer me! Please!" There was no answer. She looked up at the harvest moon in anger, cursing herself for teaching Raymond and Celine to believe in fairies. What if this flight of fancy cost the child his life? A sob escaped her lips. "Raymond? Raymond? Please come out!"

She ran faster now, away from the cluster of trees that they'd made their forest fortress and downstream to where the river widened, looking more and more precarious in the darkness. "RAYMOND!" she shouted at the top of her lungs, howling like a wolf. When there was no reply, she sunk to her knees. "Please, please. Someone. Help me." She looked at the moon in the sky again. "Fairy Godmother, if you're out there and you can hear me, help us."

Tears sprang to her eyes as she started to ramble. "He's smaller than I was when I lost my parents. I've never asked you for anything—but I'm asking now. I wish . . . I wish you were here." She heard rustling again but no one appeared.

Renée stood again, brushing the mud off her hands, anger firing her up like the lantern's flame. "FINE. I don't need a fairy's help!" she shouted at the moon. "I'll find Raymond on my own! I'll stay here all ni—"

"Help!"

Renée stopped shouting and paused. Was that a voice?

"Help me! Someone!"

The sound was faint, but clear. She looked around, her heart racing as she held the lantern out in front of her. "Raymond! Where are you?"

"Help!"

She started to run again, following the sound along the riverbank, squinting and tripping every few moments. "Raymond! Raymond! Where are you?" And then, suddenly, she saw something peculiar.

A tree had fallen and was now strewn across the riverbank, like a broken bridge, its branches and limbs extending into the water. Clinging to one of those branches, his arms wrapped tight to the branch, was her cousin. Terror was written all over Raymond's face as his small, soaked body got pushed around by the current, threatening to yank him downstream. The falls were not far, a deep chasm in the valley.

"RAYMOND!" Renée screamed, dropping the lantern and running straight to the log.

"I'm slipping!" Raymond said.

"No!" Renée said forcibly, taking a step onto the log. She stumbled. Damn bare feet! Why had she been so foolish as to leave without shoes? Her heart was nearly in her throat as she tried again, curling her toes tight against the mossy bark, feeling the spray of the water as she took another tentative step. The tree trunk bounced uneasily beneath her. "I'm coming. Hold on."

He was just a stone's throw away, but she continued to move slowly, feeling the trunk shift as she walked. Her right foot slipped slightly and the trunk waffled, a branch to her right snapping off and violently tumbling past. *That could be Raymond*, she thought darkly. She took another breath. *But it won't be. I can reach him in time.*

"Renée, please hurry!" Raymond started to cry now. "I'm scared!"

"I know you are," she said, inching closer. "I'm scared, too, but we must be brave as well. You can do that, can't you?"

He cried harder. "I don't know." Another branch snapped off beside him and he screamed.

For a moment, Renée thought he'd let go. But then she saw he was still there, still clinging on, and she tried to remain calm. "You can," Renée said, her voice firm.

He was sobbing now. "I just wanted to find the fairies. I was going to make a wish for you."

She had to keep him talking. She took another step. "A wish for me?"

"A wish they'd let you stay with Celine and me forever. That Maman wouldn't send you away. I wanted the fairies to let us live out here in the forest, just the three of us."

Renée's heart ached. "That's a very nice idea, but I'm never going to leave you, Raymond."

His small chin quivered. "Promise?"

"Promise." She was so close now she could almost touch him.

"But why haven't the fairies come to help us? Like they helped you?"

She was wondering the same thing, her frustration mounting. How could they let Raymond get swept away? "We can do this ourselves," she declared, shouting up at the blasted harvest moon. "Now listen to me."

He closed his eyes. "I'm listening."

Renée took another step. "I'm going to bend down and lock my legs around this trunk. I'll grab you once I'm in place. Do. Not. Let. Go. Not till I've told you to. Understood?" She tried to stay balanced as she slowly bent at her knees.

He opened his eyes wide. "Hurry!"

She bent lower and lower, Raymond almost in reach. Her thighs were aching as she tried to anchor herself around the shifting trunk. *Steady, steady,* she told herself till she could hold her weight no longer. She fell to her knees, feeling the whole trunk bounce. Raymond screamed again. Or maybe that was someone calling his name.

"I'm sorry I ran away to find the fairies without you," he said, his teeth chattering. The child was practically blue. "I'm so sorry."

"There will be plenty of time for all that later," she said. "Now I'm going to grab you, and you hold on as I pull you up and out of the water. It's going to be quick. Understand?"

Raymond nodded. And then she was leaning forward, the tree beneath her moving again as she reached for his right arm.

SNAP! She heard a branch—a large one that could have been its own tree—splinter off and threaten to pull Raymond away with it. The two of them screamed as she yanked him, fighting the current to pull him up onto the trunk. She pulled harder, up and up, till she felt his small cold body shivering in her arms.

"Don't let go!" he said, once the two of them were seated facing each other on the log, clinging on for dear life.

"I won't," she promised. Do you think you can stand up and lean on me?"

Her relief was short-lived.

The whole trunk was shaking now and she knew what was about to happen. Any minute, the tree was going to tear off from the riverbank and take them downstream. They had to get off this log.

"I can try."

The water tore another branch off and it hurtled by. She felt the trunk shift, the roots creaking ominously, and her panic mounted. "Hurry. Hurry."

Raymond clutched her; she winced as he tried to climb up till he was standing. She felt a moment of elation, then she heard the splintering. She quickly tried to move to her knees, her equilibrium off. The two of them looked at each other in panic, both seeming to know what was going to happen next.

Renée heard more shouting. Someone calling her name. Uncle Gaspian? But there was no time to wait. Renée knew then they couldn't both get off the log in time. It was Raymond or her. She only had a moment to decide.

Gritting her teeth, she took the boy in her arms, lifting him with strength she didn't know she had.

"Renée, no!" he shouted as she threw the boy toward the riverbank a few feet away, just as the trunk pulled free.

The second he left her arms, the trunk went flying, taking Renée along with it. She barely had a second to look over at the riverbank and see Uncle Gaspian running to Raymond, before she was tumbling toward the falls. Her voice failed her as water filled her lungs.

And for the second time in her life, she found herself falling into the darkness below.

FOUR

Renée was dying.

Of that she was certain. Her body seared with pain, battered beyond repair. She'd gone over the falls, smashing against sharp, unseen things in the dark water before winding up at the other end of the river. And now she seemed to be lying half in, half out of the water at the shore.

Renée felt cold. Bone-chillingly cold. She could taste blood in her mouth, her head felt like it was on fire, and she couldn't lift her arms. Her left leg seemed to be bent at a wrong angle, and something was oozing down her face. For a while, Renée drifted in and out of consciousness, her eyes too weak to stay open.

She was dying and no one was coming to save her.

How could they? The unforgiving river could have taken her miles away, too far for anyone to find her. Would they even bother to look? Uncle Gaspian was attending to his son. And family or not, she was an orphan he had taken pity on. Someone his wife felt was a burden. She'd been living on borrowed time.

She felt herself start to drift off again when she heard a voice.

"There she is! I found her!" She heard a gasp. "Oh no. Is she dead?"

"How should I know?"

Two voices she didn't recognize. She tried hard to open her eyes and tell them that she wasn't dead. Not yet, anyway. But she didn't have the strength.

"Can you tell if she's still breathing?"

"She's breathing. Barely."

"Poor thing."

Their voices were soft-spoken as if she were hearing them across a giant chasm. It reminded her of Raymond and the river. Raymond. Celine. Who would care for the children? She heard herself moan. If she was dying, she wanted her last thoughts to be happy ones. She thought about Raymond's laugh. Pictured Celine dancing around the children's room as sunlight streamed through the window. Maman and Papa sitting and reading to her. She would see them soon. That was something to hold on to.

"She's not going to make it."

"Don't say that!"

"Look at her."

"I'm asking if she's alive. If she's alive, I can help her."

"You can't. We don't interfere with humans' fates. You know that."

Renée wanted to speak. To let the strangers know she was still there. But the words got tangled in her mouth.

"How is this fate? The girl saved her brother. She chose him over herself."

"How do you know it was her brother?"

"Does it matter?" The stranger sounded agitated. "The point is, she saved the boy! So strange that Mother picked this fairy ring tonight of all nights."

"It's nothing more than coincidence."

"And yet the girl was calling for her fairy godmother. Do you think she actually has one?"

Renée heard a distinct growl. "No idea. Regardless, she's not your charge. You can't go around just helping random mortals."

"Why not? She's in trouble! She believes in fairies. I'm giving her a wish."

"Lune! Are you mad? To waste a wish on some human you don't even know? Besides, you're not her godmother. This is against the rules."

"This is what wishes are meant for."

Renée tried hard to open her eyes and they fluttered. Her mind had to be playing tricks on her because for a moment, she saw two small lights bobbing in front of her. *Fairies? Wishes?* Another distorted memory coming back to her at the end, perhaps?

"*Lune.* What if she's already received a wish in her lifetime? You can't grant a wish without checking with your mother first. She will be livid, and you know it."

"And this girl will no longer exist if I do nothing."

"Try to see reason!"

"It's not her time, Tresor. This human is meant to do more. I can feel it."

"She hasn't even said 'I wish'!"

"She wished for help with the boy before. That has to count."

"It doesn't!"

"It does in my book. Rules are sometimes meant to be broken!"

Agreed. Renée tried to vocalize this, but all she managed to do was gasp like a fish out of water, the sudden reaction making it feel like needles piercing her skin. The end was near. *Raymond. Celine. I'm sorry.* A tear tricked down her cheek.

"You see that? A tear. It's a sign. I'm doing it."

"Lune!"

Renée felt a sudden force push against her body, and then words, ten times as loud as the rest had been shouted into the night. "Fae! Faerie! Be! It's meant to be!"

There was a crackling sound, followed by such heat Renée thought the world around her had burst into flames. She cried out as her body warmed in a way that eerily reminded her of the momentous fire of her childhood. The heat was so overwhelming and uncomfortable, she couldn't stand it. And then, she was unconscious once more.

Heat. Warmth. Water. Voices.

When Renée awoke, she was amazed to find her pain was gone. Her body was no longer cold. Her limbs were bending in the right direction. Her mouth no longer tasted of blood. All those sensations seemed a distant memory.

She was alive.

Renée blinked hard, wiggled her fingers without wincing, lifted her legs and noticed they were no longer muddy or bruised. She was lying on something very soft that felt like fur. A quick glance down told her she was no longer wet—her dress wasn't even soiled. She felt her hair. Dry, too, and there were, surprisingly, no twigs or debris from the river. She could still hear running water.

Where was she?

Renée looked around, but her mind was moving in too many directions at once to make sense of her surroundings. The walls were covered in flowers and long green vines that intertwined like the roots of a tree. The air was humid like the worst days of summer—and the sound of gurgling was coming from a rapidly flowing wall of water. Were they *behind* a waterfall? She squinted hard. Upon closer inspection, she could see traces of a quarry behind the vines almost as if she were in a cave. A cave that somehow had thick, lush green grass and no dead leaves. How far exactly had she traveled downstream . . . to a new season?

Was she hallucinating? Was this because she hit her head? Could it be she dreamed Raymond being in peril? Maybe this was all a cruel nightmare from which she hadn't awoken. If so, why were her surroundings so beautiful?

"Raymond?" she called hoarsely. "Celine? Uncle Gaspian?"

"Shhhh," someone said softly, and Renée felt a warm hand on her arm. She blinked. Where was the voice coming from?

"You've had quite the night. Just rest. You're safe now."

"Who are you?" Her voice did not sound like her own. It was more musical somehow, more tinkling. "Also, *where* are you?"

Another voice scoffed. "One would think her first words would be *thank you*. Humans." There was a deep sigh.

Humans?

Renée sat up fast, inhaling so much air she started to cough. She blinked hard, looking at the two individuals suddenly standing next to her bed . . . which wasn't an actual bed at all. It was a cushion made up of hundreds of dandelions.

She looked at the two figures watching her—both dressed in what appeared to be thin green linen—the young woman in an empire-waisted dress, the young man in a royal doublet threaded with gold stitching. They didn't look much older than her—maybe only by a few years. Their ears had a distinctive point to the tips and appeared slightly larger in size. Both were barefoot, their skin a warm golden-brown color, and the woman had a ring of bright pink and fuchsia wildflowers in her long, curly black hair.

The woman was radiant, but Renée found she couldn't take her eyes off the young man. He was exceptionally tall with short, curly brown hair and a distinct widow's peak above his expressive, thick eyebrows. But it was his eyes—glowing amber like fire—that she couldn't stop staring at.

Renée watched the strangers intently. "Are you . . . fairies?"

The girl smiled. "Yes, we are."

"And yet you are my size," she noted, finding her voice again.

The young man scoffed, shaking his head. "So predictably narrow-minded."

"Ignore him," the girl said. "I am Lune and this is my cousin Tresor."

Her body tingled. Fairies! Real fairies! Standing in front of her. "I'm Renée Dubois," she told them. "And I'm not frightened, I'm elated to meet you both." The fée folk had saved her! Again! She clutched her chest, which probably gave them the wrong impression, but there was something about her heart that suddenly felt different—not only was it not racing in such a profound moment, she couldn't actually sense it beating at all. How odd.

"It's a pleasure to meet you, Renée Dubois," Lune said.

"I have waited such a long time for this moment," Renée said eagerly. "Although, I must admit, I'm confused. I thought fairies were tiny."

Tresor grumbled again, saying something below his breath Renée couldn't quite hear.

"We can be," Lune said brightly. She spun clockwise one time and *poof!* She shrunk down and fluttered in front of Renée's eyes with wings so whisper-thin they reminded her of tulle. "We usually make ourselves small in the human world. Easier to get around. And to escape if we're pursued by an angry house cat."

"A pet, as you call it," Tresor said tartly. "As if a human can own another creature. I will never understand that. In any case, most of the danger lies in the mortals themselves."

Lune shot him a look before spinning around again and returning to human size.

"How do you do that?" Renée marveled.

The young woman produced a long sliver of silver out of the air. "Every fairy has their own unique way of making magic. It depends on one's skill set."

"Is one of you my fairy godmother? Is that why you saved me?"

Tresor and Lune looked at each other worriedly, and Renée wondered if she'd said the wrong thing.

"I won't tell a soul, but if one of you is my fairy godmother and I suspect you are, I want to say thank you for saving my life," she rambled. "I apologize for not expressing my gratitude earlier. I heard you, but I was in too much pain to speak. I thought I was dying."

"You were," Tresor said, and Renée shuddered.

Lune nudged him. "The important thing is you're fine now. Completely healed."

"Thanks to Lune," Tresor added while Lune continued to smile.

"Healed." Renée gazed at her fingers again and waved them in front of her face. She smiled at Lune, and even Tresor, despite how miserable he seemed. "It feels different than last time."

Lune's smile wavered. "Last time?"

Renée nodded. "Yes. When you saved me as a child."

"Wait. This has happened to you before?" Tresor demanded, and gave Lune an accusatory glance.

"You don't remember?" Renée scratched her head. Her hair was dry and smooth. It felt like spun silk instead of its usual tangles. "Which one of you is my fairy godmother?"

"Neither of us!" Tresor's golden eyes darkened slightly. He took a step closer to Lune. "This is why I told you to check. She can't have *two* wishes! Which is beside the point, as you're not her godmother, and weren't supposed to grant *any* wishes in the first place."

"I—I know," Lune stammered and looked at Renée again. "Are you saying you were rescued by the fée as a child?"

Renée nodded. Was Lune going to take her wish back? Could she do that?

"And you were near death then as well?" Lune pressed.

"Well . . ." Renée started. "I wasn't dying last time if that's what you're asking. I mean, I would have died if a fairy hadn't come to my aid." Even after all this time, thoughts of that night, the screams that came to mind, made Renée wince. "There was a fire, and I was guided to safety."

Tresor took a step back. "This is odd, no?" he asked Lune. "Lightning doesn't strike the same tree twice. And we don't even know if the girl has a godmother—"

"You don't?" Renée found that news disappointing. And strange indeed. If they weren't her godmother, if she didn't have one, how did they find her?

"And now you've made her . . ." Tresor trailed off.

"Made me what?" Renée asked.

"What my cousin is trying to say is that this is all very serendipitous," Lune told Renée and shot Tresor another look. "Clearly meant to be."

"I'm not so sure about that," Renée said with a sigh. "My fate seems to be to marry a dull fabric merchant and become a stepmother." She slid off the bed of flowers. "Speaking of which, I should probably be going so I can tell the children I'm all right."

Lune and Tresor looked anxiously at each another.

"You have children?" Tresor asked, after a beat.

Renée pursed her lips and found they tasted like sugar. "Well, they're not my children. They're my younger cousins."

"Oh." Relief flooded both his and Lune's faces.

"Celine and Raymond. They're ten and seven. I am their governess. I also care for them when my aunt is feeling ill, which is often. My uncle is a merchant and on the road most days and Raymond . . ." She smiled to herself. "He can be a handful. He's got a huge imagination. He's why I was at the river tonight. I'd been teaching him about the Harvest Moon Festival, and he got

49

carried away trying to find . . . well, trying to find all of *you*. Which is why I must get home. I promised I wouldn't leave him."

"But you can't," Lune blurted out.

"Don't worry. I feel fine. Better than fine, actually." She stretched her long limbs out and felt no tightness, no cold, no bruising from her tumble. "I can manage the walk if you just point me in the right direction."

"Renée, there is something we need to explain," Lune said.

Renée smoothed her newly cleaned dress. She looked around the cave. "I'm sure you want to get back to your ball."

"And how exactly do you know about that?" Tresor asked.

"Oh, I know a lot about fée folk—fairies—what do you prefer to be called?" she asked.

Tresor looked amused. "We go by many names."

"That is good to know. I read about the festival in a book," Renée explained. "*Fairies among Us*?"

"*Fairies among Us*," he repeated slowly.

"Yes. That's where the children and I read about leaving you offerings. Maybe you found them before . . . my fall," she said, stifling another shudder. "We left trinkets along the riverbed."

"The slippers? Those were from you?" Tresor asked.

"Yes, did you like them?" Renée asked hopefully.

Tresor made a face. "If you haven't noticed, we don't exactly wear shoes." He shook his head. "This explains a lot."

"Oh." Renée frowned. He could have just said thank you.

"How many human books about fairies are written, exactly?" Tresor inquired.

"I don't know," she admitted. "But I've read several over the years."

"I had no idea humans had so much time to devote to flights of fancy," Tresor said. "What other frivolous things do humans read about? The dance of the hummingbird?"

"We study books on many topics," Renée replied coolly. "Language, history, mathematics . . ."

"And that gives human scholars a vast knowledge of what? How to destroy nature?" Tresor's eyebrows raised pointedly.

She would not take the bait. Clearly, she had overstayed her welcome. "Well, again, this has been . . . lovely. Chatting with actual fairies! But I really must be going."

"Oh dear," Lune said, blowing a piece of hair off her face. "Renée, I—"

"Thank you for everything." Renée hugged her. Lune smelled like the perfect mix of cut wildflowers on a spring day. Renée glanced at Tresor. His expression reminded her of dangerous weather, but he smelled like earth: musty and woodsy with a dash of pine. "I'll make note about the slippers when I talk to the children. They will want to thank you themselves I'm sure, so we'll leave food, perhaps? Do you like berries?"

Tresor rubbed his temples. "You talk more than any human I've ever met."

Renée bristled, unable to ignore his brusque tone any longer. "Excuse me, sir," she said, pointing a finger at his face, "but what exactly have I done to warrant such rudeness? I know you have magic and I do not, but—" Tresor smirked. "What exactly is so amusing?"

Lune placed her warm hand on Renée's arm again and instantly she felt calmer. "If you would just sit for a moment more."

"I'm sorry, but I really must go." Renée started to stride forward, and Tresor appeared in front of her. "Stop doing that!" To think she'd thought him handsome! Him telling her what she could and could not do made her boil. "I beg your pardon." She stepped around him, heading straight for the water, unsure whether she was headed toward a dead end or an exit.

This time both fairies landed in front of her, Lune's face grim, the light from her eyes seeming to dim.

"Renée," Lune said softly. "I'm sorry, but you can never return home."

FIVE

"I'm sorry?" *Never* wasn't a word Renée used with the children. Every situation had exceptions, this one included. Yes, Lune had saved her, and she was in their debt, certainly, but that didn't make her their . . . what? Fairy prisoner? "I am truly grateful for a second chance at life. Beyond grateful! But I don't think you understand—I can't stay. I have a responsibility to the children I care for. They need me."

Lune glanced at her cousin, the gold flecks in their eyes growing brighter and then dimmer. "It's not that simple."

Renée frowned. "Why not?"

"You're going to have to tell her," Tresor replied, as if Renée wasn't right in front of them.

"Tell me what?" Renée pressed. Why were they being so cryptic? Lune took her hand, and Renée felt that strange tingling sensation again, the air warming around them. The air shimmered with glowing dust.

"You were so close to death when I found you I did the only thing I could." Lune took a deep breath. "When I saved your life, I made you one of us. You, too, are now part of the fée. A fairy."

"*Part*-fairy." Tresor's voice came from behind them.

"I'm part of the fée, part . . ." Renée could not wrap her head around the words. Lune nodded. Renée felt a chill of excitement ripple through her and a small laugh burst out of her. This was unbelievable! She held tight to Lune's hand. "As in a fairy who can do magic, shrink down to miniature size, and fly?"

"You can't fly," Tresor clarified. "Or shrink—you'll stay human-sized. As for magic, we don't know what you're capable of. There are some limitations we should explain, too. Like—"

"But I am a fairy?" Renée cut him off, clutching Lune's hand tighter.

"Part-fairy," Tresor repeated.

"Right." Renée felt giddy at the thought, and she had so many questions. "Well, what do you typically do in these situations? I must not be the only—" She looked at them both inquisitively.

"There hasn't been a part-fairy in this quorum in a very long time." There was a hint of an ache in Tresor's voice, before he narrowed his eyes at Lune. "When others learn about this—"

"We won't tell them right away," Lune said dismissively.

Tresor motioned to Renée, waving his arms dramatically, causing little glittering balls of light to waft through the air. "How are you going to explain? They're going to know, Lune, just by looking at her."

"So we'll hide her for now."

"Hide her where? In case you've forgotten, there's a festival starting. A ball! How are you going to get her past the entire kingdom? Your mother is probably already looking for us."

The two were speaking so fast, Renée had trouble keeping up. Why would they have to hide her?

"My mother," Lune groaned, and held her head.

"Yes, your mother. How are you going to explain what you've done?"

"Well . . ."

"Lune."

"I'm thinking!" The fairy tapped her fingers on her waist, staring at Renée intently. "We'll move fast, have her keep her head down. Maybe I can spell a cloak to cover her lack of wings. Make her blend in."

"Are you forgetting she can't fly?"

"Right. Well . . . we will carry her. We can say she's tired and we're getting her back to her dormitory."

"Her aura is different, Lune. They'll be able to smell her."

"Smell me?" Renée felt insulted. Why was Tresor so frantic? Lune had saved her life. That was a good thing. An incredible thing.

"We don't have a choice. We can't stay in this cave for the next three days! They'll send out a search party. She's coming to the ball."

"A *ball*," Renée repeated as the word registered. "The children will love hearing stories about a fairy ball."

Lune frowned and looked at her again, taking both of Renée's hands in her own. "Renée," she said softly, "I don't think you're understanding. It's not that we're trying to keep you from your human life or your family, but you

55

can't go back to that world." She pursed her lips. "You're part of ours now. Now that you're half-human and half-fairy, the consequences of spending time in the human world are dire."

"Dire?" Renée didn't understand.

"If you spend too long in the human world, you'll die," Tresor said bluntly. "Prematurely."

Renée looked at him. Clearly, he was joking. "Die? No. *No.*" She glanced at Lune. "Die?"

Lune nodded sadly. "Time works differently in the fairy world. And, of course, fairies live hundreds of years. While you're in this realm, you will, too. But when a part-fairy returns to the human world, it seems the mortal part gets triggered . . . at an accelerated rate."

"How accelerated?" Renée asked. A tingling sensation spread across her body.

"Let me put it this way: If you tried to stay more than a brief spell," Tresor said darkly, "you might not survive the week."

Renée felt like she might throw up. "But I could return for an hour at least? How much would I age in an hour? Or for the day? So I can explain myself to the children." Lune and Tresor said nothing, and Renée looked at them both pleadingly. "Please. I can't just disappear. Celine and Raymond will think I died. They're only children. I promised Raymond I'd return."

Lune squeezed her hands tightly. "I'm sorry. I know this is a lot to process, but we can't allow it. Especially when you don't fully understand your abilities yet."

"Just give me a few moments to say goodbye!" Renée pressed. "Please." She closed her eyes, trying to concentrate on her breathing. "Grief engulfed me for years after my parents . . . I can't let Celine and Raymond live with the same guilt. If they can just know I'm all right, I'll try to make my peace with . . . losing them." She choked on the last few words.

Lune pursed her lips. "Oh, Renée, even if we could let you return to the riverbank for a short while, the children would no longer be there waiting for you."

"What do you mean?" Renée asked, letting go of Lune's hands.

"Time, as I explained, works differently here than in the human world. You've been away much longer than a night in that realm."

"How long have I been gone?" she asked, and no one answered at first. *"How long?"*

"A year," Tresor told her. "At least."

"A year?" Renée sunk onto the ground. "But I was just there. You just saved me." It was too much to handle—a near death to her body and an actual death of her old life, losing the rest of her family in one fatal moment. She could hold back no longer. She started to cry, covering her face with her hands.

"Oh, the poor thing," she heard Lune say.

"This is what you get for saving a mortal," Tresor retorted. "She can't understand our world. Maybe if she had decades under her belt like we have, she'd know what a gift she'd been given."

"She thinks she's lost everything," Lune snapped. "But she'll see in time. Renée?" Lune placed a warm hand on her back. "It's going to be all right. I promise."

It's going to be all right. Promise. A surge of anger shot through Renée, and she pushed Lune away. "If I can't leave, *you* have to go to the children. Right now. Wherever they are. Tell them I survived. *Please.* They need to know what happened."

"You don't get to give us orders," Tresor said sharply.

"This is important," Renée practically growled. "You may not understand, but humans, we care for one another! We don't just abandon each other." She was shouting now.

"*We?* Oh, you're speaking for every human, then?" Tresor raised one eyebrow.

She paused, taking this in. "I speak for myself. I taught the children to find magic in the world." She stared at a spot on the vine-covered wall, her vision starting to blur from her tears. "To love nature and believe in things that can't always be seen with the naked eye. In listening to the music of the forest or feeling the magic of a sunrise. I fear if they think I lost my life trying to save them, they'll close themselves off from finding happiness in those purest of pleasures."

Tresor studied her for a moment. "All children have to grow up sometime."

Renée stood, her body moved by the surge of anger.

"All right." Lune stepped between them. She pushed a loose strand of Renée's hair behind her left ear. "Unlike my cousin, I do understand why you're upset. And I promise you, we will find a way to check on Celine and Raymond before too long."

Renée looked at her. "You promise?"

"Yes," Lune said, and Renée believed. "But first things first—we need to get you out of this cave and slip through the ball undetected so I can figure out how to deal with my mother and explain what I've done."

"This I have to see," Tresor quipped.

"Oh, you're helping me, cousin."

If Lune's mother was anything like Aunt Olivia, Renée understood her hesitation to admit she'd done something wrong. And truthfully, if she was going to find a way to see to it that someone looked out for the children, she had to be agreeable. "All right," she said, holding her hand out to take Lune's. "I trust you."

Lune smiled. "Good. You'll need something proper to wear." She produced a wand out of thin air. "Fae! Faerie! Be! It's meant to be!"

Seconds later, Renée found herself looking down at a dress as luminescent and wispy as a spiderweb. The iridescent shade made it appear a dozen colors at once, but in her mind's eye it was the palest of purples, featuring layers and layers of tulle that swished when she moved. A matching lightweight cloak kissed her shoulders. She'd never seen anything so delicate. "I love it," she decided, her voice lightening.

"Good." She and Lune grinned at each other.

A tinkling of bells sounded and suddenly all the flowers in the cave turned toward the noise.

"The ball." Lune swore under her breath. "We have to hurry." She grabbed Renée's hand, hurrying them through the cave while Tresor shrunk down and flew past. "We can't let Mother beat us there!"

Lune's pace quickened and Renée struggled to keep up. As they rounded a bend, she noticed the cave narrowed into a long hallway. Water dripped down the rocks and puddled on the floor where water lilies drifted by. Renée paused.

She closed her eyes, the nightmare of what just happened coming roaring back. She could almost hear her own screams—or were they Raymond's?—the sensation of tumbling head over feet, the frigid water threatening to swallow her whole. She tried to remind herself this was different—barely a puddle. She was safe with Lune and even Tresor. Tentatively, she stepped forward and found the water surprisingly warm. She rushed through it to the other side and breathed deeply.

"Are you all right?" Lune asked, glancing back before taking off again. The cave path seemed to be heading upward now, the water receding.

"Humans know how to run. She's fine," Tresor's tiny voice sounded like it was coming from somewhere near her right ear. She scratched at her head, wondering if she could knock him out of the way.

"Just ignore him," Lune said as Tresor returned to full size. "He's as unhappy with humans as he is fascinated with them."

"Hardly," Tresor fired back, reaching the cave's exit. Renée could see it was daylight already beyond the cave. Tresor fixed his eyes on Renée, his stare so piercing she felt her cheeks burn. "Mortals, in my experience, are impulsive, selfish creatures." He paused for a moment, studying her. "You, however, are a unique specimen—you saved that child thinking nothing of yourself. Foolish, yes, but selfish, no."

"Specimen?" Renée lifted her chin defiantly. "I'm not a bug, thank you. And I hardly would call saving someone's life foolish." She turned to Lune. "Do my new fairy skills allow me to turn him into a toad?"

Lune stifled a laugh. "That might be an improvement." She touched the crown of flowers on her head to make sure it was straight. A butterfly flitted out as if it had somewhere important to be.

"I'd prefer if you didn't," Tresor said dryly. "You two may need my help." He stepped into the sunlight, a glow washing over his face.

60

Renée felt herself inhale sharply. The young man was even more breath-taking in daylight. She felt like she was staring at the sun. He caught her staring, and she quickly looked away. How could someone so handsome be so insufferable?

"Even if, dear cousin, you already knew our path was clear," he added.

"Amusing," Lune said testily, and grabbed Renée's arm again. "He is referring to my gift. I'm a seer," she explained. "Like my mother. Most think that means we know everything that's going to happen before it happens."

"Do you?" Renée frowned. The power sounded equal parts intriguing and exhausting.

"Not unless I want to and even then, it can change. I don't test the theory. No one wants to know everything. But sometimes I see flashes without my *bulle*. Like when I found you, I could sense something intriguing about your future, a special flame ignited."

Renée swallowed, the word *flame* making her feel uneasy. "Bulle?" she asked as Lune, too, moved to the edge of the cavern and looked out. All Renée could see was sky.

"Later." Lune gently pulled her forward, out of the cave into the light. "First, let's get you to the ball."

SIX

So this was the land of the fairies.

As Renée emerged from the cave, the world laid out in front of her. It resembled home, yet felt different, like a watercolor. For one, the colors were more vivid. The green of the forest practically glowed fluorescent. The sky was violet, the clouds a stark but stunning contrast in pink, round and fluffy meringue. The entire land seemed to sparkle. In the distance, a snow-speckled ridge of mountains stood, a turquoise lake reflecting its beauty below.

Even sounds were amplified here. Was this a fairy power? Renée touched her right ear, tuning in to whispers intermingling with laughter and birdcalls. Back in Aurelais, the world had been readying for fall, but here it felt as if the land had awakened to an orange and yellow spring, birds she couldn't identify calling one another as they flew by at breakneck speed, darting in and out of lush, flowering trees connected with vines like canopies. And the flowers . . . she'd never seen species like these before.

Renée reached down to touch an electric-blue bud waving in the meadow. The flower retracted at her touch, then just as swiftly curled around her finger. She jumped.

"It likes you already," Lune said.

Renée gently pulled her hand away, unable to stop staring at the veritable rainbow of vegetation around her. She stepped forward, her legs tickled by knee-deep, thick green grass. Her eyes found an enormous castle in the distance, bright white, with several pillars and what appeared to be a glass atrium. Around the compound, the sky seemed to glitter with orbs of light. *The fée.* "Is that where the ball is?"

"Heavens no," Tresor said. "This festival is held there." He pointed upward.

Renée followed his gaze "There is another castle of the fée in the sky?"

He smiled slyly. "Not exactly."

"Ready?" Lune asked. Taking Renée's stunned silence as a yes, she gently held Renée's left arm. Tresor took her right. This close, she got another whiff of pine and tried to brush it away as he looped his arm through hers. His wings fluttered.

"I thought you only flew when you were small," Renée said.

"We're fairies. We can do whatever we'd like."

Tresor's face was so close she could touch it if she had her hands free. Not that she wanted to touch that stubble on his chin in the least.

"Besides," Tresor added, "if we shrunk now, how would we explain why you're a different size?"

Renée looked straight ahead. "Let's go thennnnnnnn!" They took off without warning, the rushing air making her scream. Tresor laughed as they rose over treetops, then swooped low over the lake; she could almost touch the water with her fingertips. The air where they flew sparkled with fairy dust.

Magic.

Renée had goose bumps. As they soared up and down, the wind whipping at her face, making her eyes tear, her hair billowing out behind her, she felt a childlike urge to squeal, much like Raymond used to do when she'd run down the hill with him high on her shoulders.

Raymond.

The thought of him sobered her instantly. She heard his small voice as she tried to reach him. *I'm never going to leave you, Raymond* she'd vowed as the tree splintered and started to give way. And now she'd been gone—what did Lune say? A year. No one would be looking for her now.

I'm still here, she thought, wishing somehow they both could hear her across time, space and—clouds.

Lots of clouds.

Renée braced herself as they flew straight at a large gray one. They passed right through it and she felt nothing more than a faint mist.

"We're fine!" Lune reassured her. "Just trying to stay out of sight."

Tresor snickered.

"Thank you, Lune. How was I to know you could fly through a cloud?" Renée groused at the fairy's cousin. Out of the corner of her eye, she saw movement and turned her head. "Oh!"

Below them were fairies haloed with auras of all colors. Some skipped across clouds, others were dancing on giant floating leaves. The glitter dust lit up the sky, a sky that seemed to be suspended in twilight, sun and moon both visible high above. Lanterns bobbed among the clouds. Their glow was no flame, however. As Renée peered closer, she noticed swarms of fireflies.

A gust of wind blew, and Renée watched as a group of fairies in shades of oranges, green, and brown zoomed past, landing on a dense cloud. When she looked up again another pod flew by, riding the back of a sparrow. The strains of a violin and a trumpet sounded, and more stunning, sparkling fée spilled onto the clouds below, starting to dance. They turned in pairs, spinning across clouds in a waltz.

It was real.

It was all real.

The fée had their own world and not only was she witnessing it, she was part of it. She was one of them. Half of them? Whatever Tresor wanted to call it—she was here now, too. How she ached wishing the children could be there.

"Look how beautiful they all are!" She watched the fée swing through the air. "And the music! That sound. Oh, I could watch them dance all night!"

"We cannot do that," said Lune, frowning.

But she had so many questions. "Do you have balls like this all the time?"

"Too often," Tresor complained. "The fée like any excuse for a fête."

Renée saw nothing wrong with that. A celebration was wonderful. Her aunt and uncle never hosted parties. Just a few select acquaintances on occasion. And of course, the disastrous dinner with Monsieur Valliery that never happened. "They look happy. Joyful."

"You're overthinking this," Tresor told her.

She ignored him and watched a fairy thrown into the air by her partner. "But why is no one wearing shoes?"

"We have no need for them," Lune said simply.

"I told you, those slippers you left us were a waste," Tresor said, and Renée started to fume again.

"Let's wait here for a moment," Lune yelled to Tresor as they came in for a landing on a vacant cloud.

The surface felt squishy, like Renée could bounce on it. It held fast, even though parts of the cloud appeared translucent. She scrunched her toes up tight, trying to remember every detail of this sensation.

"Now we need a plan," Lune said as they each let go of Renée's arms, and she tried to balance on the moving cloud. "We want to be seen, but not *seen*, and that will be tough because any second your devotees are going to try to whisk you away and I don't think I can fly Renée alone. You'll need to fight them off."

"You exaggerate, cousin," Tresor said, his eyes scanning the sky like a bat.

"I do not." Lune caught Renée's eye. "This one has many admirers, none of whom he gives the time a day."

"I'm busy," he said flatly. "And they're all so . . . chirpy. I don't like fawning and I despise matchmaking."

An indelicate snort escaped from Renée. Tresor gave her a curious look. "Sorry. I meant I understand your plight. No one wants to fight off an unwanted admirer," she admitted, thinking of Monsieur Valliery. "But can we stay and watch for just a bit longer? I've never been to a ball before and it seems a pity to waste such a beautiful gown," she said, admiring her new dress.

66

Lune paused, and Renée could see her considering it. Perhaps she didn't want to miss the festival either. "One song," Lune said. "But then we really must go."

"Thank you," Renée said, her eyes on the cloud above.

Hundreds of fairies soared through the air, looking like a multicolored blanket taking flight. It reminded her of the hot-air balloons Uncle Gaspian said he'd once seen on a trip. *Imagine! Being able to fly and see the world from new heights. Who would have thought it possible?* she recalled him saying. And now here she was in a world where flying didn't require a basket or a balloon.

She heard the first chords of a waltz and clapped with delight as fairies moved in time to the music. Many of them danced around tall poles, holding on to multicolored strings, reminding her of St. John's Day celebrations of years past. Though Aunt Olivia did not condone the dancing, she insisted they bring embers of the fire home as a talisman to keep bad luck away. As Renée watched some of the fireflies whiz by, she thought about reaching out to grab one for luck. But maybe she didn't need luck in this strange new realm where the sun and the moon shone in joint company, the sky always in a perpetual state of dawn and dusk—the colors of the world both orange and blue at the same time depending on how she blinked. And who knew? Perhaps such an action would offend here.

"Do all your festivals take place in the sky?" Renée asked.

"No, but for this one, it feels important to be as close to the guest of honor as possible," Tresor told her, pointing up to the moon. He looked at Lune. "We should stay for another moment, then come up with our excuses."

"Flight fatigue?" Lune suggested. "Rotten radish?"

Tresor shook his head. "As if either would keep anyone from the Harvest Moon Festival. We need something better."

"The first night is very popular and can get a bit out of hand," Lune explained, "which is why I was glad Mother asked Tresor and me to take a solo mission to the human world to—"

"Incoming," Tresor said gruffly.

"There you two are! I was starting to get worried." A fairy with a green aura landed before them. White flowers loosely cascaded from her head to her toes, wrapping around her limbs and her green dress like jewelry. A ring of pale buds sat on her head.

"Iris! Hello!" Lune said nervously.

Iris's emerald eyes took in Renée with interest. "Who's this?"

"She's new," Tresor said, taking Renée's arm again.

Lune eyed Renée meaningfully. "Hello!" Renée attempted a smile. "I'm Renée Dubois."

Iris frowned, swatting a fly away from her face that had the bad sense to be flying in her path. "Dubois? I don't know any Duboises in our quorum."

"Iris is my mother's handmaiden." Lune gave Renée a pointed look. "If there is anything you want to know around here, Iris knows everything. *Everything.*"

Ah. She was similar to Rose, Aunt Olivia's favorite servant. Renée understood. "That sounds helpful. It's lovely to meet you, Iris."

Iris flew closer, her green eyes sparkling. "Your dialect is different. Where are you from?"

"Renée's from the Upland region." Tresor spoke quickly. "She recently came to join our quorum."

Iris's nose twitched. "Margarite didn't tell me about any new transfers. What training group is she in? Classes start next week."

"It's all been very sudden," Lune chimed in. "I'm sure Mother meant to tell you, but . . . Oh? Tresor? Do you hear that? I think that is her calling for us now."

Iris glanced at them suspiciously. "I don't hear anything."

"She's about to," Lune said solemnly. "We should really take Renée over to greet her before the feast. See you later!" Lune and Tresor picked Renée up again and started to fly off.

"Lune! I will need her papers!" Iris called after them.

"That was too close," Tresor hissed as a pack of fairies approached like a swarm of bees.

"Tresor!" A fairy dressed in orange grabbed his arm. "You haven't danced with me yet."

"He promised me a dance at the next festival," said a young man in yellow.

"No, me!" crowed one with a crown of pink roses on her head that matched her rose-toned dress.

"My apologies, but I can't dance with anyone right now," Tresor said just as one managed to yank him free.

"Oh, my." Renée felt her body start slipping as Lune attempted to hold her up with only one arm. Looking down, she saw she was thousands of feet in the air and gasped. *Don't look down.* Panicking, Renée reached out, trying to take hold of something that would steady her. Tresor swooped in, grabbing her so quickly, he lifted Renée into his arms.

"Oh!" she said, inhaling sharply. She was face-to-face with him now, their chests touching, and she did the only thing she could think of. She placed her arms around him as if they were about to dance. He caught on and wrapped his arm around her waist. Renée felt like she couldn't breathe.

"My apologies," Tresor said to the other fairies, his eyes on Renée. "As you can see, I already have a partner this evening." Renée felt her face warm. Tresor looked at the others. "But please save me a dance tomorrow."

The other fairies did not look appeased.

"Who is that?" asked the orange one, coming closer to their pairing.

"I've never seen her before," the yellow one replied.

"I like your dress," the orange one told her, lifting a layer of the skirt and rubbing the fabric between her fingers. She smelled like peaches.

"Thank you," Renée said, pleased. "Lune made it."

"Lune?" The orange one looked from Lune to Renée. "You didn't make your own?"

"I . . ." Renée held tight to Tresor's shoulders and glanced over at Lune, whose expression was fraught. She could feel Tresor's hands on her lower back, and she tried to steady her breathing. "I'm not from here."

"Where are you from then?" asked the red fairy. The closer she got to Renée, the stronger the scent of peppers was. "What is your name?"

"I . . ." Renée let go of Tresor without thinking and immediately started to fall. Tresor and Lune each grabbed one of her arms, holding her steady again.

"What's wrong with you?" the red one asked.

"This is Renée Dubois, from Upland, and she has a damaged wing, poor thing," Lune said quickly.

"Yes, she's on the mend, so we're making sure she doesn't overexert herself," Tresor told them.

"Damaged wing?" the yellow one repeated, and Renée could sense he didn't believe them. He flew in closer and sniffed the air. "She seems different, doesn't she?"

The other two fairies came in closer, and Renée could feel herself start to perspire. Did they say fairies could smell humans?

"Aster, Amb, Lilith, you're being rude," Tresor tried, but now all three fairies had surrounded Renée and were touching her hair, her dress, her cloak, breathing in her aura, which was clearly different from their own.

Suddenly, the red fairy tugged at Renée's arm, the one Lune was holding, then pulled off the lightweight cloak, exposing her wingless back. The fairy gasped. "She's mortal!"

The yellow fairy covered his mouth with his hands while the orange fairy's wings started to flap at an alarming rate.

"It's all right," Renée said, panicking as more gathered round. "I'm one of you! Well, part-fairy. I was saved by Lune," she added without thinking. Lune turned white as a sheet.

"Saved by . . . But, Lune, you're not a godmother!" the yellow fairy shouted. "That's against the rules! You should know—your mother made them."

"Please," Lune begged, looking around. They were starting to cause a scene. "Let me explain."

"Tresor, did you help her with this?" the orange one sputtered.

"I think you should stop panicking and listen to Lune," Tresor said as other fairies tittered. It was too late. More fée surrounded them. There was a ripple of voices as the music stopped.

"A human is here!"

"Part-fairy!"

"Does Margarite know?"

Renée wasn't sure what to do. Her whole body began tingling again. Lune wouldn't make eye contact with her.

The orange fée flew over and continued her tirade. "How could you do this? We haven't had a part-fairy since . . . since . . ."

"She'll betray us all. Like Jules!" shouted the red fairy.

Who is Jules? Renée wondered as Lune and Tresor landed her onto a nearby cloud.

Two fairies began to cry. Another started to shake. Renée couldn't understand. This reaction seemed extreme.

"What happened?" asked a pink fairy as he approached the cloud.

"Lune made a part-fairy!" another shared.

"I mean no harm," Renée tried again, but it was too late. The fée were clearly upset, all of them descending on the cloud, which seemed to dip lower due to the weight, or maybe it just felt that way to Renée. Her breath started to come fast, and she closed her eyes, trying to find a solution. The ball, the dress, her beautiful entrance to a world she'd longed to see for so long had turned sideways so quickly.

"We have to find your mother," Tresor was saying to Lune.

"It's too late. They're not going to let us leave without an explanation," Lune said, looking around. "We should— Oww!"

One of the fairies lobbed something at Lune, and Renée reached down and picked it up. It was a red pepper. Now the fée were throwing things? This was getting out of hand. "Please!" she tried. "I am a friend! I make slippers for the fée all the time."

Tresor shook his head. "Don't mention the slippers."

It wasn't as if anyone heard her anyway. The fairies' voices seemed to grow more brash. Fluttering birds squawked. An owl hooted in what Renée felt was a ridiculously hostile manner, and it was all too much.

"Please stop!" Renée tried again, the pepper in her hand getting crushed slightly by her grip, her eyes springing with tears, before she finally burst. "STOP!" she screamed, and she, Lune, and Tresor were thrown backward, nearly tumbling off the cloud as something large and red rolled away, threatening to crush a dozen fairies in front of them.

Fée shrieked and tumbled out of the way. Tresor grabbed Lune and Renée and helped them up onto the cloud to see what had happened. Once the dust settled, fairies stood around in shocked silence, pointing.

A red pepper as large as a boulder was sitting in the middle of the cloud where they'd all just gathered.

Tresor looked at her. "How did you do that?" he whispered.

"Me? I didn't do anything!" Renée swore, before looking down at her hand and realizing the pepper she'd been holding was gone.

"You did," Lune said not unkindly.

Renée stared at her hands. Had she just done magic? Actual magic?

"Did you see that?" a young fairy exclaimed. "She made the pepper grow ten times in size! Without a wand."

73

"Impossible!" an older fairy sputtered. Others started to comment now, too, looking at Renée curiously. Some seemed terrified, others intrigued.

"What is the meaning of this?" said a clear, ringing voice that quieted the scene.

"The queen!" Renée heard someone whisper.

Suddenly, the fée were making a path for a woman backlit by wings that glowed bright like the sun.

"Mother," Lune whispered.

SEVEN

THE FAIRY BEFORE RENÉE WAS BREATHTAKING. HER SKIN SHIMMERED A LOVELY mix of silver and gold, flickering before Renée's eyes. Unlike the other fée, she had two sets of wings—one small, one large—that flapped behind her, leaving her curly reddish-brown hair in a perpetual state of breeze. She wore a gown that reminded Renée of a nightdress, with thin straps that exposed the parts of her skin that weren't adorned with flowers. A matching crown of baby's breath and wildflowers rested upon her head, filled with flapping butterflies. She didn't look much older than Lune or Tresor, but she had an air about her that seemed ancient.

"Mother, I—" Lune started to say, but the fairy put her hand up.

She turned to address the rest of the fairies on the cloud. "Everyone, please go back to your festivities," she said, her voice as soothing as a late summer's breeze. "It's the harvest moon and the only thing any of you should be thinking about is celebrating this glorious gift nature has given us."

"But that girl with Lune." The orange fairy gestured to Renée, her finger waving wildly. "Did you see what she did with that pepper? How did she turn it into a weapon without training? Or a wand?"

The expression on Lune's mother faltered slightly. "All will be explained in due time." The fairy in yellow started to protest and she cut him off. "Please don't make a fuss about one rogue pepper. Go dance. Eat. Sing. I, for one, cannot wait to join you. But first, I must take a moment and speak with my daughter and nephew in private." The butterflies in her crown stopped flapping, waiting for the other fairies to disperse. Lune's mother kept smiling encouragingly till the last one was gone. It was a moment before the music began to play again. Then the carefully crafted expression fell away, and Lune's mother turned to look at them.

"What happened?" she growled. Lune tried to cut in, but the fairy kept talking. "I asked you to accompany your cousin, since you just earned your wand . . . which is perhaps something we should rethink." Lune let out a small gasp as her mother went on. "It was to be a simple expedition near a well-known fairy ring. Plants, soil, mineral deposits. I did *not* ask you to bring back a human specimen!"

There was that word again. Renée cringed.

"I know this wasn't part of the plan," Lune started. "But you also told us when to go, and when I saw her in trouble, I thought for a moment—"

"You thought what?" Sparks fluttered around her mother like lightning. "It's one thing to help a human, but who said you could bring one here? You know it's expressly forbidden! How could you do this to me? *To Tresor.*"

He put his hand up. "It's all right."

"It is not!" the fairy thundered. "Lune, explain yourself. Is this about something you saw in your bulle?"

"No! I just had a feeling she could be important."

Her mother's nostrils flared. "A feeling?"

"Yes, a sense she was meant to be here. Mother, I didn't have a choice. There was an accident at the river's edge. She saved her cousin and almost died. I couldn't let that happen. You don't understand. Her destiny lies with us. I can feel it." Lune crossed her arms, the aura around her flaming red.

"You think I don't understand destiny? That's rich, Lune!" Her mother's aura flashed the same crimson. She glanced at Tresor. "And what were you doing?"

"I tried to stop her, Auntie," he said emphatically. "I knew how you'd react."

"Are we never to trust another human again?" Lune argued. "I know when something feels wrong, and leaving Renée to die wasn't right. Our two worlds are connected. We can't fear mortals. Not if we want to survive."

"We've surviving just fine," her mother seethed. "No thanks to your error in judgment."

So she was a specimen and an error in judgment? Renée knew better than to interrupt, but her stomach was churning.

"She called on us," Lune explained, and her mother faltered. "The boy did, too, and when we didn't come, she sacrificed herself to save a child! This is a life worth saving. And look at what she did to that pepper! With no training! I've never seen anyone transform a vegetable before, have you?" Her mother didn't answer. "There is a reason she's here. I know it."

Tresor folded his arms across his chest and held his stance. "You want to believe there is a reason for everything."

"And you care about no one but yourself!" Lune proclaimed.

"Enough!" the queen snapped. Her rosy-pink lips puckered. "You're causing a scene." Both Lune and Tresor quieted as the strains of a violin swelled in the distance. "I expected more from both of you, but . . ." She sighed.

Seeming to sense her opening, Lune nudged Renée forward. "Mother, if you'll just meet her. This is Renée Dubois."

Renée dropped into a curtsy. "It's an honor to meet you, Your Majesty." The queen did not respond. "I'm not here to cause any problems. If it helps, I did offer to return to my world, but Lune explained that would be . . . ill-advised. However, if there *is* by chance a way I can go back, I could take my leave at once."

Maybe if the queen was that upset with her being in the fairy realm, there was a way to undo Lune's action. Could she be dropped back before everything happened and do things differently? Or if not, could she join the children somehow now that they were older? No matter. She'd find them if given the chance.

The queen froze—her wings stopping mid-flap, her expression going cold. She looked right at Renée, then away again. "She is not supposed to be here." Her voice was strained. "Take her back."

Renée's eyes flickered to Lune, who frowned. "Mother," Lune said. "You know the consequences of such an action. I can't. She won't survive."

Margarite was quiet for a moment. Even the butterflies in her crown seemed to hold their breath. "I guess we have no choice." Her voice was strained. "The girl stays with us."

Lune's shoulders relaxed. "Thank you, Mother."

"Yes, thank you," Renée said quickly. "I'm grateful that Lune saved my life. Very grateful! I didn't mean to cause a rift among the fairy quorum, much as I have enjoyed my short visit here. The ball has been lovely."

Renée glanced at Lune, wondering what to do. Lune nodded ever so slightly as if to say, *Keep going*, so Renée barreled on. She pulled at a strand of her brown hair and found a flower had somehow weaved its way into it. "I'm not sure who this other part-fairy was everyone was worried about, but I'm not like them. I can assure you. For one, I've long been an admirer of fairies. I leave the fée gifts near the river by our château all the time."

Tresor coughed. "Slippers," he told his aunt. "She read we like them in a book."

"A book?" the queen repeated slowly.

"*Fairies among Us*," Renée explained. "The children in my care—my younger cousins—love the fée as much as I do, and we've always wanted to meet one. Actually, I have." Margarite's expression faltered once more.

Lune jumped in front of her. "Me! She means me. Today."

Apparently, Lune did not want the queen to know about her childhood encounter. "Er, yes. Lune. And Tresor. In fact, Lune said she would help me find a way to check on home in the human worl—"

The queen's expression hardened. "You would do well to not press the issue of crossing realms again."

"I—I apologize," Renée said meekly.

"Tell me something," the queen said. "The pepper: How did you enlarge it?"

"I don't know," Renée admitted. "I didn't even realize anything had happened at first. I just got so angry they were throwing objects at Lune that I threw it back. I'm sure that's not the fairy way, but—"

"See?" Lune cut in, looking at Renée appreciatively. "She has a gift."

Tresor snorted. "How is transforming a pepper a gift?"

Despite his knock, Renée couldn't help but feel pleased with Lune's assessment.

The queen studied them once more, the butterflies in her crown peering closer. "Perhaps, but for now, it would be best if she did not make a spectacle of herself. Understood? I'll address the quorum."

Renée's skin tingled. She had a second chance at life—a more fulfilling chance than her future had been if she'd been married off to Valliery. If the choice truly was this or death, she was incredibly lucky. *I am to be a fairy. An actual fairy.*

Impulsively, Renée grasped the queen's hand. Margarite's skin felt surprisingly warm.

"Renée," the queen continued, removing her hand, "you must understand—there are many in this kingdom who will fear you simply for what you are. You will have an uphill battle to win them over. I don't envy your journey, no matter what my daughter thinks." She looked at Lune. "Take her to the dormitory. Nelley will meet you. And she's going to need to be placed."

Lune threw her arms around her. "Thank you, Mother! Thank you!"

"She's your charge now, Lune. Remember that." Margarite flew away and the butterflies trailed along after her.

"Thank you!" Renée shouted. "You will not regret this. I don't do anything halfway and I have so many—"

Tresor grabbed Renée's arm. "Thank you, Aunt Margarite! We'll see you at the festival!"

Lune hurried to Renée's other side. "That didn't go as badly as I thought it would. At least Mother didn't turn Renée into a hummingbird."

"Yet," Tresor murmured, his gold eyes on Renée.

He was still holding her, which, despite her best efforts, was very distracting.

Renée heard whispering. Several fairies stared down at them from a cloud above.

"Remember what your mother said. Maybe we should take our leave before there's another incident," Tresor suggested.

"Good idea," Lune agreed. They jetted into the air without warning, Renée between them. The wind picked up and the trio descended below the clouds, away from the festival and toward the glimmering structure Renée had seen in the distance.

As they neared the grounds, Renée could see what she had thought was one castle was actually a village, with several manors clustered together. Each abode was linked with glass walkways; the buildings almost ten stories high. Together they formed a square with a large courtyard in the middle. Every stone building looked similar—high peaks and turrets, stained glass windows, and lots of ledges where birds and fairies alike lounged. Renée watched as fairies came and went through large open windows in each manor.

"Does anyone use doors here?" Renée shouted to be heard over the wind.

"They can," Lune yelled back. "Most prefer to fly instead of taking the stairs, but we do have them."

Ivy trailed up the walls and curled around a clock tower in the court-yard, where dozens of fairies were congregating around fountains. Some were splashing around inside, jumping on massive lily pads. It was the most beau-tiful place Renée had ever seen.

"Welcome to Daffodil Hall," Lune said as they came in for a landing on a large balcony several stories up.

They touched down, and Tresor and Lune let go of her arms. Renée imme-diately pulled Lune closer again, enveloping her in a hug. "Thank you." She turned to Tresor and paused. There was something about touching him again that felt too intimate. "And thank you . . . for . . . helping Lune, I suppose."

Tresor smirked. "Awfully big of you, Dubois."

"Tresor, what if she doesn't like being called by her family name?" Lune inquired.

"It's fine," Renée said. She found she strangely liked the way *Dubois* sounded in Tresor's voice—strong, sturdy, honored. So unlike her aunt's address.

Tresor stared at Renée, and she felt heat creeping up the back of her neck. Tresor seemed flustered, too. "In any case, I don't suspect we'll cross paths much now that you're here."

"We won't?" Renée stared at him and he stared back. Despite Tresor's arrogance, she felt oddly sad to see him go.

"I suspect you'll be placed in a different area of study than mine."

Renée frowned. "Placed?"

Tresor seemed like he wanted to say more, but a bell chimed on the clock tower, interrupting him.

"You better head back," Lune said, starting to sound impatient.

Tresor was still staring. "I won't say it was a pleasure meeting you, but I will say it was interesting, Dubois."

Renée threw him her brightest smile. "Likewise, Tresor-who-hates-mortals."

He sighed. "I never said I *hated* mortals. I just . . ." He shook his head and seemed to think better than to get into a lengthy explanation. He placed his hands in his pockets. "Good luck."

"Thank you. I look forward to meeting you again once I've mastered how to turn you into a toad," Renée crooned sweetly.

Lune snorted.

Tresor's eyes twinkled. "We'll see about that." Then he spun once, and disappeared in a glittering ball of gold light.

EIGHT

"I THOUGHT HE'D NEVER LEAVE," LUNE SAID, TAKING RENÉE'S ARM AS GLITTER lingered in the air where Tresor had just been. "I just hope he didn't make your first day too uncomfortable."

"Uncomfortable?" Renée stepped over a carpet of rose petals to follow Lune through the large window. "Why would I be uncomfortable?" She chuckled nervously, giving herself away.

"I know Tresor's my cousin, but he can be rather crotchety. And irksome! He's younger than I am, but he thinks he knows everything."

Renée's eyebrows raised. "How old are you?"

"Only eighty-seven," Lune said with a sigh.

Renée wanted to ask if this meant she would live to that age, too, and how long that would take in this peculiar place with its own sense of time, but Lune was moving on to the cavernous room before them. Flowers covered the ceiling, the floor, and draped the walls like paint. The scent was overwhelming. Renée caught a whiff of jasmine and honeysuckle. Maybe a hint of orange blossom.

She followed Lune to the giant atrium at the center of the room, feeling as if she were back outside. A supersoft green moss grew on the floor where a rug would be. Ivy decorated the walls and formed a canopy of wildflowers above their heads. Butterflies and birds flew in and out, chirping or buzzing with information to share, sometimes landing on furniture, other times on branches.

Lune stopped to prune a flower. "Wait till you meet Nelley. You're going to love her. She's our house mother. Nelley? Are you here?"

There was no answer. Other than the chirping, the manor was quiet.

Lune took off, flying past the endless levels dotted with curved windows. One that was lit up caught Renée's eye, displaying two floating beds with almost a dozen mattresses stacked on each frame. Several cabinets and paintings lined the walls at unusual heights. A mirror nearly touched the ceiling. A writing desk was held tight by the branches of a tree that seemed to grow out of the walls.

"Nelley!" Lune yelled from high above. "Maybe she's—"

As if in answer, a warm light suddenly flashed, and a woman appeared out of thin air.

The fairy was shorter than Renée and had a head of cropped white hair hidden beneath a robin's-egg blue hooded cloak. She appeared older than Margarite, or Iris, or any of the fairies Renée had encountered so far. In human years, she'd place the woman around seventy. But in the fairy realm, who knew? In her left hand, she held a tarnished silver wand.

"I'm here. I'm here," she croaked.

A small group of butterflies flew down to perch on the wall next to her, waiting, watching. The nearby flowers seemed to flourish at the sight of the fairy and turned their buds toward her.

Lune zipped down to join them. "I was getting worried."

Nelley waved her wandless hand at Lune. "Pfft. Worried. Can't a fairy disappear for a bit without the whole quorum whipping into a frenzy?"

"Sorry," Lune apologized. "You're just always here when we call."

Nelley touched Lune's cheek, her tone softening. "I was checking on a potential charge. Took me a minute to get back." She spotted Renée. "Ah, there she is. Hello, Renée."

Renée did a double take. "You know who I am?"

Nelley nodded, her blue eyes twinkling like stars. "What happened? Did Tresor give you some lip? Or was it Margarite?"

"How do you—" Renée started.

"I'm your house mother," she said by way of explanation. Her pale pink lips curled into a cupid's bow. "You've had an awfully hard day, child." She opened her arms. An invitation.

The butterflies stopped flapping and watched Renée. So did the flowers.

While Renée gave many hugs—to the children, to Anne when she snuck her pastries—it had been a long time since someone had offered her one. Suddenly, she missed her mother more than anything. She missed the children. She felt guilty that they were mourning her when she was alive and with the fée. The sound of Celine's and Raymond's laughter echoed in her head. Renée leaned into Nelley's embrace and started to weep.

"Shhh." Nelley patted the back of her head. "It's all right." The older fairy smelled like freshly washed linens and a hint of strawberries.

"She's having a difficult time understanding she can't go back to the human world," Lune told Nelley.

"Of course she is. She didn't get to say a proper goodbye." Nelley understood.

Renée wasn't sure how long she clung to Nelley, but Lune stood by quietly till Renée was all cried out. When she was finished, Nelley tilted Renée's chin up toward her own.

"You're going to be fine. Just fine. And so will Celine and Raymond. I promise you."

"But how do you know . . . ?" Renée started, wiping her eyes with the back of her hands.

"Child, house mothers know everything about the fairies in their care. My official job is fairy godmother." Her eyes twinkled. "But I've lived so long, I'm equally good at house mothering." She gave Lune a pointed look. "There isn't much that gets by me."

"Mother told me to go with Tresor, I swear," Lune told her. "The trip came up so quickly I didn't have time to tell you where I was going." She glanced at Renée. "And then, when I found Renée, I couldn't leave her there. Not like that."

"Of course." Nelley pulled a handkerchief from thin air and gave it to Renée. "This one is going to do marvelous things."

"I appreciate your optimism." Renée dabbed at her eyes. She had to admit, between the cry and the hug, she was feeling a bit better. "Are all fairies seers? Is this something I can learn, too?"

"Oh, I'm not a seer—I don't have a bulle—but I work with seers very closely," Nelley told her. "Our role in the fairy world is based on our disciplines. The Grand Verre knows how each fairy is best suited to help nature and the worlds at large."

"It is a magic mirror embedded in the waterfall below Marseille Mountains," Lune explained. "It's helped fairies find their way for centuries. You'll be taken to it when you start your training."

Renée tried to follow this logic. "A mirror decided Lune was going to be a seer and that you belonged as a house mother?"

"Well, it knew I was going to be a fairy godmother. I run the program with Greta. You'll meet her later. But I chose to live in Daffodil Hall, and eventually became house mother. A lot of the older fairies do." Nelley patted her hand. "This is a lot to take in at once, I know, but you have so many wonderful experiences ahead." Her face lit up. "Wait till you learn magic!" Her eyes widened. "Oh, forgive me, child. I know you already have had your first brush with enchantment—I heard all about the pepper."

Renée couldn't believe Nelley knew all this. "I don't know how I did that. Everyone seemed quite alarmed."

"Vegetable transformations aren't the norm," Nelley told her. "You might be the first I've heard to try it."

"Is it . . . frowned upon?" Renée asked.

"Not at all. But fairies around here get a bit jittery about new things." Nelley hooked her arm through Renée's. "They'll come around."

"With training you'll be able to do loads," Lune said. "Help flowers bloom, heal wounds, manipulate light, even— Well, I shouldn't say."

Lune and Nelley exchanged another pointed look.

"What is it?" Renée asked. "Did you see something in my future?" She paused. "How do you see things anyway?"

"Show her, Lune," Nelley said encouragingly.

Lune pulled out her wand—it was shiny green with flowers carved into the shaft. "Fae. Faerie. Be. Meant to be." A small round bubble appeared in the air in front of her, bobbing up and down as if it might pop at any moment. Renée watched curiously as the colors inside changed, moving like clouds.

"When there is something seers want to know, we call on our bulles to show us the way," Lune explained.

Renée longed for one of her own. "Can you check on the children for me? Better yet, do you see me visiting Celine and . . . Celine and . . ." For some strange reason, Celine's younger brother's name escaped her. "Celine and . . ."

"Raymond," Lune supplied.

The name came roaring back to her all at once as did the face of the little boy. How strange. "I can't believe I forgot him."

"It's a limitation of being part-fairy, I'm afraid," Nelley told her. "You may be forgetful sometimes and being forgetful can be a dangerous thing for a fairy. Along with the rapid aging in the human world and the inability to fly." Renée must have looked alarmed, because Nelley patted her hand reassuringly. "Not to worry. We will train your mind to be strong!"

"Training. Yes." Renée nodded. "I'm sure that will help. So, back to Celine and *Raymond*," she said, pronouncing his name clearly. "Does your bulle see me visiting the children again? Even just once?"

The fairies shared another look.

"What the bulle shows isn't a guarantee of anything," Nelley said gently. "Nothing is set in stone. We see different possible paths. Especially with humans. And the bulles' track record with part-fairies is limited. You're our first in a very long time."

It wasn't a no. She'd have to cling to that hope.

"Now why don't we show you to your room," Nelley suggested. Lune took hold of Renée's other arm, and they leapt into the air. "I assume you're staying with Lune." They flew several floors up.

"Absolutely," Lune said. "I promised Mother I'd keep an eye on her as she settled in."

"*I'll* keep an eye on her," Nelley instructed. "You simply be Renée's friend."

Lune smiled at Renée. "That I can do. I've lived on my own for fifty years and it can be so lonely!" As they passed a magnolia tree growing out of the wall, Lune plucked a flower from it. A new one grew right back in its place. "But with you here, I know we're going to be thick as leaves—pardon the fairy pun."

Renée felt a tingling sensation in her arms again. Was this magic? "I do, too. And I just know I can win over the other fairies. Like your mother."

"She's a tough nut to crack. Been through a lot. Like you, I'm afraid," Nelley said. "But you won't see much of her. She has her own manor and rarely visits Daffodil Hall."

She waved her wand and a thread of glitter seemed to lead from the wand to a glass atrium on top of a building across from them. It reminded Renée of a greenhouse. She only knew of a few families wealthy enough to have them;

Uncle Gaspian sometimes spoke of a botanist who used a greenhouse to grow medicinal plants.

"And Tresor? Where does he live?" She looked out the nearest window at the rest of the fairy village.

Nelley coughed.

"What?" Renée asked.

"Nothing," said the older fairy, looking away. "Just some pollen in my throat."

"Tresor has a room in Prickly Pear Hall," Lune told her. "But he usually hides out at his parents' old home in the southern ridge." She pointed out the window to the homes nestled in the countryside that Renée had spotted earlier.

Renée stifled a yawn. When was the last time she'd slept?

Nelley's eyes narrowed. "Bed!" she said firmly.

"But I still have so many questions."

"You can ask them tomorrow," Nelley insisted as she and Lune helped Renée up several cushy mattresses stacked on top of one another.

"Is this too high?" Before Renée could answer, Lune was already waving her wand. She tapped the comforter and multiple mattresses disappeared one by one till only four remained. "There! That's better." Lune tapped her wand again and a small step stool appeared, tall enough to allow Renée to climb in. "You should have no trouble now. I've already talked to the flowers—they won't bother you."

Nelley fluffed the pillows.

"Bother?" Renée tried not to sound worried as a hydrangea inched closer to rest on her shoulder. The bed was softer than the cloud they'd stood on at the ball, and it smelled like lavender.

"Sometimes they can get a bit clingy. They like to curl up with me while I sleep, but they know to leave you be," Lune said.

"Once you have a wand, you'll easily be able to communicate with nature and animals on your own," Nelley added.

My own wand. "When will that be?" Renée asked as her eyes began to flutter closed.

Nelley chuckled. "Patience, child."

Renée fought the urge to drift off, but the blanket was so soft and inviting. Several flowers curled onto the bed. She felt safe. She felt warm. It had been the longest day. Still, something was gnawing at her. "One last thing."

"Just the one," Nelley said lightly.

"Why is Tresor so mistrusting of humans? And who is Jules?"

The flowers started to retract. Nelley paused.

"All in good time," Nelley said finally. Her voice already sounded further away. "Just go to sleep, child. Sleep."

As Renée drifted to sleep, she was certain of one thing: She'd been given another chance at life. And she wouldn't squander it.

NINE

"Now don't be nervous," Nelley said as she fussed with the ring of daffodils nestled in Renée's hair.

"But this is a big moment," Renée said, trying to still her fidgety knee. "The Grand Mare and all that."

"The Grand *Verre*," Lune reminded her as she fluffed the skirt on Renée's new apricot gown.

"The Grand Verre, *Verre*, *Verre*," Renée repeated to herself, trying to commit the word to memory. Try as she might, she couldn't fight the hazy fog that seemed to descend on her out of nowhere, at the most inconvenient times. In the past few weeks, she'd mispronounced the word *fork*, couldn't recall the name of her favorite maid in her uncle's home (*Anne, Anne, Anne*), and almost—*almost*—forget the name of her favorite book (*Fairies among Us*). Worst of all was the afternoon she almost ate poisonous berries, having forgotten which ones that grew in the garden outside Daffodil Hall were safe to eat. Nelley stopped her just in time, but what if Nelley hadn't been there? Renée had no idea how frustrating this part-fairy limitation would be.

"We should head over," Nelley told her.

Renée took her now familiar stance, arms out at her side, ready for Nelley and Lune to fly her. But this time Nelley shook her head, pulling out her wand and pointing it at the window on the balcony. A stream of sparkle shot out, and then a swirling circle of light appeared.

At the other end of the light was a waterfall and mountains. Renée looked at Lune, gobsmacked . "Is this a portal?"

"No. It's a shortcut," Lune said. "It works for especially enchanted places."

Renée hesitated half a second, then she stepped through the light, expecting to feel . . . well, she wasn't sure what—a burning sensation? Her body waffle or shimmer? Instead, it was as simple as opening the kitchen doorway at Uncle Gaspian's and walking outside. Except this time, she was now in a meadow with tall grass, the sky above a mixture of swirling blues and oranges. A few yards away she could see the mountains and at the base a waterfall where dozens of fairies in rainbow-colored robes were waiting on either side of a stone-lined path. Along the walkway waved the most vibrant wildflowers Renée had ever seen.

"I don't see the Grand Verre," Renée whispered, looking for a mirror.

"You will," said Nelley, taking one of Renée's arms as Lune took her other. "When the ceremony starts."

Renée was suddenly so nervous she thought her legs would give way. "Can you go over it again? Just one more time?"

"When a fairy comes of age, they stand in front of the Grand Verre, and their future self is reflected back to them, specifically the type of magic they shall cast most often," Nelley explained. "That's how we know what they are meant to do, their fairy discipline, as it were."

Renée frowned. "And what if the Grand Verre is wrong?"

"It's never wrong," Lune said. "It was made by the seers of yore and the magical waters of the Marseille Mountains. It's as old as this dirt beneath our toes. The Grand Verre knows how each fairy can do their part to protect nature. And how nature can best serve each fairy. It's a sacred relationship. What the Grand Verre tells us, we follow."

"But didn't you say future-telling isn't exact? What if there are multiple paths for one's discipline, too?" Renée wondered. "Or what if a fairy grows tired of the work she's doing and is ready to do something new?"

"I haven't seen it happen before," Nelley admitted. "Then again, you're not like most fairies."

Renée smiled, sensing Nelley's warmth behind her words. "In any case, I already know what I'm meant to be," Renée went on. "A fairy godmother."

Lune and Nelley glanced warily at each other again.

"That's admirable of you," Nelley started. "Many fairies do not wish to travel between worlds."

Lune bit her lower lip. "And, of course, you remember what we said will happen if *you* cross to the other side?"

"I do, but I've decided we can find a way around that," Renée told them, her eyes on the water up ahead. "I was a governess in my other life. I'm good with children. People. Animals. I care about nature. The human world's relationship with it. I would make a good fairy godmother. Even if I was only able to cross over a few times."

"It's a rewarding job but draining, too," Nelley said. "Trying not to get too attached. Knowing your time with a charge is limited—even for fairies who have endless visits to the mortal realm. Realizing that sometimes what you want and what's better for the world are two different things." She sighed. "I love being a fairy godmother, but there are many wonderful jobs for a fairy to choose from that aren't so emotionally draining."

Renée wasn't worried. She knew godmother was the right discipline for her. She anxiously eyed the fée lined up in front of the shimmering water, dressed in robes. Each one raised a wand at the water as if ready for something.

"What are they doing?" Renée wanted to know.

"Summoning the Verre," Lune explained.

They took their places next to a group of younger-looking fairies wearing satin suits and pastel dresses adorned with flowers, talking and laughing among themselves, some perhaps a little too loudly. Renée knew immediately they were waiting to be assigned, just like her.

"The Elders let the Grand Verre know a new group of fairies is ready," Nelley added. "Normally new fairies come alone, but we knew you'd have questions. That's why I came along with Lune." Her blue eyes were a bit guarded, if warm. "I know the last few weeks haven't been easy. You have had a lot to adjust to. And I'm, well, I'm . . ."

"You're my house mother," Renée said, trying to hide the rising emotion she knew was coming if she thought too hard about Nelley's kindness. "I appreciate you being here with me."

"Good." She could almost hear the smile in Nelley's voice. "I don't want you to worry about a thing. Even the appearance of Margarite."

"The queen is coming?" Renée looked around worriedly.

"She'll be here any moment," Lune said.

Fairy dust started to flutter through the sky as if it had heard them talking. Seconds later there was a bright light and then the queen appeared. Her expression was so fierce she reminded Renée of a sudden summer storm, the kind that blew in out of nowhere, bending trees like taffy and making even the most level-headed human quake. Renée couldn't help being taken with the queen's dress; layers of pink tulle fabric were interwoven with fresh flowers that she also wore in a crown on her head. Iris landed next to the queen, a scroll and a quill in her hands.

"Welcome," Margarite said, her voice soft but firm. "Today we invite young fairies to join the ranks of those who walked this earth before them. They will learn the unique ways they will give back to nature. One by one, I ask you to come forward, stand before the Grand Verre, and learn your destiny."

There was murmuring among the fairies. Renée felt tingling all up and down her arms.

"Open the Grand Verre," Margarite commanded.

All at once, the caped fairies lowered their hoods, lifted their wands higher, and pointed at the waterfall again. A burst of light projected from each wand, crossing till they formed one beam that bounced off the water and back, bathing everyone in brightness. Renée shielded her eyes. When she looked back, the water had frozen. Then it began to shimmer iridescently and reflect the scene on land—the Elders holding their wands.

A young fairy stepped up and the crowd stilled, watching. At first, the Grand Verre only showed her reflection, her broad stance, her cerise shift, the twitch of her wings. Then the water started to waffle again, and the same fairy was shown flying alongside blue jays and eagles, among a complicated web of clouds.

"Anastasia, you are a future sky architect," Margarite said as Iris quickly took note. "Congratulations."

The group before them broke into polite applause. The young woman turned with pride and received a royal-blue robe.

Next, a fairy in green walked up to the Grand Verre. Moments later the water shifted and then the same boy appeared sitting in a meadow, in conversation with a deer.

"Jasper, you are a future animal whisperer," Margarite said as someone handed the fairy an amber robe.

One by one, fairies took a step up to the frozen waterfall and awaited their fates. There were far more fairy jobs than Renée even knew. Nurturing naturalists who communed with the earth. Fairies gifted with song who led orchestras of birds and crickets, others who gardened and farmed. Fairies who had the gift of healing and fairies who wrote soliloquies. None, however, were called to be godmothers. The closest they came were human-fairy relations positions, which seemed like a specific type of seer, watching the human world from afar to make predictions.

Finally, it was Renée's turn. Nelley gave her hand a squeeze, and Lune smiled encouragingly as Renée walked past the Elders. She stopped at the base of the waterfall, her toes curled over the edge. Then she took a deep breath and stared at her reflection, studying her wild hair, her freckled skin. No one would know she was no longer mortal if it wasn't for her chiffon dress or the faint glow that surrounded her. *I want to be a godmother*, she thought. *I am meant to help humans.*

The water began to waffle, and Renée held her breath.

Her reflection smiled back at her, then disappeared.

Renée blinked. Had this happened with the others? She glanced back at Nelley worriedly and heard fairies whispering. Someone gasped and started pointing.

The water rushed down the side of the mountain straight at the Grand Verre and stopped right before the sheet of glass. Then images started to appear in rapid succession—Renée talking to a horse, petting its mane. Her kneeling at a tree, picking up a small yellow slipper. Her pointing out a fairy ring in the grass to Celine and Raymond. Renée felt tingling again. Was that her just a few weeks ago? Why was she being shown her past instead of her future?

There was more murmuring, which sounded almost like a wave, voices growing louder. More water flowed down the mountain and the Verre started to waffle again.

"It's all right," Margarite assured the group. "The Grand Verre is just taking its time."

But the water kept shifting, moving from one image to the next—past and present. Did it just show an image of her waving a wand? Why was she working with a giant pumpkin? Before she could understand what was happening, there was a rumble and the water burst forward like a geyser, soaking Renée.

Lune and Nelley came running, and Nelley quickly used her wand to dry Renée off. "Are you all right?" Lune asked worriedly.

"I've never seen the Grand Verre do that before!" Renée overheard a fairy say.

"It's her part-fairy nature—she's broken the Grand Verre!" cried another.

Others gathered round, talking in hushed tones and staring at her. Renée tried to stay calm.

She glanced at Margarite. Her mouth was in a tight, thin line. "I'm fine," Renée told everyone, her eyes on the queen. "I don't know what happened. Did I do something wrong?"

"The Grand Verre is unsure," an Elder declared. "It doesn't know where to place the girl. You must decide, Margarite."

Renée looked at Margarite hopefully. *Godmother. Godmother. Godmother.*

Margarite stared at her pensively. Iris held her quill at the ready. Finally, Margarite waved her wand and a beige robe appeared. "Welcome to the fairy ring corps, Renée. Report to training at once."

TEN

RENÉE TOOK THE ROBE FROM MARGARITE AND PUT IT ON. SHE TRIED NOT TO appear disappointed.

While beige could be a lovely color—it reminded her of mushrooms, the tone of Raymond's hair, waving wheat fields—this robe was dull, almost colorless. It needed something. Ribbon, certainly. Why did only some fairy robes have ribbon? How lovely this would look with a pop of brightness. Maybe yellow like the dress she was wearing.

Just like that, a yellow daffodil from her crown of flowers extended its stem and curled around the collar.

"Much better," she told the flower, hoping it could understand her. The flowers certainly seemed to be attuned to what she was thinking. She looked left, then right. Most of the other fairies, now wearing various colored robes, were staring.

Renée smiled, hoping she seemed friendly. The fée turned away. Nelley and Lune had rushed off, leaving her alone, once the Grand Verre had placed her. . . . Well, it hadn't exactly placed her, had it? Margarite had. And that was fine. She would be the best fairy ring creator this world had ever seen.

"Which way to fairy ring study?" she asked the flowers. A vine from her crown came down and pointed its leaves to the right. "Wonderful." She started to go back the way she'd come through the meadow when Lune and Nelley caught up with her.

Lune placed a hand on her arm as her wings fluttered along behind her. "I'm so sorry, Renée. I rushed off to talk to Mother about what happened and your placement, but I couldn't get her to reconsider."

Renée kept her eye on the path up ahead. She could see the manors and dormitories in the distance. "Don't worry about me. I'm fine!" Renée wasn't sure she wanted to admit what just happened was unnerving. Had she somehow broken an ancient fée mirror just by standing in front of it? "I'll do what I was assigned and then when I master this skill, I'll move on. No one is meant to do just one thing in life."

"Well, that is one way to think about—" Nelley stopped short, listening for something Renée couldn't hear. Even so, Renée's arms started to prickle.

"I must go. A charge needs me. Good luck with training," Nelley said, waving her wand above her head in a clockwise circle, before there was a flash of light and she disappeared, leaving fairy dust in her wake.

Renée stared at the shimmery particles. "So that's it? She appears in the human world now?"

"No, she has to open a portal, but . . . Well, let's focus," Lune said, hurrying alongside her. "Are you sure you're all right with what just happened? And your assignment?"

"Why wouldn't I be?" Renée tried to stay positive. "Margarite must feel I would be good at this fairy rings corps if she gave me this assignment."

Lune made a face. "Yes, well . . . I just thought you might be more upset. You have so many feelings. It's not the most valued trait here, to be honest. You might have noticed fairies are not the best at expressing our emotions."

Renée thought of Tresor. "I have gotten that impression. And I may be a tad disappointed, but I can turn this all around. I'm sure of it!" She smiled. "And you and Nelley don't seem like other fée. You are both so affectionate."

Lune lifted a delicate shoulder. "Nelley and I are compassionate. Maybe it comes from being a seer and her being a godmother. But others aren't as in touch with their feelings. Most fairies believe any emotion besides joy is useless, more trouble than it's worth. They think humans are a little ridiculous when it comes to all that." A bell tolled in the large clock tower in the manor courtyard, and Lune left the conversation there. "Anyway, I just want you to be content with what you're studying."

"I will be! Fairy training in itself is exciting, and I'm familiar with fairy rings." Renée touched Lune's arm. "They're a little dangerous, no? *Fairies among Us* said that mortals who stepped in one would dance until they died."

Lune blinked twice before she burst out laughing. "What a wives' tale! No, the rings are beacons for any fairies headed to the human world. For godmothers, or scouts—those who inspect the area beforehand. So they know it's safe. The human-fairy relations task force uses them, and the diversion tactics team practices in rings when they're doing evasive maneuvers." Her face turned serious. "When we shrink, we can appear to be prey, so it's important to learn how to avoid being a sparrow snack."

"Good idea," Renée agreed. "So my job seems very important. I will do it well."

"I'm sure you will. Ah, we're almost there. Hurry now!" Lune shrunk down and flew ahead, reaching the door to a large castle in the center of the square. She materialized full size again. "Welcome to Faerie Training Academy!" She opened the door slowly and Renée walked inside, feeling reverent and thrilled all at once.

Above her, dozens of fairies were walking, flying, and floating around a great hall at least ten stories high. At the very top was a glass dome that allowed dusty light to cast a glow over the entire building. Balconies on each floor jutted out of the walls at various levels, where classes appeared to be taking place. Renée read floor signs with interest—human-fairy relations, fairy management, living off the land, fairy *mis*management, wand repair, portal malfunction, fairy archive society, and a department of fairy fashion. She didn't see anything about fairy godmothers anywhere. Where did they practice?

Lune flew ahead of her. "We have over fifty divisions here for the purpose of tutoring newly-of-age fairies in their fields of study and helping others complete upper levels of coursework in magic, spells, flight, and wand instruction."

"Wand instruction," Renée repeated enviously.

"You'll get there. You'll need to take the stairs each day, unlike the others. They aren't easy to find." Lune tapped a wall and a staircase swiveled out of the wall. "On second thought . . ." Her wand appeared in her hand. "Fae! Faerie! Be! It's meant to be!" A small cloud appeared under Renée's feet, and she was floating alongside Lune.

"That phrase . . ."

Lune grinned. "My magic words. Words are powerful, especially those catered to your type of enchantment. As you find your way around the world and connect with all of nature's gifts, your own magic words will come to you. They can be long. Short. Spoken. Sung. There really aren't any rules." She took Renée's arm again as they flew upward. "Okay, level one has some of the basic fairy skills—forestry, tracking. Your fairy ring classes will also be here."

There were two tree-covered balconies where fairies in dark green robes practiced spells. ("You see a bear! Fly above it!" a trainer was calling out on one balcony.) On the other balcony a group of fairies in brown robes were magically placing tulips on a pillow of soil in circular patterns. ("Leopold, how do you expect them all to get equal watering that way?" a teacher scolded.)

They continued to ascend, spotting fairies poring over books as large as a table. Three fairies worked together to turn the page on a book marked *Fae-Story*, while three more were talking to books with blank pages that appeared to be filling with text.

"Fairy storytelling is on this level," Lune explained, "along with deciphering runes and the archives."

Renée perked up. "Are there archives about godmothers?"

"Those are kept in the library," Lune said. "Every godmother mission is recorded—both the wishes they succeeded in granting with positive outcomes and the ones that . . . well, didn't go as planned."

Renée wanted to ask more, but Lune was already floating them to the next level, where a group of fairies were working on spells using wands. She could hear them calling out commands as a group, sparks of glitter surrounding them. ("You need a flower to bloom—NOW! Transform that vine into a tree—NOW! Disappear—NOW! Quicker!")

On the next level was animal training. Renée watched as a fairy was attempting to converse with a piglet, while another appeared to be having a full conversation with a group of goats.

"Protectors and healers add small bits of magic to all realms," Lune explained.

Renée read a small gold sign with interest. "Fairy concoctions?"

"You didn't think humans came up with the concept of dessert, did you?" Lune asked continuing upward.

The next level showcased a group standing on a cloud ten times the size of Renée's, while fairy teachers called out directions:

"You're light like air!"

"The breeze is flowing around you, and look!"

"That's it!"

"Give your wings a rest!"

"You can float!"

They passed several more floors—fairies working on potions, practicing spells, learning how to spot wrongdoing, learning how to find good, and testing out magic words. There were so many different fairy skill classes, Renée wasn't sure she'd remember them all.

Renée looked around. "What about Tresor? Where does he study?"

"He's on the botany floor, nearest the atrium at the top because they have the best light. That's where the fairy godmothers are, as well."

Renée tried not to look too interested. "Are we visiting that level?"

"I want you to see the fairy scouts first."

They soared over to a classroom that looked like a grassy knoll. It was dotted with little dewy pools that shimmered with glimpses of mortals. Renée could have watched the scouts work all day. She loved hearing every detail about them looking for humans in need. Renée wondered if she couldn't be a godmother, might she become a scout? At least then she could be able to see Raymond and Celine for a moment while she was searching for potential charges. Was that how someone had found her as a child?

"And this is my level," Lune said, coming in for a landing on a balcony where fairies were standing in front of tables staring at iridescent bulles. "Seer studies. I've been working here the last twenty years, but I don't attend regular classes anymore. Only when I need refreshers." She sighed. "I miss it though. Maybe I should sign up for another seeing eye course."

"What does your vision show you?" a fairy was asking the group as she floated around the room, her wings fluttering fast as she went table to table. "Really concentrate. We need to see the truth, not what we want to be true. There is a difference." The fairy looked up and spotted Lune, winged her way over. "Hello, Lune." She had purple eyes and hair that fell to her shoulders. She eyed Renée with interest. "And Renée Dubois. You've caused quite the stir."

A tinkling bell rang, and fairies put away their bulles and flew into the air. They crisscrossed the air in front of her and it was all Renée could do to keep from getting in their way. A pack of female fairies she recognized from the ball knocked into her as they flew to another level. Another familiar fairy flew straight at her. Her expression was strained.

Iris appeared, waving her wand in front of them. "You should be in class by now," she said stiffly, as Renée's little cloud started traveling downward at an alarming speed.

"Have fun!" Lune said, waving to Renée.

"But how do I . . . Where is my—" Renée started.

"Down there!" Iris and Lune shouted together as Renée plummeted faster and faster.

ELEVEN

Renée did not like feeling out of control.

Not being able to fly had been more of a problem than she anticipated. Using her own two feet to go everywhere in this fast-paced land was proving to be difficult, but she didn't want others to always fly her around either. She'd have to master her own magic, and fast.

"Excuse me! Coming through! Sorry!" Renée shouted now as she continued to descend.

"Watch it!" snapped a fairy as Renée's right leg clipped their wings.

"Don't you know how to fly?" griped another.

"No!" Renée yelled back, making the fairy gape in recognition.

Yes, she was the new resident part-fairy. Make way! Coming through!

Finally, the floor started coming up fast, and Renée braced herself. But her body slowed down and she softly hit the ground of the first-level balcony. A gold sign on the door told her she was in the right place: FAIRY RING STUDIES.

"First class," she said to herself with excitement, brushing herself off and pushing her way into the classroom.

A dozen fairies turned.

"Hello!" She waved. "I'm Renée. It's nice to meet you all."

The other students looked away, whispering with their heads close together, their pointy ears twitching.

Renée chose not to let it bother her. This was a chance to learn how to make a proper fairy ring, something Margarite seemed to think she'd be good at. She was going to prove herself worthy of her estimation.

She looked around the room. The scent of wet earth greeted her, the air thick and humid. On one side of the class lay vegetable beds with signs identifying various types of mushrooms. The walls of the classroom had been spelled to evoke the morning sky.

An older fairy in spectacles and a beige robe flew to the front of the room. His name magically appeared on the wall in a loopy scrawl: *Mr. Agaricus.* "Take your rocks, please."

Fairies zipped around the room, gathering in pairs to sit on large stones. By the time Renée walked to the front, every rock was taken.

"You can sit with me," said a small voice in the back.

"Thank you!" Renée hurried over to the fairy perched on a mossy stone in the last row. "I'm Renée."

"Oh, I know," she said. "I'm Peony." She shook Renée's hand. She had shimmery gold skin and wild blond hair that couldn't be tamed by the flowers woven into her curls. Renée could see her dress underneath her robe had a tear in the skirt, and there was mud on the hemline and all over her legs. Making fairy rings was clearly a messy job.

Peony raised her voice. "Unlike some fairies, I'm not afraid of mortals." A few of their classmates glanced over.

"Thank you," Renée whispered.

Peony smiled. "My great-grandmother was a fairy godmother and her stories about the mortal world were magical. With the limited years humans have, they sure do a lot."

"We're quite motivated," Renée agreed.

"My mother said when she was a girl most fairies *wanted* to be godmothers. It was the discipline every fairy hoped the Grand Verre would say they were destined for." Peony made a face. "But that was before . . ."

"Jules?" Renée guessed.

Peony's green eyes widened. "No one really talks about him."

"Why?" Renée leaned forward on the rock. "What did he do?"

"All right, class," Mr. Agaricus called over her, his voice flat. "Can anyone tell me the difference between a false morel mushroom and a puffball mushroom?" No one answered. "Anyone?"

Renée's hand shot in the air. Mr. Agaricus consulted the scroll in front of him, then looked up again. "Ah. Ms. Dubois. Our newest student. You know the answer?"

"I do. Hello! A puffball mushroom is round and creamy white in color. They are mostly harmless and sometimes can grow as large as a watermelon and appear pear-shaped."

A few fairies looked over at her with interest.

"And how do you know this?" Mr. Agaricus asked.

"We kept a vegetable garden at home. In the human realm," Renée explained. "Our cook loved all types of mushrooms and squash. Cucumbers. Tomatoes. The children and I would harvest them."

Mr. Agaricus blinked. "Very good, Ms. Dubois." He looked at the others. "Then you must also know that mushrooms are the most important vegetable there is. You will use them to create your fairy rings, homing beacons for those fée making the treacherous journey across realms."

Renée pictured the fair folk traveling the countryside looking for rings. She didn't want to hurt Mr. Agaricus's feelings, but it seemed like the rings should be constructed by many types of vegetables. They needed color. And flowers to give the rings a certain je ne sais quoi! Maybe she'd suggest this after a few classes.

"Now who can tell me what the fungus that produces small threads is called?" He looked around.

The other thing that occurred to Renée as Mr. Agaricus continued to discuss fungi was how she had seen exactly two rings in the human world. One on the grounds of their home when she was a child. And the ring near the river that she and the children visited. Who were those rings created for? It couldn't be a coincidence that she'd lived near a fairy ring at both of her homes and been saved twice as well.

Mr. Agaricus cleared his throat and picked up one of the samples on the rickety desk in front of him. "Now let's go through every species of mushroom—in all realms— alphabetically."

"Ooh." Renée sat up straighter. "This is exciting."

Peony looked at her. Her hands were resting on a book called *The History of Fungus*. "You think?"

"Yes!" Renée gushed. "I didn't realize how important our jobs were. We'll be traveling to the human realm to place the fairy rings ourselves."

Peony side-eyed the others, making sure no one heard them. "That's the part everyone is worried about. The first day we go out on assignment, there will be several meltdowns. I'm sure most will sit the trip out, sending their ring through the portal instead and hoping it gets where it needs to go, instead of placing it there themselves. Even if they only enter the human world for a bird's song, everyone is panicked that they're going to jump through and not be able to get back."

"Why wouldn't they want to see the human realm? If only for a moment?" Renée asked. The queen had probably intended for Renée to send her rings through the portal, instead of going herself, and a bird's song was not a lot of time. But it was a start.

"Because of what happened when . . . you know."

Renée nodded, but of course she didn't know. She wondered if she could tactfully ask Peony for more information about the part-fairy called Jules.

Peony looked around. "Personally, I'm surprised to see so many students here. Usually, fairies make an appeal to Margarite to be in a discipline that has little to do with the mortal realm."

Renée frowned. "I can't believe others wouldn't want to visit, even once. There's so much beauty there. And the people . . ." She thought of Celine and Raymond. "There are some wonderful humans."

"Are there?" Peony seemed curious for a moment, but then she quickly shook her head. "Oh, we're not to engage with the humans, of course." She looked down at her dull robe. "That's why we wear these—to blend into the surroundings. Though it does nothing for my complexion." She glanced at Renée's robe, the collar adorned with yellow flowers. Flowers had even worked their way down the robe, making the fabric look patterned. "I like what you've done with yours."

"Thanks." Renée touched a bud and it rested on her hand.

Peony straightened her shoulders. "Maybe I should adorn my robe, too. I just discovered my magic words this week. . . ." She glanced at Mr. Agaricus. He had his back turned to the class as he inspected mushrooms and continued his lesson. She closed her eyes. "Fleur! Fleurs! Fleurir!"

Renée watched as Peony's plain robe began to sparkle and suddenly a white flower sprouted from the robe, near the shoulder.

Peony grinned. "I was hoping for several, but considering my magic words are still so new, one flower will do."

"It's wonderful," Renée agreed. "I can't wait to learn my magic words and spells."

"They're challenging, but there's no better feeling than when you get a spell right," Peony told her. "My cousin Mona is in plant science and she's working on one that helps plants thrive in difficult climates. The other day, she spelled a dragon fruit so it would grow in the snow. I'd love to do that."

"You should take that class next," Renée suggested.

Peony's smile wavered. "It doesn't work that way. We all have spell courses, flight training, and diversion tactics, of course, but we can't pick specialty lessons." She sighed. "We must pursue the discipline the Grand Verre decides for us."

"And what if the Grand Verre sees several options for your future?" Renée pressed.

Peony looked pensive, a pout forming on her bright pink lips. "Well, that would be impossible."

Renée shook her head. "It's not. It happened to me. This morning."

"Really?" Peony's white flower turned to look at Renée. "The Elders must have panicked."

"I wouldn't know," Renée admitted, watching as Mr. Agaricus flew several mushrooms around the room. "We left quickly. But my point is, once we know how to make fairy rings, we should be able to try out a new program. One can be good at more than one skill, don't you think?"

Peony looked up at the cloudy ceiling pensively. "Hmmm . . . I never thought of it that way before."

A bell rang.

"That's all the time we have for today," announced Mr. Agaricus, sounding bored. "Please proceed to your next class."

Renée paled. "I'm not sure what mine is."

"Don't worry. We travel as a group," Peony said, gathering her books. She offered Renée her hand. "Next is spell work." She pulled a face. "With Ms. Sneezewood."

TWELVE

Renée might have been excited to meet Ms. Sneezewood, but the teacher did not appear to reciprocate the sentiment.

"Why don't you take a seat in the back," Ms. Sneezewood said, using her wand to wave to a table that was set several feet apart from the rest of the class. "And when you're practicing, perhaps you should face the wall in case we have any . . . mishaps."

Peony raised her hand. "Ms. Sneezewood? Doesn't Renée need a partner?"

Ms. Sneezewood faltered. "Uh, yes. That is true. We do work in pairs here." She coughed. "What is the first rule of memorizing spells?" she asked the class.

"If unclear, say the spell loud for all to hear," the class repeated, their voices a flat murmur.

Renée applauded. Everyone turned.

"Yes, Renée?" Ms. Sneezewood's expression was tight.

"Sorry." Her voice felt too high. *Don't say anything*, she told herself. But she couldn't help it. "I was just thinking about how, when I was a governess, I made up funny little songs to teach the children to remember important details. So I might add something like *'Use your voice, in all its shades. Practicing aloud is brave!'*" she sang, her voice soft, but growing stronger as she played with the words. The flowers on her robe gazed up at her. Buds all around the room looked over. Ms. Sneezewood gave her a look.

"And to remember to do so with a partner, perhaps, *'Spell together, mind the weather, the magic will be swayed!'*" Renée continued.

Peony burst into a round of applause, but Ms. Sneezewood did not look pleased. In fact, Renée was pretty sure she saw the teacher's nostrils flare. "My version has worked fine for the last fifty years," she said. "Not that you need to memorize anything in here. I don't expect you'll be able to master many spells in my class. Part-fairies, in my limited experience, are quite absent-minded. We wouldn't want you forgetting how to float up to a cloud, and plummeting to your death."

Renée paled thinking of her swift descent earlier that morning. "No, that does not sound pleasant." Despite this, she wondered if perhaps her little ditties could be a way to combat her new forgetfulness. Maybe Nelley could teach her some memory spells. It didn't sound like Ms. Sneezewood would be very helpful in this department. "I'm sorry to have interrupted."

Ms. Sneezewood smiled stiffly. "Take your seat in the back, Renée."

"I'll join her," Peony offered. "We can be partners."

Ms. Sneezewood waved her off. "Suit yourself."

Renée trudged to the back of the classroom. The last table was closest to the balcony, so when she looked out, she could see fée in other classes across the way. Some laughing, others talking. Clearly eager to learn. That's all she wanted.

She sat down and exhaled. One of her flowers seemed to curl under her chin. "Thank you," she told the daffodil as Peony took the seat next to her.

"I liked your song," she told her. "What does it matter *how* you learn a spell as long as you learn it? Don't let Ms. Sneezewood bother you."

Renée perked up. Peony was right. "Thank you! That's what I was getting at."

There was a rap of a wand at the front of the room. Ms. Sneezewood cleared her throat. "Let's return to the spells we were practicing yesterday. As I mentioned, fairies without wand pairings will need to concentrate more on the task at hand. For simple spells, this is easy. You're probably already doing many of these things without realizing it. Perhaps seeing family members do the same. Focus solely on what you want to happen and it will. Let's start with a simple one," Ms. Sneezewood instructed. "Close your eyes and signal fairy dust to gather around you, letting nature know you are at work."

Renée looked around in wonder as fairies at every table closed their eyes and began to glow, glitter surrounding them like an aura. It was the same effect Lune and Tresor had when she first met them. But how did one do that? She turned to ask Peony and found her new friend already glittering, dust sparkling around her like fireflies, her expression one of utter concentration.

Close your eyes, Renée instructed herself, and then what? Ask dust to appear? *I am a fairy*, she tried. *Fairy dust materialize!* She opened one eye. Nothing was happening. She sighed, sensing she was being watched. *Fairy dust appear! Appear!* It didn't.

"Well done, *most* of you," Ms. Sneezewood said, her eyes landing on Renée's sharply. "Now please demonstrate a float. Remember, even if your flying skills are preliminary, all fairies can float with minimal effort."

Students all around the room, including Peony, began to rise, hovering a few feet off the floor. Did she even bother trying to do the same? Lune and Nelley said she couldn't fly. But could she float with a spell? Renée closed her eyes again and tried imagining herself in the air. *I'm weightless! I'm one with the sky!* She opened her eyes and looked down. Her bare feet were still firmly on the ground.

"Wonderful!" Ms. Sneezewood told them. "Now we're going to try something that combines both spells—levitating an inanimate object." This caused a twitter around the room.

Peony looked at Renée. "This is a tricky one. Don't worry if you don't get it right away."

Renée nodded. If her other spells hadn't worked, this one had little chance of working either.

Ms. Sneezewood waved her wand. "Trees! Fly! Free! That's me!" she shouted, and suddenly there was a sunrise-colored peach in front of each student.

Everyone applauded, including Renée.

"I want each of you to concentrate on lifting the fruit off the table." Ms. Sneezewood closed her eyes and the peach in front of her started to rise, till it was at the same height as her head. "I don't expect you to raise it very high your first time. A thimble's distance is enough."

Renée gazed at the peach in front of her. *Rise!* she told it, to no avail. *Lift!* That word didn't work either. She thought about the previous two lessons. *Fairy dust, help us float*, she tried. No luck. She looked around the room. Fairies at several tables had managed to make their peaches hover. Ms. Sneezewood was walking among the desks issuing praise.

She looked over at Peony. Her eyes were closed, and her lips were moving. Her fruit started to waffle and then began to roll. Renée caught it from falling off the table. "So close!" she said encouragingly.

Peony sighed. "How is it going for you?"

"Not well." Renée heard laughter and looked up.

"Peter! I didn't say to eat the lesson! We are using that peach again!" Ms. Sneezewood scolded.

Most of the fairies had their peaches bobbing in the air now. Peony and Renée were the only ones who couldn't make the spell work. Ms. Sneezewood's eyes narrowed as she spotted Renée again.

"She's coming over," Peony said. "Look like you're working hard."

Please, peach. Renée tried again. *Even just a twitch!* Still nothing. Peony, however, was getting her peach to shake again. Then it started to float into the air before smashing back down on the table, bruising the fruit.

"It worked!" Peony crowed.

"Again," Ms. Sneezewood said by way of praise.

Peony placed the peach in front of her again and closed her eyes. This time the peach began floating up till it reached her shoulders. Renée applauded.

"And you? Anything?" Ms. Sneezewood asked, an almost smug smile on her blue lips.

Renée shook her head. "I'll keep trying."

"Right. Well, as I said, part-fairies do have trouble with spell work."

Renée felt her face grow hot as the teacher walked away.

Peony turned to the wall where baskets of fruit were nestled in large wooden boxes. "Here," Peony said kindly. "Try a strawberry. They're smaller." She placed one on the table in front of Renée.

Renée narrowed her eyes. *Strawberry . . . fly . . . strawberry!*

"Don't stress," Peony said. "My mom said it took her weeks to learn how to open a window. Finally, she realized spells worked best when she danced as she cast them. Works for her every time."

Dancing, Renée thought, swaying back and forth as she concentrated. *Strawberry, float! Float, please!* It didn't move. Renée sighed, trying not to feel too disappointed.

"Strange. I've heard of radishes being prickly, but not strawberries." Peony tapped her long fingernails against her waist. "Should we try something else?"

"I guess it couldn't hurt," Renée decided. She glanced at the fruit boxes. Beneath the strawberries was a bruised pear, lopsided and almost overripe. "How about this one?"

"Try it!" Peony placed the fruit on the table and Renée stared at it.

Okay, pear. Let's see if you can fly. We'll do this together, all right? If I am to prove myself worthy of this education, if I am to see Celine and Raymond again, I need your help, Renée implored with her mind.

The pear stayed where it was.

Renée frowned. If dancing or attempting to connect with a piece of fruit wouldn't work, she would try something else. She thought back to the beginning of the lesson. What would happen if she sang to it?

"Use your voice, in all its shades. Practicing aloud is very brave. Floating is fun. Floating is free. Pear, take to the air for me," she sang softly. The pear started to rock.

"It's working!" Peony cried, rushing to stand next to Renée.

Renée kept going. *"Floating is fun. . . ."*

Her voice grew stronger, clearer, and the pear reacted to it, lifting into

121

the air a few inches. Around the pear was a glow of fairy dust popping and glittering.

"Keep going!" Peony shouted, and others in the class turned to look, including Ms. Sneezewood. "Singing works for you!"

Renée felt goose bumps. She was doing it. She was casting a spell! She didn't care if she was the only one singing to a piece of fruit. If it worked, she'd do it every time.

"Floating is fun. Floating is free. Pear, take to the air for me!"

The pear continued to rise, lifting higher till it rose to eye level. Renée grinned at Peony. Her new friend's expression faltered.

"Is that pear getting bigger?" Peony asked, starting to retreat.

Renée looked back. "Oh my." The pear was indeed growing, doubling to the size of a watermelon within seconds.

"That's enough now, Renée!" Ms. Sneezewood shouted.

"I'm not sure how to stop it," Renée said anxiously. She wasn't sure what spell to use to reverse the damage either. Nervously, she started to sing her song again.

"Floating is fun. Floating is free. Pear, please stop growing for me!"

The pear just got larger, bloating to the size of the table.

"Renée . . ." Peony panicked, taking a few more steps back. Renée grabbed her hand. She was worried she'd fall off the balcony if she kept going.

"Shrinking is good. Shrinking is grand. Pear, become the size of my hand!" Renée tried.

The pear refused to listen. The table cracked as the pear outgrew the space it had been in. A chair crumbled beneath the giant pear's weight. It would destroy the classroom in mere moments.

Fairies all around the room began to notice. They started shrieking and flying out the windows in a panic. Peony pulled away from Renée and looked for somewhere to turn. Ms. Sneezewood came running.

Ms. Sneezewood aimed her wand at the fruit. "Arrête! Arrête!" she tried, but it was no use.

Renée couldn't catch her breath. She heard fairies screaming and saw the fée from the other balcony pointing and shouting. "Move out of the way!" she called to the stragglers. But it seemed the pear was the one that listened instead. Seconds later, the fruit ricocheted toward the balcony, straight at Peony.

"No!" Renée cried, rushing for the first friend she'd made in the academy, and pushing her out of the way just as the pear crashed. The motion sent Renée free-falling off the balcony.

"Help!" came Peony's shout. "She can't fly! Someone help her!"

Renée could hear others screaming as she fell through the air, reaching uselessly for something to grab on to. This wasn't like last time when Lune helped cushion her flight down. She was going to crash and there was nothing she could do to stop it. Just as Ms. Sneezewood had predicted. She closed her eyes tightly and felt something slam into her.

Someone wrapped their arms around her midsection as the hit sent her and the other fairy tumbling head over feet. They landed hard on the ground. The pear flew past them, crashing into the ground and cracking it, rocking the surrounding buildings.

Renée turned her head to see her rescuer and recognized the gold eyes immediately. "Tresor!" She failed to hide her surprise.

"Dubois." He gave her a satisfied smile. "So we meet again."

THIRTEEN

Fairies swarmed on the scene, talking at once and hovering over the absurdly large pear. Tresor was still planted firmly on top of her, as though the fruit were still a threat.

"Could you please get off of me?" Renée asked, trying hard not to make eye contact. He smelled like pine and his close proximity was making her skin tingle.

"Right, yes. Of course," Tresor said. He picked himself up, offering his hand. Renée couldn't help but notice he was dressed in a white shirt that was only half-buttoned.

"I can stand on my own, thank you," Renée said, smoothing her dress with a shred of dignity even though every eye was on her. Renée glanced at the fruit wedged into the ground beside them. How had this happened again?

"Renée!" Peony flew in and threw her arms around her, hysterically crying. "Fairy be! Are you all right? I can't believe you saved me instead of worrying about yourself. You can't fly!"

"I guess it's a good thing I can," Tresor said cheekily.

The group of fairies she had seen following Tresor at the ball rushed over to see what was going on.

"Tresor saved her! That girl is so lucky she almost got killed by a pear," one of them said.

"I know," another said with a sigh.

"I wouldn't need his help if I could fly!" Renée snapped. The fairies gaped at her. "I certainly don't need this . . . this . . ." She stared at Tresor, trying to think of the appropriate word to describe someone so infuriating and egotistical (whether he smelled good or not).

"Savior?" he tried, and the other fairies beamed contently. "Fée in shining armor?"

It burned Renée how much he was enjoying this. "I could have figured out how to cushion my fall on my own, thank you!"

Tresor raised his left eyebrow. "Really? And you were waiting for the right moment, then?"

Suddenly, Ms. Sneezewood flew in to survey the damage. She looked mutinous. "Renée Dubois, we cannot have fairies mis-spelling and causing disasters! Peony could have been killed! And what are we supposed to do with this oversized rotten fruit now?"

Renée's cheeks burned. Suggesting a dozen pear pies did not seem wise. "I'm sorry, Ms. Sneezewood. I'll clean this all up."

"Ms. Sneezewood, it was her first day," Peony said, trying to placate the instructor. "And she's bleeding." She pointed to Renée's left knee, which had blood trickling down it. There was a very nasty gash right above it as well.

If there was one thing Renée was not good at, it was blood. Anne always handled bandaging the children if they got a cut or scrape. The sight of red made Renée sway. "Oh—oh, I'm fine." Clearly, part-fairy or not, she could still bleed.

"Tresor? Would you help Renée take care of that, please, before she stains our beautiful floor?" Ms. Sneezewood asked, shooting her one last look of disapproval for almost getting herself killed on her first day of class. "Then she can return and get rid of this mess."

"Yes, Ms. Sneezewood," Renée said miserably.

Tresor placed a hand on Renée's back. She jumped at his touch. "Sorry," he said. "I was just going to fly us out of here. Unless you'd prefer to levitate. Since you don't need any help."

"We can fly, thank you," Renée said stiffly.

Tresor pulled out his wand, muttered something under his breath (did his magic words include the word *vine* or *divine*?), and they were airborne, flying fast past the other fairies, toward the now-empty balconies near the top level.

She hadn't had a chance to explore this area with Lune. The sunlight was much brighter here, warming her skin as they touched down on a balcony covered in vines. Across the way was a much larger balcony that was hidden by vine-covered gates with big blue letters made from iron: *F* and *G*.

Fairy Godmother.

Renée felt her skin begin to tingle.

"Why are we up here?" Renée asked as Tresor walked ahead through the brush and disappeared. Renée followed, noticing the heavy foliage that concealed bright oranges. Beyond the tall grass was a pumpkin patch and a pear tree. There was also a row of apple trees and cucumbers as large as her arm. The balcony was clearly a trick to the eye because the pumpkin patch seemed to extend several acres.

"This is the botany balcony. I have some ointment here that will clear that wound up." Tresor returned with a jar of what appeared to be oil mixed with large leaves. He knelt beside her. "Can you lift the hem of your dress please?"

Renée firmly pressed her hands against the soft fabric. "I beg your pardon?"

"So I can put a salve on your knee and bandage you up?"

Her cheeks started to flame again. "Oh. Right." Renée pulled her dress hem up an inch. She wasn't sure she could look down at Tresor while he did this.

He opened the jar and poured the liquid into a wooden bowl. Next, he added several herbs and used a pestle to grind them up. Then he gently applied the salve to her wound.

Renée looked away, feeling slightly woozy at his touch.

"I heard you gave the Grand Verre quite the challenge," he said, blowing on her knee to dry the ointment.

She inhaled sharply. "It could see I'm able to do many things in this province. Not just one."

"Starting with fairy rings."

She watched him wind a bandage around her knee. "Your aunt picked that one. And for someone who dislikes mortals so much, you sure know a lot about what's happening to me."

He shook his head and opened another container. It smelled like lemons. "I don't dislike you, Dubois." His voice was softer. "And neither do the others. They're just scared, especially to see you in training. We haven't had someone like you here in a long time."

Renée frowned. "Are you saying I shouldn't be allowed to learn magic?"

"Not at all." He looked up at her. "Quite the contrary."

She felt a little tingle ripple across her arms and she broke eye contact. "What is that salve made of?" she asked, changing the subject.

"A mix of lemon balm, burdock, calendula, and mullein, with some apple thrown in. The acid in the apple keeps the mixture from turning." He waved his wand over the rest of the concoction in the bowl, and it poured itself back into the empty container.

"Fascinating. How did you figure out how to combine these ingredients?"

"I study botany." He put a lid on the container and placed it on a tree stump. "My job is to learn about plant life, fruits, and vegetables. How they interact with everything in their environment. Like learning what plants and herbs when mixed together make the best treatments."

"Do you enjoy it?" She noticed his discarded dark green robe near his other tools.

He paused. "The Grand Verre felt I was meant to be a botanist."

Renée picked up on his tone. "And you don't?"

He wouldn't look at her. "I didn't say that."

"You didn't say you enjoy it, either," she said lightly.

"Did you enjoy learning how to make fairy rings?" The question felt like a challenge.

"I'm sure I will," she said, lifting her chin. "Fairy rings are valuable tools for fairy godmothers, and I plan on making the most spectacular fairy ring the queen has ever seen."

He chuckled. "Fairy rings always look the same. That's the point." He stood, offering her his hand again. This time she took it. "There is no need wasting effort on making one fancy."

Renée walked around the vibrant garden. "How is making something beautiful wasteful? A fairy ring that enhances nature and is beloved by all feels right to me."

"The queen's not going to change her mind—about any of it." Tresor had his back to her now. She could see him busy cutting herbs. The second he clipped one, the leaves magically reappeared. "If I were you, I'd devote my energy elsewhere."

Renée ignored him and looked across to the other balcony and saw a group of fairies in blue robes. Nelley was standing in front of the gates waving students inside. "How long must they train before they start journeying between worlds?" she asked, motioning to the godmothers.

"Even godmothers can't go on assignment without consulting seers first." Tresor moved a large vat of mushrooms from the table to a grassy knoll a few yards away. "No godmother goes on assignment without checking the appointment chamber first. If you and Lune aren't godmothers, what were you doing in the human world the night you found me?" she asked.

"There are fairies who must make brief visits to the human world for their work, but all crossings are approved by my aunt first. She was the one who insisted Lune accompany me," he explained.

"So there *are* exceptions to the rules," Renée guessed.

He sighed. "Yes, but those exceptions are limited. As are portals. There are very few now and only the queen can open a new one. She's the one who opened the one in the cave that led us to you that evening."

"Really?" Renée asked, curious. "Are you saying that portal isn't always there?"

Tresor gave her a sharp look. "Don't worry yourself about portals. *You* should not travel to the human realm, because of how your human body will react."

Renée scratched her cheek. "I know. That's why I find it so curious."

He cocked his head to the side. "Find what curious?"

"That your aunt would allow me to work on fairy rings. Why send me to a discipline that has anything to do with the human world at all?"

Tresor frowned. "I'm not sure. Maybe because those who work on fairy rings don't *have* to travel for their work, strictly speaking? Regardless, crossings to the human world are limited. Even fairy godmothers must work with seers to rule out immediate threats before traveling between worlds."

Renée didn't understand. "Threats?"

Tresor's brow pinched. "A charge placing a trap, for example."

"Why would a charge want to trap a fairy?" The idea seemed preposterous, but the moment she saw Tresor's expression she knew she was wrong.

"It happens," he said softly. "That's why my aunt closed most of the portals. There are only a few that remain all the time, like the one in her office and the one in the fairy godmother chamber."

"But there are two portals?" Renée asked, unable to hide her curiosity.

He gave her a look. "Don't get any ideas. I don't know what my aunt would do to you if she found out you had snuck access to a portal."

Renée looked down at her patched knee. Her first training had not gone as planned, but she wasn't about to give up. Maybe she'd have to work harder than any fairy who'd ever trained before if she wanted to learn spells, but she'd do it. She'd learn magic. She'd be granted a wand.

She looked up at Tresor again, her mouth forming a thin line. "I don't need to *sneak*." She thought of Celine and Raymond. *Raymond, Raymond*, she repeated to herself. *I will see you both again.* Renée smiled. "When the time comes for me to cross over, everyone will know about it."

FOURTEEN

Months flew by like days, weeks seemed like hours. When Renée wasn't in class, she was practicing spells with Peony, peppering Lune with questions, or trying to get Nelley to tell her more about Jules. "I really think it would help to know more about part-fairies that came before me," Renée would say.

But Nelley was good at being evasive. "No need sharing something that might distract from your training, dear. You worry about your own journey and let me handle the gossips."

But gossip, the fae folk did. And fête. From what Renée could tell, there were fairy soirees almost nightly. Peony went to many and begged Renée to join, but without an official invitation, she felt strange doing so. She decided improving her spell work was key to establishing herself in the fée community.

In private, away from prying eyes. And so Renée gravitated to the one place where she could practice in peace: the library.

Renée had never been to a library in the human world. Maman and Papa's few tomes had been lost in the fire, and Uncle Gaspian's manor had a couple of books for the children's studies, or ones her uncle would bring back from his travels. Here in Faerie Province, there were books on every subject one could dream of. If there was any place that could help her learn more about honing her magic, it would be here.

Like everything in the fairy realm, the library was stunning. It was a dozen stories high, a glass dome twinkling at the top, with shelves that extended all ten floors. Made perfect sense for the fée, but for a trainee who hadn't yet learned to levitate, it made research a bit complicated. She couldn't reach a single book above her head without using one of the rickety ladders attached to the shelves or asking the librarian, Lady Opus, for help. Every time Renée wanted a book, the woman had to fly up and down the room retrieving tomes. ("Here," she finally said the other evening. "Read this book on levitation. *That* is the first spell you should master.")

"Hello, Lady Opus!" Renée greeted her now, placing a few books on an empty table (as usual, she was the only one there. Outside, she could hear the festivities starting. They'd provide just the right amount of background noise.)

Lady Opus stopped her. "I'm off to Blossom Bright's party, so I won't be able to fetch books for you today."

They both looked over at the nearby ladder warily. The first time Renée had used it, a rung had broken off when she was midstep. The wood was quite old and was extremely brittle. Of course, there had been no reason to update it till now.

"All right," Renée said with fake cheer. "A bit of exercise will do me some good."

Mrs. Opus didn't return the optimism. "If you fall, no one is here to catch you," she said, grabbing her things and flying out the window. "Just remember that."

"Of course," Renée said as Lady Opus flew away. "Have fun!" She decided this was as good a time as any to try levitating. She closed her eyes and tried singing about taking flight. *"Flutter! Feet! Float! For me!"* She thought the rhyming would help. It didn't seem to make a difference. She waited to feel some tingling.

Ms. Sneezewood said there would be tingling.

There was no tingling.

All the library books said that spells came easier once a fairy found their specific fairy magic words, but Renée hadn't come up with anything that worked. She suspected not having magic words was holding her back. Peony's *Fleur! Fleurs! Fleurir!* had only gotten stronger. Lune's phrase was also made up of words that started with *F.* Nelley's was an old riddle.

It didn't help that Renée couldn't even request a wand till she passed the Wand of Enchantment test, which she'd heard was a doozy. Maybe she'd grab one of the pre-wand training books on this visit. But she also needed to read up on fairy ring design. And she figured, while she was alone, perhaps she could find some sort of record about Jules. Lune had said the library contained extensive archives, after all.

Outside, music was beginning to play, the strains of a flute and a violin making Renée long for an evening nap. Reaching for the ladder, she began to climb and didn't look down. That was the key. Move quick, find the books, and get back to ground level. The fairy ring design books turned out to be under *F* instead of *R*, so she found those a few levels up and tossed them to the floor instead of trying to carry them. (Lady Opus would be horrified, but desperate times.)

She wasn't sure where information about Jules would be shelved, however. Renée moved slowly, eyes scanning the section headings. Maybe *human* under *H*? Or *mortal* under *M*? She bit her lip, proceeding another few rungs before she heard a snap. A rung went flying below her foot and for a split second she panicked, gripping the railing, yelping despite her best efforts not to.

She heard a gravelly voice. "Renée Dubois, what in the love of fairies do you think you're doing?"

Renée winced. "Hi, Nelley."

The fairy flew over to the ladder and hovered in the air beside her, looking aggravated. "Child, what did I tell you about playing with heights, after the pear incident? These ladders are as old as me. They're decorative."

Renée moaned. "Lady Opus is at a fête, and I needed a book."

Nelley's eyes crinkled. "Didn't want to attend Blossom Bright's party?"

Renée said nothing, pretending to study a shiny spine in front of her.

"Ah." Nelley sighed gently. "You weren't invited."

"It's fine." She lifted her chin. "I've been to many parties. And I have work to do."

Nelley's fairy dust swirled around her. "Oh child. They'll come around."

"I hope so." Renée looked up. "Can you help me get to the *M* section? I need a book on . . ." She paused. "Making fairy rings."

"*M* huh?" Nelley pulled out her wand and did a spell so Renée could float. "Those books are under *F.* Which you knew, because you already tossed them on the floor."

Renée let go of the rung. "Were you spying on me?" she asked, her eyes on a book in front of her called *Myths vs. Facts about Elves and Fairies.*

"I was alerted that there might be trouble," she said simply.

Renée smiled. "You and Tresor are two peas in a pod."

Nelley smirked. "That boy has more heart than you think. It's why he— Now you're going to get me saying things I'm not supposed to. Can we float to the ground level, please?"

Renée looked up at the *M* section high above and tried not to be disappointed. She'd had such high hopes for the evening. Her mind went to the children again and her heart ached. "I guess. If there's nothing up there about any other part-fairies. Particularly ones named Jules." The flowers on her robe seemed to quake at the sound of his name.

"Don't upset the mums," Nelley scolded. "They only bloomed yesterday."

Renée started to descend fast. "Sorry."

Nelley zipped over. "Are you coming down on your own?"

"I—I am!" Renée realized. "But I didn't do anything. It just happened."

"Interesting." Nelley scratched her chin with her wand. "Let me ask you: When the pear started to enlarge, what were you thinking about?"

"Celine and Raymond," she admitted. "How I used to teach them, how I wanted to see them again."

Nelley's fairy dust began to glimmer. "Then your power may have something to do with the children. . . ."

Renée's arms began to tingle. Was that it? "But I thought I had to say something to make it work, ideally my magic words."

"That's how most fée enchant." Nelley's blue eyes sparkled and her thin lips curled into a small smile. "But you are not most fée. Perhaps the way you enchant is a combination of words and memories."

Celine. Raymond. It wasn't hard to think of them. She was getting used to Faerie Province and was excited by what she was learning, but she still missed her cousins every day.

Nelley waved her wand and all but one of the books flew onto the table. "I want you to try something. I want you to try picking this book up with magic."

"I can't." Renée panicked. "What if I accidentally make it grow to the size of this room?"

"Then I'll be here to shrink it. Think of the children and this book and make it rise."

Renée squared her shoulders. "All right." *Celine. Raymond. Book.* The book began to waffle.

"Keep going," Nelley instructed.

"Celine. Raymond. Book. Celine. Raymond. Book," she sang, watching the book start to rise, then fall again just as quickly. Rise. Fall. The book didn't lift more than an inch before tumbling down again. She sighed, putting her arms down. "Oh well. At least the book didn't chase me out the window."

"No. It didn't." Nelley scratched her head. Then she waved her wand and the book turned into a pear. "Try it now."

Renée groaned, tripping over the newly transformed fruit. "Not another pear. I'll just make it explode and then Lady Opus will have my head for destroying a library collection that has existed hundreds of years."

"Try a thousand." Nelley waved her wand at the pear again. "Don't be nervous. I'm here if anything goes wrong. We're collecting knowledge, learning what connects with you."

Renée sighed. It was an interesting technique, something she might have thought of during a particularly tough lesson as a governess. Renée squared her shoulders again and stared at the piece of fruit. *"Celine. Raymond. Pear. Celine. Raymond. Pear."* The fruit started to roll then rock back and forth.

"Keep going," Nelley encouraged.

"Celine. Raymond. Pear." The pear rocked faster and suddenly it began to grow. *Oh no*, she thought. *Not again.*

"Keep going!" Nelley pressed.

"Celine. Raymond. Pear." The fruit grew to the size of the book it used to be. Then the size of a lamp. It kept growing, soon becoming the size of a boulder as Renée kept singing.

"Stop!" Nelley shot a burst of light at the pear, and it returned to normal size. "Fairy be, that was incredible! How did you do that?"

"You mean almost destroy the library? I don't know," Renée quipped.

"It's fascinating. Fairies usually need a specific spell to grow things that rapidly and even then, it is complicated." Nelley grinned. "That's what's so wonderful."

Renée didn't understand. "Enlarging fruit and creating killer pears? What would be the point of that?"

"It's a new skill! Where's that wild imagination of yours, child?" Nelley cried. "Maybe you'll need to use an apple to make a hut if your journey takes you too far from home. Or zucchini to craft boats in a pinch." She grabbed Renée's arm. "Don't you see? You're doing magic no other fairy does! The pear wasn't a fluke!"

Renée's arms began to tingle, Nelley's excitement contagious. A cucumber boat. An orange cave. A carrot as a mode of transportation in the rain . . . "You're saying I can actually do magic?"

Nelley laughed and kissed the top of Renée's head. "Yes, child! You're trying magic that's never been done before!"

At this news, Renée took Nelley's arms and began to swing her around. "Can we show the queen? Perhaps she would reconsider if she knew . . ."

Nelley stopped short. "The godmother business?"

"Yes," Renée said. "You saw the Grand Verre. It said I could do many things. Why couldn't I train as a godmother as well?"

Nelley hesitated. "It's not a simple answer. And I don't want to disappoint you. You have many talents, child. But godmother . . . that ask is nearly impossible. Even before Jules took so much from the queen."

Took. That word was new. "What happened, Nelley? What is it the queen distrusts about humans? How can I change her mind?"

Nelley looked sad. "She lost so much. The path to changing her views on this will be a rocky one."

"I'm not glass. I can take it," Renée said fiercely.

Nelley held her gaze. "Good. Because if you're going to succeed, you'll need to be better than any fairy that has come before you."

FIFTEEN
Lune

WHEN LUNE RETURNED FROM BLOSSOM BRIGHT'S PARTY, SMELLING OF bonfire and with powdered sugar still on her lips, Renée wasn't in their room.

The practical side of Lune knew there was no reason to panic. How far could Renée get without wings? Despite all her practice, magic wasn't coming easy. She hadn't even learned to levitate yet. (*Could* she? Lune wasn't sure.) She had promised her mother she'd look out for the girl.

When Lune asked her mother if Renée was in the right discipline, given the Grand Verre's confusion, her mother had bristled. "All fairies are perfectly suited for one area of study," she'd said. "Clearly her part-fairy status confused the Verre. That's why I intervened. There's nothing more to it than that."

But Lune wasn't sure. When she found Renée by the river, she'd had an inkling the girl was meant for more. The river wasn't where her journey ended. And when she'd consulted her bulle later that night, when Renée was fast asleep on the other side of the room . . . a not insignificant prophecy had appeared. A prophecy Lune had only shared with Nelley.

"Renée?" Lune called now. No answer. *Hmmm* . . . Lune flitted through the air, searching the common areas of the dormitory—the garden, the lounging patios, the honey drip tearoom—keeping an eye out for Nelley as well. She'd know where Renée was. But the house mother was nowhere to be found in Daffodil Hall, either.

Lune closed her eyes, wings twitching. Consulting her bulle wouldn't help. The object only showed snippets of what might happen. Or, if she focused, what was happening in real time. But she had to have a location. A tingling deep in her gut told her that she was missing something.

She took off out the window, soaring over glass rooftops. She glanced down over the library, one of Lune's favorite buildings in Faerie Province. Maybe that's where she was. Renée loved how the light filtered in through stained glass windows; how ivy had found its way inside, trailing from floor to ceiling, yet somehow knew not to extend too far and disturb books.

Lune flew through an open window and didn't spy Lady Opus. She frowned. That was strange. Lady Opus never left the chamber unguarded, and she doubted Mother knew Lady Opus had left early. The library was sacred. Not only did it contain books, but it had records on human encounters, charges, potential wishes, and detailed accounts of fairy history. Even the most unpleasant parts.

Mother didn't like anyone but godmothers looking at stories about humans, and even then, after all that had happened with Jules, she didn't grant requests to read old records lightly.

Lune heard a laugh and looked down.

Renée and Nelley were dancing around on the ivy-covered stone floor.

"I have unique magic!" Renée was shouting. The flower blossoms followed her, swaying in delight.

Lune stopped short, fluttering in mid-air. "You have unique magic?" Lune repeated, now excited.

Renée and Nelley looked up, brightening as soon as they spotted her.

"She has her very own specialty!" Nelley whooped.

"A specialty!" Renée parroted. The flowers around her began to grow and bud, their vines slinking toward her.

They are so taken with Renée, Lune thought. She made a note to ask Tresor. He was a botanist; maybe he'd have a theory as to why.

"Tell me everything," Lune said, coming in for a landing beside them. "Did you learn how to levitate? Can you summon fairy dust? Talk to squirrels?"

"Nope. I can't do any of those things," Renée said, sounding happy despite this news.

Lune was confused. "Well? What can you do?"

Nelley and Renée looked at each other, and Renée laughed harder.

"I can transform fruits and vegetables!"

Lune blinked. "I'm sorry?"

"She can enlarge them! *Purposefully!*" Nelley said. "Which means she can use them for other things. Temporary shelter! Turn them into a table, or a soft peach into a bed. The possibilities are endless. No one else has done that before, have they?"

"Er, no." Lune wasn't so sure this one spell was the breakthrough Nelley thought it was, but she didn't want to discourage them. "That's . . . great!"

Renée's brown eyes widened. "Want to see me do it?"

"All right," Lune said slowly. "This isn't going to be like the pear, is it?"

"Not at all." Nelley placed a peach on a table next to them. "Renée has things under control. Show her."

Lune watched as Renée closed her eyes, concentrating, and singing under her breath. Within seconds the peach started to rock and grow, a sparkly haze surrounding the piece of fruit. She stopped her song and the peach halted, frozen at the size of the table. That's when Nelley used her wand to shrink it back to size. Renée grinned at Lune triumphantly.

"Well done," Lune said, amazed. "Your first intentional spell!"

Renée frowned. "I wonder if it has anything to do with my garden back home—I mean in the human realm. I planted vegetables and my uncle said he'd never seen such a bounty from a little patch. Maybe the skill is related?"

"Maybe." Lune wasn't sure there was a connection, but she wanted to be positive.

"There's so much I want to learn," Renée gushed. "Even beyond spells. Identifying parts of Faerie Province, for instance. Learning what animals are allies of the fée. And all the types of flowers that can aid a fairy." She picked up one of the books on the table and pointed to a hand-drawn flower on one of the yellowed pages. The bud was white and resembled a teacup, cushioning a ring of golden stamens in the center. "It says this flower can help a person grow several inches *and* cure hiccups!" Renée studied the writing, squinting hard to read the fine print. "The gan-la-mee-a."

"Gannelmera," Lune and Nelley corrected.

"A flowering tree," Nelley explained. "We have several in the greenhouses if you want to see one up close, but you should be forewarned—it isn't as friendly as other flowers. It bites."

Renée frowned. "Flowers can bite?"

"Yes," Lune told her. "When a plant can grant a wish, it comes at a price. Leaves a scar even magic can't remove."

"Do not use gannelmera! Do not use gannelmera . . . do not use gannelmera," Renée whispered over and over, closing her eyes, trying to commit the rule to memory. "What flowers should I befriend, then?"

Nelley picked up a large tome and dropped it on the table with a thud. "There are more than forty thousand species. Some are good in potions, some are poisonous, others fragrant, some only bloom once, others bloom annually. There are flowers who thrive in daylight and ones in moonlight. If we tell you about all of them, we could be here for weeks."

Renée's eyes widened. "Forty *thousand*?" Some of her newfound momentum seemed to deflate a little. "How am I going to remember them all?"

Lune noticed Renée's shoulders were starting to sag. She was a bubbly thing, and from what Lune could tell in the time she'd known Renée, the girl was very driven. That would serve her well. But Lune also knew the brightest fires burned out the quickest.

"I study so much, but sometimes I forget what I've read an hour before," Renée added, a note of discouragement in her voice.

"I told you—the more you practice, the more you'll sharpen your mind," Nelley reminded her. "You will get there."

Renée nodded, her hands tensing. Flowers curled around her shoulders. "I just want this to work. I want *all* of it—the risks you've taken, not being there for my cousins—to be worth it. Growing produce aside, this all seems to come so much easier to everyone else."

Lune frowned. There was that human emotion again. Just a moment ago she was brimming with joy, and now the threat of a sudden tear storm. But as she watched Renée's eyes blaze, she noticed the peach on the table start to rise.

"Are you doing that?" she whispered to Nelley.

"No," Nelley said. Her blue eyes widened as the peach kept levitating without Renée noticing. "Fascinating." She flew to Renée and clutched the girl's hand. Then she looked at Lune. "I think she's ready for some news about them. Don't you think?"

"You have news of Celine and Raymond?"

The peach shot up fast and Lune heard a tiny ping as it hit the atrium ceiling. Renée looked up. "How did that happen?"

"You did that," Nelley said with a chuckle.

"I did?" Renée blinked.

Nelley nodded. "At first, we thought sharing what we learned about Celine and Raymond might upset you, but now I wonder if it would help."

"Agreed," said Lune, smiling softly at Renée. "She has a right to know."

"Know what?" Renée pressed. "Are they all right?" The more she talked, the more the flowers around her began to wind around her legs. Books on the ground began to rumble and rise.

Lune tried not to stare. Clearly, Renée was capable of more than she had realized. "They're all right. *And* someone appears to be watching over them."

Renée's shoulders rose. "They have a godmother?"

"We think so," Nelley said, nodding. "When Lune consults her bulle, she can sense fairy dust surrounding them."

Renée's eyes welled up once more, this time gratitude shining in them. "Oh, thank you for telling me this. Can you find out who their godmother is?"

Lune and Nelley looked at each other and wondered.

It wasn't against the rules, was it? "We are in the library," Lune started to say. "And every charge *does* have a file."

Renée's interest seemed piqued. "That means I have a file, too. Can I see it?" she asked Nelley.

"Your file? Maybe—" Nelley started to say.

"Nelley," Lune warned. "Mother won't be happy."

"Pishposh. What she doesn't know won't hurt her." Nelley flew up to an upper level.

Renée locked eyes with Lune. The girl would not give up. Lune smiled. She liked that about her. "Let me help." She flew off, too, leaving Renée below.

"Thank you!" the girl called up to them.

Lune opened the closest records cabinet high above the towering bookshelves. A black puff of smoke emerged that made her choke. The ivy around the cabinet shrunk. Lune read the label—*Villains in Need of Hope*—and closed the drawer.

"This is exciting! I can finally thank my godmother properly," Renée was saying. "I've always sensed her nearby. That's why I called to her when Raymond . . . well, that night."

"Peculiar that you would have been saved twice," Nelley mused, opening several drawers at once with her wand and peering inside. "And also strange that I've checked the *R* and *D* files now twice and there is nothing on a Renée Dubois."

146

"How can that be?" Lune wondered. Every charge had a file. How could Renée have been visited—multiple times no less—without one?

"So, fairy godmothers can only appear once to their humans?" Renée asked. "But they still watch over them? Even after the wish is granted?"

"They can visit more than once. It's complicated, but they do keep track of their charges, even post-wish." Lune opened a drawer marked *In Peril*. Dense fog seeped out.

Nelley closed a drawer marked *Wars and Famine*. "Of course, there's not much we can do after a wish is granted. That's why we're always so careful with them." She looked at Lune, lowering her voice. "There are no files on her."

"Or Celine and Raymond," Lune said, her skin tingling. "But I *know* I saw them with a fairy!"

"What are you two whispering about up there?" Renée called.

"Just comparing notes!" Nelley shouted back, accidentally opening a file drawer marked *Siren*. A piercing shriek filled the large room. The flowers wilted, and glass panes started to crack. Nelley quickly closed the drawer. The two flew back down to Renée empty-handed.

The girl looked at them. "Nothing?" Renée asked, and the flowers started to slink back toward her. Flowers could never stand to miss out on good gossip.

"No files," Lune confirmed, looking over her shoulder as several flowers seemed to bloom out of nowhere at this revelation. "I don't understand. There has to be a reason I was able to hear you when you called for help."

Renée thought for a moment, then her face broke into a wide smile. Flowers around her grew buds instantly. "That's all right."

"It is?" Nelley asked.

"You saw the children being protected," Renée noted. "And we know I have someone looking out for me, too. That's what's most important—someone here seems to care a great deal. Even if it isn't necessarily the fée way. What could be a greater gift than that?" Renée added.

Lune shook her head, confusion giving way to awe. This girl was going to be all right. Better than all right. She was going to shine. She could feel it. Prophecy be damned. "Nothing," she replied. "Absolutely nothing."

SIXTEEN
Renée

For the first time in her fairy life, Renée had an audience.

While they waited for Ms. Sneezewood's class to start, other students gathered round the table, clamoring to see Renée work.

"How are you doing that?" asked one.

"Do it again. Can you?" asked another, her wings smacking the girl behind her in the face.

Flowers slowly wound their way around the table legs and crawled onto Renée's table to watch, too.

"She can show you," Peony said proudly. "Do it again, Renée."

Renée had been honing her fruit and vegetable spells for weeks, always with Lune, Nelley, or Peony there to supervise, per Margarite's request. When one of the culinary fairies had admonished Renée for using too much of their bounty, Lune had started smuggling out the discarded and spoiled produce for her to enchant instead. Renée found overripe gourds worked the best. To avoid further waste, she'd started using their seeds to grow her own little hidden vegetable patch behind Daffodil Hall.

Now Renée stared down the squash on her desk. Taking a deep breath, she thought of Raymond running through a meadow. She pictured Celine carefully carrying a small thimble of milk for the fairies. She heard Uncle Gaspian reading to the three of them from *Fairies among Us*. Slowly the gourd began to tingle and glow. *"Grow, honey,"* she started to sing, her voice soft. *"Please don't flee! Grow, little sprout. I have no doubt you can be, all you want the world to see."*

Fairies gasped as the gourd grew and grew, its vines starting to lengthen over the edges of the table, the gourd turning from yellow and green to a soft orange before it was the size of the window. Then it stopped, gracefully curling its vines into a braided pattern upon the workspace.

The fairies around her began to clap. Renée had never heard such a delightful sound.

"Is that a pumpkin?" a male fairy asked.

"A giant pumpkin," said Peony, who'd already seen this magic at work several times.

A girl frowned and placed her hands on her hips. "Why would anyone need a pumpkin this large?"

"I'm not sure, but isn't it pretty?" Renée asked, patting it fondly. It was pale peach and had a squat, flattened shape with a long, light brown vine. Unique, like her.

"It kind of resembles a musk cucumber," said the first fairy again.

"No, it's definitely a pumpkin," Peony insisted.

"Regardless, it's a beauty," Renée told them all, and the gourd grew a few more centimeters in size as she cooed at it. "Look at that! Do they normally grow that quickly?"

"Not at all," said another fairy, removing her hood and coming closer to see the progress. "Pumpkins are some of the most stubborn produce in Faerie Province." She looked at Renée suspiciously. "What's your secret? It's the singing, isn't it?"

Renée brightened for a moment. "I do think the singing helps, although I haven't tried it with other spells. Only on edible objects so far." She scratched her chin. "I might have to look into that. Perhaps botany will be my next area of study."

The fairy's nostrils flared. "Fairies don't choose new disciplines."

Renée grinned. "That's what they keep telling me." If she had her way, she'd try every type of class she could wiggle her way into.

A bell tinkled and fairies scattered quickly, but Peony and Renée had nowhere to hide. This was their assigned table, which meant Ms. Sneezewood flew through the balcony and found a mutant gourd dominating their workspace.

"What is this?" she asked disapprovingly.

"Renée can enhance fruits and vegetables," Peony said with pride. "Isn't it lovely, Ms. Sneezewood?"

The teacher's lips curled into a deep frown. "When would we have the need for a giant gourd?"

Renée was prepared for this question, thanks to Nelley. "Maybe we could use it for . . ." She cleared her throat and started to sing. *"Fee fiddle dee, I would love if you became a seat for me!"*

The gourd began to sparkle and then it started to shake before it started to glow bright and transform in front of their eyes into an orange rocking chair. Peony cheered while the rest of the fée gaped. Ms. Sneezewood just glared.

"Clean it up," she said, flying off to the front of the classroom. "You're going to need your workspace for more important things than gourds today."

Renée tried not to be disappointed, but clearly her emotion came through loud and clear because the pumpkin immediately started to shrink . . . as did her confidence. "I thought she'd be impressed," she said quietly.

"Well, *I* am," Peony said loyally. "Something like that would look splendid in Daffodil Hall. I bet Lune and Nelley would agree." She smiled shyly. "What you're doing is amazing—learning new spells. Trying new things. Wanting to do more."

"You think so?" Renée asked.

Peony's eyes widened. "I do. It makes me wonder . . . I mean, I don't know if it would work for me, too, but it kind of makes me wish that maybe . . . Just maybe . . ."

"Go on," Renée said, moving closer to hear her.

"That maybe I could try a discipline other than fairy ring crops, too," she said, looking relieved to have gotten the idea off her chest. "Like tailoring?" She pulled back her beige robe and revealed a lily-white dress underneath with a beaded bodice. "I've been playing around with designs for a dress for the Summer Solstice Ball."

"Oh, Peony! It's beautiful!" Renée gushed. "You made that?"

She nodded. "I know it needs work, but—"

"It's perfect. I'd love to wear one of your dresses someday," Renée told her.

"Really? Thank you." They smiled at each other.

Ms. Sneezewood cleared her throat loudly.

"Oh. Here. Let me help clean this up." Peony closed her eyes, and her lips began to move. Seconds later, the pumpkin vanished.

Now it was Renée's turn to applaud. "You're getting really good! Maybe we shall take botany together."

Peony beamed. "I'm not going to get my hopes up. Still, we have other things to celebrate: Are you going to the Summer Solstice Ball?"

"I don't usually attend the soirees," Renée said, not mentioning her lack of invitations.

"It's in two weeks' time." Peony's green eyes brightened. "Which means we have much to prepare. New dresses, the perfect floral accessories, and of course, dates." Renée started to protest. "At least that's one thing you don't have to worry about."

"I don't?"

Peony gave her a knowing look. "Tresor is going to ask you."

"Ask me? To the ball?" Renée sputtered. "Don't be ridiculous! Tresor cannot stand me."

"*Sure.* That's why he appeared and saved you from a certain fall to your death." Peony placed her hands under chin. "He likes you."

"No." Renée shook her head even as she felt her skin start to tingle. "He doesn't like"— she dropped her voice to a whisper—"humans. In general. Or part-humans."

"Well maybe someone's changed his mind," Peony teased. "Why do you look so worried? Aren't you excited? Everyone wants to be courted by Tresor."

Renée thought of the disgruntled fairies she'd encountered on her first night and chewed on her quill. "Oh, I know."

"He's quite the catch," Peony said wistfully. "Impossibly handsome, talented, son of the former queen, nephew of the current queen, a smile that could light the sun for a thousand years."

Renée almost choked on her quill. "Did you say son of the former queen?"

Ms. Sneezewood rapped her wand on her desk. "Ladies, is there something more important than learning about magic words?"

"Sorry, Ms. Sneezewood," they said in unison.

"Thank you." Ms. Sneezewood raised her wand and a teacup appeared in front of each pupil. "There are a few of you who have already found your magic words. If that applies to you, please practice using them. For everyone else, we shall concentrate on discovering that phrase that will channel your intention in its purest form." She waved her wand. "Trees! Fly! Free! That's me!" Ms. Sneezewood's teacup began to fly around the room, passing each student.

The fée applauded.

"I was born in an oak tree and spent my early years flying over the forest, so those words made sense for me. Which speak to you? Try different ones out."

Renée stared at the teacup on the desk in front of her and willed it to move. She thought of some of her favorite things. "Beets! Butter! Bees!" she shouted. Nothing happened. Darn. She really did love beets. She thought that would be a winner.

"Try something else," Peony said encouragingly.

"All right." Renée crossed out the catchphrase in her notebook and went to the next one on her list, feeling disappointed. She took a deep breath and stared at the teacup again. "Dragonflies! Daisies! Dates!" Again, there was no change.

"Watch me," Peony said, and stared at the small, bone-white teacup. "Fleur! Fleurs! Fleurir!" Renée's teacup soared, then gently drifted back to the table.

"Celine! Raymond! Gaspian!" Renée shouted at the cup. It didn't move. Ms. Sneezewood was walking around the classroom now.

"Maybe you should sing it. That worked for the other spells."

"Yes, good idea." Renée concentrated extra hard and took a deep breath. *"Brave! Bread! Birthdays! Bold!"* she sang. The teacup raised two inches then fell again.

"Singing is definitely key for you, but the words aren't exactly right," Peony noted, glancing at Ms. Sneezewood growing closer.

Renée groaned and crossed out the phrase. "I really thought I had something with that one. It was the letter *B*. That felt right." Renée glared at the teacup.

Peony thought for a moment. "I know alliteration is often the way to go, but—and don't be mad at me for saying this—it sort of feels like you're just combining words at random."

"I suppose," Renée said dejectedly as flowers wound their way around both her arms. "But I like the words *bold* and *brave*. And who doesn't like bread? Or butter?"

"True, but do they make you think of wonder? Of enchantment?"

"No." Renée sighed. "What if I can't find the right ones?"

"You will. It took my maman five years to come up with a phrase."

"Five years?" Renée tried not to look as aghast as she felt. How long was that in human time?

"Yours won't take that long," Peony said quickly. "Just remember: The words combined should evoke power. A tingling from your ears to your toes. And they don't have to make sense to anyone but you. They can be gibberish. When you want the magic to flow through you, this phrase should be on the tip of your tongue. That's what you're looking for."

All the flowers and vines wrapped around her looked at her again.

Not actual words. Renée looked at the teacup. She focused on her breathing. Channeled the ache in her heart, her love and sorrow for the children. *"Fiddle-de-de!"* she sang.

For a second, she thought she saw the teacup wobble. It stopped just as Ms. Sneezewood got to their desk.

Her tsk was loud enough for the entire balcony to hear. "As I said, some of you will not be ready." She smiled venomously. "Or ever ready."

Renée felt her cheeks warm. Peony shot her a sympathetic smile, but the other fée were whispering and looking over. Renée could imagine what they were saying. *There goes the strange mortal again. She'll never truly master magic.* And that burned her up inside. She could do this. She felt it in her bones. There was clearly something she was missing, but what? She allowed her frustration to course through her, her determination interweaving with it. She knew the words were there, just waiting to appear.

Immediately, she was reminded of Raymond and Celine jumping out at her in a game of hide-and-seek. *"Boo,"* she sang. The teacup spun around.

Renée and Peony looked at each other.

"*Boo, boo, boo!*" Renée sang, and the teacup spun more but didn't rise.

"You're getting closer," Peony said encouragingly.

"Maybe I need more than one word?"

"Probably," Peony agreed.

But what word? Or words? "*Bread-boo! Bakery-boo! Banana-boo!*" she sang. Banana boo sounded silly. She could picture Raymond laughing.

You're trying too hard. Have fun with this, a voice in her head seemed to say. And she realized then what she was lacking. Fun. Silliness. It's what worked when she was with the children. She was overthinking it. A tingling began in her arms and stretched down her body to her toes as she remembered a moment with them from their last day together.

"*Wisp! Wisp! Shush! Shush! Listen, hush. Wisp-shush-whisper!*" they'd sang together. It was such a silly little phrase, but the memory filled her with longing. It came from a place of love, and her magic words had to do the same. If she were teaching the children magic, what would she suggest? Renée racked her brain trying to find a memory. *Please let me remember.*

She controlled her breathing, closed her eyes, and heard Raymond laughing.

"*Boo! I'm a tiger!*" Raymond would pretend.

"*Boo! I'm a bird! A baby bird! Tweet!*" Celine had said, *jumping from behind a tree.*

"*Baby bird! Baby bird! That's silly!*" Raymond laughed at her and, of course, Celine had gotten vexed.

"*Make him stop, Renée!*" Celine demanded.

She popped out from behind a tree and started to sing. "*Boo who! Look at me! I'm a bibbidi-bobbidi-boo!*"

Both children started to laugh.

"That's not a real animal!" Raymond said, doubled over.

"It is!" Renée had insisted. "A bibbidi-bobbidi . . ." She snuck up on him and Celine and jumped at them both. "BOO!"

They both shrieked and started running.

Renée felt her fingers start to tingle. Her whole body warmed. Her breathing was shallow as she stared down at the teacup and started to sing. *"Bibbidi-bobbidi-boo!"*

The teacup shot into the air so fast, Renée and Peony both ducked. Then they watched in wonder as the cup circled the room, causing the students and Ms. Sneezewood to look up in confusion.

"What is going on?" Ms. Sneezewood demanded.

"Renée is doing it! She found her phrase!" Peony cheered. "Show them!"

"Bibbidi-bobbidi-boo!" Renée sang, and for good measure came up with a string of gibberish. It was fun. Very fun. She could hear the children's giggling in her ears.

She could also hear yelling.

All the teacups had formed a circle in the air and were following Renée's orders, swirling around the room she sang. But it wasn't just the teacups. Notebooks, a vase of flowers, someone's apple, and Ms. Sneezewood's wand had taken to the air, too, and were now flying fast around the room as Renée continued singing her nonsense. The rest of the fairies watched her in wonder. Ms. Sneezewood looked gobsmacked. Fairies on other balconies flew over.

"Keep singing!" Peony said in excitement.

Fairies started to duck and race for cover as the teacups and other items spun faster and faster. Nelley and Lune had appeared and were watching with a mixture of shock and amusement. For a moment, she was sure she saw Tresor fly into view, but it was hard to concentrate when she was trying to keep her magic going.

Ms. Sneezewood flew at her and Peony. "All right. That's enough now," she said, sounding nervous. "Make it stop."

Renée stopped singing, but the items kept flying. She frowned. *"Bibbidi-bobbidi-boo!"* Nothing happened. The items spun faster.

"I said, make it stop, Renée Dubois!" Ms. Sneezewood admonished.

Renée felt a tingling again. She glanced sideways at Nelley and Lune. She felt her brow starting to perspire. "I don't know how," she said meekly.

"Well, I can't! You stole my wand!" Ms. Sneezewood yelled at her.

"She didn't steal it," Nelley said hastily, looking worried as she flew over to intervene. "The magic just . . . well . . . whisked it away."

"I don't care how it happened. How do we end the spell?" Ms. Sneezewood said.

Nelley raised her wand. "Zinnia, zinnia!" she tried, but nothing happened.

Lune jumped in. "Fae! Faerie! Be! It's meant to be!"

Some teacups spun off the balcony, shattering against the floor, against walls. Renée winced as Ms. Sneezewood shot her a look.

The intact teacups gathered in the middle of the atrium, and fairies began flying haphazardly trying to avoid the commotion.

"This is not good," Peony said, standing close to Renée.

Renée felt a rising sense of panic. *"Bibbidi-bobbidi-boo!"* she tried again, but the teacups kept spinning. Someone was going to get hurt. Why weren't her magic words working?

Nelley shot a stream of light at Ms. Sneezewood's wand, to no avail. A group of fairy godmothers appeared and chanted a spell together, but that didn't work either.

"Her magic is too strong," Ms. Sneezewood said to Nelley.

"Run for cover!" a fairy yelled, and a few started to scream.

Nelley flew to Renée's side and put her hands on her shoulders. "You are the only one who can fix this, dear."

"You heard Ms. Sneezewood. I can't. I don't know how," Renée yelled over the commotion, feeling desperate now. "The spell has taken on a life of its own."

"So you need to make another one," Nelley instructed.

Renée nodded and rushed to the end of the balcony. *Please listen and stop. Stop at once*, she begged the flying objects. She opened her mouth and started to sing loud. *"Bibbidi-bobbidi, bibbidi-bobbidi, bibbidi-bobbidi-boo!"*

The teacups and notebooks froze for a moment, then dropped fast, sending fairies flying out of the way, screeching as the crockery shot past all the floors and landed on the ground level with a thunderous crash. Renée winced.

Everyone turned to look at her.

"I'm terribly sorry! Truly! I don't know how I did that," she tried to explain, appealing to irate Ms. Sneezewood. "I didn't know a nonsense phrase could be so powerful."

"Renée Dubois" came a new voice, chilling in its measured tone.

Renée turned.

Margarite was hovering above the balcony, her aura bright red, the butterflies in her crown of flowers fluttering fast. "In my chambers. At once."

SEVENTEEN

Renée's knees shook as she exited the academy with Nelley and Lune. They kept assuring her all would be fine, but she could feel their fear as they clung to her. *The queen's going to banish me*, Renée thought. A loud thunderclap seemed to agree.

Nelley frowned. "It's not supposed to rain this week, is it?"

Renée looked up. It almost never rained. And when it was going to rain in Faerie Province, there were numerous announcements made by the seers because fairies had trouble flying in wet conditions.

Lune frowned. "No. That's strange." Her eyes flickered to Renée, who looked away.

She swallowed hard. *I won't cry*, Renée thought, but she wanted to. Clouds quickly moved across the sky. In the courtyard, she could hear windows shutting. The wind had picked up.

"Let's fly," Nelley said, sounding nervous.

"You're coming with me?" Renée asked.

"Of course," Nelley told her. "We will help explain what happened. I'm sure the queen just wants assurances that you aren't trying to cause harm."

"I'm not! I don't know what happened!" Renée screeched, and a gust of wind blew them sideways. She looked at Lune. "Do you know why my magic is so strange?"

Lune grimaced. "Your magic is different than ours . . . but I'm not sure why."

Renée fell silent. Would the queen send her back to the human world? If she did, what would be her fate? They kept telling her she couldn't survive there long. Would she age out of this life within a week? Days? She shuddered and felt tears spring to her eyes again. *Stay in control*, she told herself. Losing her composure would certainly not endear her to the queen.

"What I mean is that I knew your transition to being a fairy wouldn't be without strife. But I saw you eventually thriving here, which you are," Lune said.

"And?" Renée prompted, sensing there was more.

"And I know no one's future is set in stone," Lune added gently. "Life is what you make of it, and your destiny could go multiple ways."

"What exactly did you see, Lune?" Renée heard her own voice crack. Her fingers were tingling. She couldn't believe she hadn't asked Lune this before.

Lune gave pause, her wings fluttering fast as they flew Renée closer to the queen's quarters.

"Might as well, at this point," Nelley said gravely. "It might help her with your mother. It's all right. She can take it."

Lune seemed to compose herself before looking Renée's way again. "When Tresor and I heard the commotion that night at the river between you and your cousin, Tresor was certain it was a trap."

"A trap," Renée repeated, thinking of her conversation with Tresor in the botany atrium.

"Humans have trapped fairies before," Lune said worriedly. "But I sensed you were genuinely in need of help, and I couldn't leave you. Later, when I consulted the bulle, I realized who you were. Who you could be."

Renée leaned in closer, desperate to understand. "And who was that?"

Lune's voice was strained. "Someone with fire. Someone who could destroy or inspire us all."

Destroy or inspire? Renée's stomach dropped. Those were two completely opposite things! Of course she didn't want to destroy Faerie Province. Did anyone actually believe she did? Or that she even could?

Celine and Raymond grounded her at home, but she'd never really belonged with them, not with Aunt Olivia always plotting her exodus. She didn't want the same thing to happen here in Faerie Province—others actively wishing her gone. There had to be a way to convince Margarite that she could take the best of what she'd been as a mortal and combine it with feé power.

Rain started to fall fast now, soaking them through.

"Thank you for telling me the truth," Renée said softly.

"Of course." Lune looked up and frowned again.

Nelley quickened their pace. "Hurry, dear."

The Fairy Queen's residence was smaller than the other châteaus in Faerie Province, but its architecture was unmatched. There were two towers that seemed to touch the clouds, looking out over the whole valley, with multiple turrets covered in ivory that reminded Renée of the castle on the hill at home. One wing even had a greenhouse on the roof. Renée squinted hard to make out a vast variety of flowers growing inside the enclosure.

A flash of lightning made her jump, and the trio zoomed under a turret. As they landed and pulled open the doors to the château, Renée paused, unsure what she was seeing.

Was it raining *inside* as well?

Three fairies, including Margarite's, handmaiden Iris, were flying back and forth placing buckets around the foyer, trying to catch the water, and shouting directions. As Renée stepped inside, she felt water slosh over her feet. Thunder roared above their heads, and two of the fairies dropped their buckets and flew away.

"Lune, do you have any idea what is going on with this weather?" Iris demanded.

Lune wiped water off her face. "I've never seen this happen before."

Iris grimaced. "Your mother is not going to be happy. This is going to destroy the summer solstice decorations. I'm going to try to find someplace safe to place these scrolls," she said, grabbing giant banners in her arms. "You three try to stop the manor from flooding." She waved a wand and two dozen new buckets appeared on the floor.

"Will do," Renée jumped in, moving buckets to optimal locations while Lune and Nelley fluttered in and out of the room. When Iris returned, she looked pleased.

"I'm glad to see you can do something right," Iris said pointedly to Renée. "The queen isn't too happy about what happened in the academy."

"I can explain," Renée started, just as the wind picked up out of nowhere and threatened to blow them all out the door.

"Fairy be!" Iris shouted.

Iris and Nelley clung to a pillar while Renée and Lune grabbed hold of a statue in the corner, and Renée prayed she wouldn't topple it.

"One moment!" Lune said. "I think I know what's going on. If I'm right, the gust should die down soon."

As predicted, the wind died down, and Lune looked at Iris. "Can we please bring Renée into Mother's office and wait for her there? The next storm will be blowing in any moment now."

"How do you know we're going to get another storm?" Renée asked, suddenly wishing she'd read up on Faerie Province weather patterns.

Lune looked up at the ceiling and pursed her lips. "I think I've figured it out." She glanced at Iris again. "And it's better for everyone if we go into the office."

Iris glanced at Renée warily. "You're supposed to wait out here till she arrives. She's already in a mood today, as you know."

As another clap of thunder boomed, they all looked up. Renée heard shouting.

"I'm telling her this was your idea." Iris opened the office doors.

"Thank you, Iris," Renée said as Nelley and Lune each took one of Renée's arms and led her toward Margarite's chambers.

Iris just looked at her. "Good luck. And whatever you do, do not touch the portal!"

Renée stilled, inhaling sharply as she saw the office before her. She'd forgotten what Tresor had said about the portal being here. She gazed at the office's wood-carved doors, her body tingling. There were numerous symbols, drawings, and letters etched into it. She traced her hand along them, wondering what they all meant. The portal entrance was so close she could almost feel it. A way to the other realm. While there was a large part of her that longed to find it, another part of her pictured Margarite tossing her through for all eternity, and she shuddered.

"Don't worry. It's hidden," Lune said, nudging her inside the office.

"And no one is crossing today," Nelley added. "At least the queen's room will be dry. It's enchanted to block unwanted spells."

An enchanted room, Renée thought, marveling at Margarite's power. *What if she turns* me *into a bucket?*

Margarite's office was massive, with large windows looking onto a garden. Ivy trailed along the walls and flowers seemed to bloom upside down from the ceiling, making Renée a little off-balance. Flowers turned to look as she walked along the edges of the room, avoiding the thick grass that served as carpeting by the queen's desk. Lanterns and wooden bookcases lined each wall.

"Why don't you take a look around?" Nelley suggested, her voice falsely bright. "There are so many wonderful artifacts in here, and I need to speak with Lune privately."

Renée knew they were worried. "All right." She stepped away to walk among the bookshelves, trying to calm her nerves as she looked at the weathered spines. These tomes appeared far older than the ones in the library, the gold on the covers all but rubbed away. But there weren't just books on display. Around the room were small fairy sculptures, intricately patterned vases, a variety of painted wands encased in glass, and a giant glass case with an antique blue robe inside.

Was that the first fairy godmother's robe?

Her fingers tingled at the thought. A clap of thunder rattled the room. The storm sounded closer.

With Nelley and Lune still whispering, Renée kept wandering. She stopped in front of several maps on the walls. She couldn't tell what they were of—maybe Faerie Province? Or the human realm?

In the center of the room sat a large desk, empty aside from a blank scroll, a calligraphy inkwell, and a tiny painting of two female fairies. She picked it up. The painting appeared to be of a young Margarite, her skin golden and glittering, and an older girl the spitting image of Tresor—the same golden eyes and beautiful brown skin, perfectly curled hair, an identical smirk. There was no telling how old the fairies were—they looked eternally young—but they certainly looked happy. Her finger traced the image of Tresor's mother. *What happened to you? Why won't anyone tell me?*

Outside the door, Renée heard new voices.

"Auntie, you know this is the future she wanted for me."

"*Before!* She wouldn't want it now. She'd want me to protect you. How can you even ask this of me?"

"Because it's what I want. You can't hide me here forever. You have to let me live."

Renée felt her skin tingle. She recognized those voices. Was that Tresor? And Margarite?

"And what have *you* been doing to 'live'? Hiding in the botany lab? I know for a fact a dozen lovely young fairies have invited you to the Summer Solstice Ball and you've turned them down. Take Hyacinth, for example. Strong fairy lines. Good sense of character. She'd be an excellent match."

167

Renée heard Tresor sigh. "Auntie . . . if I go to a silly ball, I will choose my own date, thank you very much. What I care about is my discipline. You know where I belong."

What did Tresor mean? Renée wondered. There was another loud clap of thunder.

"Do I not have enough to worry about? Please, child. Let us honor her memory today and not argue. We can discuss this later."

"All right, Auntie, but—"

"*Tomorrow.* If you have a date for this summer solstice, we will talk."

He laughed. "Oh, we're bargaining now?"

"We're always bargaining, child. Let's hope the girl you saved in that room knows how to do the same."

Renée felt her stomach sway. Lightning flashed.

The door jingled and Renée quickly put the portrait back on the desk just as Lune and Nelley hurried to her side.

Renée held her breath at the sight of the queen and her nephew. Margarite was dressed in a sage gown with a wide skirt and a pink flowered bodice while Tresor still wore his green robe. Another crack of lightning lit up the hallway behind Margarite. She stared at Renée, her face strained and pale; the gold in her eyes dull. Tresor, however, didn't look as serious. If Renée wasn't mistaken, she thought she saw him wink.

"Renée Dubois?" the queen's voice echoed.

She smiled nervously. "Yes?"

The queen flew across the room and sat behind her desk, frowning at the portrait of her and her sister, which she angled ever so slightly. She turned her attention back to Renée. "Well? What do you have to say for yourself?"

"I'm sorry?"

"You don't sound very sure," Margarite pointed out as Tresor moved to stand next to Lune and Nelley.

"To be honest, I'm not sure what I'm sorry for," Renée said, and Margarite's eyes flashed dangerously. "I mean, sending the teacups careening off the balcony and flying haphazardly around the academy was not ideal, obviously—"

"This is not your first offense," Margarite interrupted. "There was of course the pear incident. And your insistence to take new classes . . ."

"Yes," Renée said. "The Grand Verre showed me doing many things, and I want to try them all. I want to help change the way Faerie Province looks at humans that have become fairies." She glanced at Lune, but her friend's brow furrowed.

"Humans that have *become* fairies?" Margarite's voice shook as another clap of thunder rumbled outside. "You didn't *become* anything. My daughter granted your wish to live, which is odd considering I was told you were so close to death you couldn't actually make a wish—"

"Mother, please," Lune tried to cut in.

Margarite wouldn't let her. "Instead of saving your human life, she gifted you a fairy life. Without my blessing! *That's* how you wound up here. You haven't *become* anything but a nuisance."

Renée blinked, trying to stave off the tears that suddenly threatened to fall.

"Margarite, please," Nelley begged. "You're being too harsh on the child."

"Am I, Nelley? She was reckless, impulsive, and arrogant in her magic." Margarite looked at Renée stonily. "Need I remind any of you what we've been through before? What we lost because of her kind?"

"My kind?" Renée repeated.

"Yes," Margarite seethed, and then glancing at the portrait on her desk again, her face fell. "I want to be open-minded, but I see too much of him."

"Auntie, be fair. She's not arrogant," Tresor tried.

"And she's not reckless either," Lune tried, too. "*I'm* reckless. I'm the one who insisted we save Renée. Tresor is the arrogant one." She gave him an antagonizing look, and he shot one right back.

"Maybe it would help to explain—" Nelley started.

"No." The queen laced her fingers together and looked at Renée. "We shall stay focused on the matter at hand. Renée's appearance here has turned this province upside down. Fairies are frightened."

Renée's lips felt dry. She heard a low rumble that shook the château as she opened her mouth to respond. "I'm trying," she said, her voice shakier than she intended.

Margarite scoffed. "This is you trying?"

Renée bristled and another clap of thunder rolled through. She couldn't help thinking Margarite was behaving like Aunt Olivia. All bluster, no kindness. Couldn't she put herself in Renée's shoes and wonder what it was like being an outsider?

"Your Majesty, learning how to live among the fairies I've loved since I was a child is not easy. But I sit in the library night and day practicing my spells, learning the rules of this world, even when I still don't understand why you fear humans so. And to be honest, Queen Margarite, I'm not putting in all this effort for you." The queen's expression sharpened. "Yes, I want to fit in here, but what I really want is to make the children I left behind proud."

Renée could feel her voice growing stronger. "For them to somehow know losing me was worth it. I'm just trying to learn how to be one of you."

Margarite relaxed, and sighed. "Be one of us . . . as if becoming a fairy is something you can learn."

"But—" Renée tried.

"Humans think the world is theirs for the taking," Margarite continued. "That they can go anywhere they like and take any resource they want without consequence. Well, here there are consequences." Her tone hardened. "For every action there is a counteraction. You not learning the proper way to do magic could cost Faerie Province. Part-fairies are also doomed with forgetfulness! What if you'd cast the wrong spell and been eaten by a cario vern plant?"

Renée tried not to look alarmed. "Eaten?"

"Or interfered with godmother work between two kingdoms agreeing to a peace treaty?" Margarite continued.

"I would never do that," Renée swore. "I would never hurt anyone."

Margarite gave her a look. "Another part-fairy said that, too, before taking everything from us."

That's when it occurred to Renée: Margarite was never going to believe her words. She needed to see action. But how did she show Margarite what she was capable of when she couldn't even control her magic? Outside, the rain started to fall in sheets. Wind rattled the windows.

Margarite whirled around to her daughter. "And what is this storm? Today was supposed to be beautiful."

Lune motioned to her friend. "Ask Renée. She's the one causing it."

"M-me?" Renée stuttered.

Lune smiled softly. "I don't know why I didn't see it before. You're an empath." She looked at her mother. "She feels with every inch of her being."

"That's why her magic is so different," Nelley realized. "It's tied to her emotions!"

"Because she's feeling every spell she casts?" Tresor looked at Renée with interest now, too.

"Yes," Lune said, and reached out a hand to squeeze Renée's. "You just have to be open, Mother. Give her a chance. Please."

Margarite pounded her fist on the desk. "But that's not what the fée do! Look at all of you! Don't you see what's happening? She's already changed you all. Your fondness for her is interfering with your judgment." She glanced at Tresor, whose expression was hard to read.

Lune stepped forward. "I'm not ashamed to admit she's my friend." Her face brightened. "I know Renée is meant to be here."

"Is she? Or has she come to destroy us all?" Mother asked, and Renée felt her confidence waffle. "I'm sorry. I think having a part-fairy among us again so soon is too difficult." The queen blinked rapidly. "This isn't what I wanted, but keeping Renée here is dangerous."

Wasn't that what Lune's bulle had said? Destroy or inspire? Had the queen seen it, too?

Prove yourself. "I am not leaving," Renée vowed, and a thunderclap echoed so loud the entire room shook. "I'm sorry someone hurt the ones you love, but I deserve a chance." Her voice softened. "Please do not discard me because of another's actions." She stood up straighter and strode to the queen's desk. "I know I can do this. Please. Just let me show you I belong here."

Margarite's eyes flashed. "Oh, you're going to have to do more than that."

She waved her wand and the doors to the study flew open. A dozen fairies in rainbow-colored robes, the same ones that had summoned the Grand Verre, flew in.

Margarite's smile bordered on a dare. "You're going to prove it to all of us."

EIGHTEEN

As lightning continued to flash (courtesy of Renée's own doing apparently), a group of fairy godmothers gathered round the queen's chambers. Their faces were grave, which only made Renée more nervous.

"Elders who serve on the fairy council, I have asked you here today to decide the fate of one Renée Dubois, the half-fairy who my daughter saved," Margarite told them.

"Hello again." Renée gave a little wave. "I would like it known that I did not ask to become part-fairy. Though I am honored to be here."

Tresor coughed, suppressing a grin. Renée could see the queen's nostrils flare, and Renée wondered if steam was going to come out of them. Taking a quick glance around the room, she saw that everyone seemed to have the same pinched expression.

"What are the charges?" asked one of the Elders.

"Her magic can't be controlled." Margarite motioned to the window. "This storm is her doing. As is the pear that almost crushed several fairies, and this morning's teacup incident. All results of her unruly magic. I fear allowing her to continue training with us could be disastrous."

"Or she could be a wonderful ally." Lune jumped in. "Someone who has walked two worlds and knows what it's like to be a human and a fairy. Someone who can help Faerie Province understand the other realm better. To help us see the shades of all mortals, not just the mistake of one."

"A mistake that could have eliminated Faerie Province," Margarite reminded them. "When I became queen, I promised I would never allow anything like that to happen again. And yet here we are. . . ."

"Please," Renée appealed to the Elders. "My intention is not to harm. I only want to learn. I've always been fascinated with fairies, grateful for the impact they've had on my life. Now I want to be part of it. That's all."

"Ah, but you don't just want to be a part of the fairy world." Margarite tested her. "I'm told you want to become a godmother yourself."

There were whispers from those in attendance.

"That's true," Renée admitted. "The Grand Verre saw me doing many things and I want to try all of them. If I'm not right for the job, then I'm not right, but at least let me take classes in all areas and see." She looked around at the Elders. "No fairy should be stuck in one discipline. We should be able to explore, craft multiple talents."

Margarite scoffed. "What has happened in the few classes you've taken so far? You've caused chaos."

"So what are you proposing? That we sentence her to death by returning her to the human world?" Nelley tutted. "You can't do that, Margarite. And I know you. You wouldn't."

"No." Margarite's expression softened. "I am not that cruel. But is it so wrong for a queen to worry about her fae? I must protect what we've built here." She glanced at Tresor. "I won't lose another fairy on my watch to a human." She took a deep breath. "Therefore, Renée, if you are to stay, we will be limiting the magic you attempt. And you must be more careful."

"I will be," Renée promised, instantly relieved that banishment was off the table. "I promise."

"No new spells unless someone like Lune or Nelley is there to supervise. We can't have any more incidents."

"Understood. I promise," Renée said, bouncing on her toes. The next words were on the tip of her tongue and she couldn't stop them. "Does that mean I can continue trying new classes, too?"

Tresor coughed. Margarite threw up her hands. "Really child? After I just gave you a stay of execution, you're asking about godmother lessons? Absolutely not. I can't allow it. For many reasons. Need I remind you, as a godmother, you would be returning to that world and would face very real consequences each time you crossed?"

Nelley cleared her throat. "That's true. But Lune is right—Renée has had two lives. She understands both worlds. Who better to know how a godmother works? As for the crossings, we could try to help slow the effects."

"*Try*," Margarite pressed. "You don't know that your methods will work."

176

"Does that mean we shouldn't attempt it?" Nelley asked.

Margarite stared at Renée pensively and Renée wondered if they'd gotten through to her. "It's a big risk."

"What's the harm in more study, Auntie? Shouldn't we all be allowed to practice potential disciplines that suit us?" Tresor asked, and for some reason Renée knew he meant himself as well.

"It's only fair, Margarite," said one of the Elders, turning to Renée to look at her. "Child, we already know you can do magic—whether it is what others here can do or not, spells can be mastered." She cocked her head. "But there are some things that cannot be taught. You take a fairy ring course, do you not?"

Renée could feel her fingers tingling. "I do."

The fairy waved her wand, and a patch of grass grew in the center of Margarite's office. "Create one now. Your way."

Renée felt the tingling travel through her body. She glanced warily at Lune and Nelley, who nodded encouragingly. Margarite was stone-faced.

This was a test. Her chance to prove she could master a fairy discipline.

Renée got to work, walking through the tall grass and thinking of the magic she'd need to make it just the right height to see a fairy ring in the woods. She imagined walking through the forest by Uncle Gaspian's manor and stumbling upon the fairy ring. She knew it couldn't look like the one they'd found or the ones she'd seen in class. This had to reflect her unique talent, her own point of view. To wow the queen, it would need to be extraordinary.

She prayed this time she could control her magic. *"Bibbidi-bobbidi-boo!"*

she sang, thinking of the children and the length of the grass. It shortened to half an inch, the green in each blade growing a deeper green in the process.

The room was quiet as the Elders gathered closer to watch her work, but Renée tried to ignore them.

The rings she'd been taught to make were done with mushrooms, which was all well and good. But if she could add flowers . . . she mused, plucking one off her robe. *"Bibbidi-bobbidi-boo!"* she sang again, thinking of the yellow of spring chicks and the blue of a summer sky, the red in her old toy rabbit and the pink slippers Anne favored.

The flowers on her robe grew and brightened, and Renée plucked them off one by one. She placed them on the grass, forming a heart instead of a circle. With another *"bibbidi-bobbidi-boo,"* she produced radishes and carrots, carved to look like flowers, the orange and purple bright against the green grass rug. She laid them out one by one, standing up every few feet to check her work.

She could hear whispers behind her. She was keeping their attention, but she wasn't finished. Not yet. It needed something more.

"Bibbidi-bobbidi-boo!" Renée sang, her voice louder this time. Birds flew in from the office door, and the butterflies in Margarite's crown rushed forward, each creature taking up residence on a different piece of the ring so that the whole ring seemingly came to life.

"Bibbidi-bobbidi-boo!" she sang a final time, and now the ring started to sparkle and glow, fairy dust shooting through the air.

Renée turned around in triumph.

The Elders applauded, coming closer to examine Renée's work, each one whispering to another.

"This is the most beautiful fairy ring I have ever seen!" gushed one.

"If you can do this with flowers, radishes, and carrots, imagine what you could with other resources," said another. "You are talented, child. You certainly deserve to engage in more studies!"

Lune hugged her. "Well done."

Renée beamed.

Tresor appeared at her side and gave her arm a squeeze. "Nice work, Dubois," he whispered, and she felt goose bumps on her neck.

Margarite walked over to examine the work and the group quieted. "What is that?"

Renée paused, wondering if this was a trick. "It's a fairy ring."

"Fairy rings are round," Margarite said tersely. "And made of mushrooms. Not carrots or radishes. Why is this one shaped like a heart?"

"This is a new design I've been thinking about," Renée said.

Margarite sounded agitated. "I'm sorry?"

Renée carried on. "If these rings are a representative of the fairy world, shouldn't they be as magical as fairies are?" Renée addressed the Elders in attendance. "Radishes are useful. As are carrots." She picked one up as proof. "Most vegetables that grow in the ground showcase the versatility and beauty here in the province. Give the fairy ring a little something extra and humans will see, just by looking at it, that it was made by something otherworldly. Plus, a pretty ring also enchants the experience the fée have when using one as a landing guide."

Margarite's nostrils flared. "Humans are not supposed to know for certain that we exist. We're an idea! A flight of fancy! That's how we stay hidden and do our work. We don't *want* the whole world to have proof of us," she sputtered.

"Don't we want humans to believe there is still some magic in the world?" Renée asked. "Because if there is magic, then there is hope that anything is possible. A beautiful fairy ring would show them that."

The Elders looked from Renée to Margarite. Outside the window, the dark clouds were beginning to clear away. A ray of sunlight shot through.

"Fairy rings solely exist to be beacons. They don't need to prove anything. Do you know what would happen if humans had veritable proof we were here?" Margarite's voice was growing louder.

"Yes," Nelley said, stepping forward. "But we can't let our fear of what happened in the past keep us from moving forward. When the fairy godmother program started, our mission was to bridge Faerie Province with the human world, to protect both realms." Nelley glanced at Renée. "In the short time I've known her, I've found Renée to be a person who is kind, who loves our world as much as her own, and who puts others before herself. Isn't that what a godmother does? Bridge the gap? Usher in kindness and hope everywhere? The more these things exist in the world, the better it is for all of us. Didn't you once say as much to me?"

"That was long ago." Margarite thought for a moment. "I do believe in the program, but being trained as a godmother is a vocation the Grand Verre gives to few. Fewer since we lost my sister. Not many can handle that calling."

"Then let us prove there are more godmothers out there waiting to be trained," Tresor interjected.

Renée felt her stomach flip again as the room fell silent. The queen looked like she was going to be ill. The butterflies, now back in her crown, even stopped flapping their wings.

"I vowed to protect you," Margarite said to Tresor, the words strained. "This discipline requires . . . I can't ask of you . . . after what happened . . ."

"You're not asking. I am," Tresor said. "My future, much like my mother's, lies in this area. I know being a godmother is my calling. If only you'd let me embrace it. Please, Auntie."

The queen was quiet, staring at him for a long time. The Elders looked at one another, shuffling slightly, their robes swishing as everyone waited for an answer. Renée wasn't as patient.

"Your Majesty, you have two fairies in this room simply asking you to consider allowing us to learn more," Renée said. "You've seen what we both can do. What is the harm in letting us at least *try*? Doesn't the human world and Faerie Province need more fairies willing to dedicate their lives to helping everyone? Let's remind everyone of the magic the fée provide."

"Yes!" a fairy cheered spontaneously.

Several others began to shout out their approval as well. Some started to lift from the ground and let their wings flap like applause.

"Say yes, Margarite!"

"Vive les godmothers!"

"Quiet please! I've made my decision." Margarite cleared her throat and the Elders' merriment died out. Margarite addressed Renée and Tresor directly. "You both may take classes in other disciplines—*if* you can keep up your work in your regular coursework as well. Renée, your magic will still need supervision. And that does not mean either of you will automatically become godmothers at the end of the training. But perhaps you will learn the cost of such an endeavor this way."

"Thank you, Auntie," Tresor said, bowing slightly.

"Thank you!" Renée felt her whole body hum. She wanted to scream with happiness. Her throat burned with gratitude. "You won't regret this."

Margarite's eyes were as sharp as a lightning bolt. "For your sake, I hope you're right." And then with a wave of her wand, she was gone.

NINETEEN

"Splendid presentation of the fairy ring," said an Elder in peach, rushing to shake Renée's hand. "I can't wait to see what you do in my divination class."

"And in my class on the human ecosystem," said another in an indigo suit, pushing her way forward.

"The last time Margarite let two fairies enter the godmother training program was at least sixty years ago," said a third, his wings fluttering.

"You'll need to be on your best behavior," said one flying over to join. "All eyes will be on you."

"Be punctual, finish all your work, create new spells!" piped up the first Elder. "And make sure you don't do anything godmother-related without permission."

"I will. *We* will!" Renée corrected herself, looking at Tresor. "Thank you. Thank you all so much."

With that, the Elders began to file out of the room, flying to destinations unknown.

Lune threw her arms around Renée. "You were so impressive with my mother. Instead of being reprimanded for the teacups, you got her to let you take new classes." She shook her head. "I did not see that coming."

Renée hugged her friend back. "Maybe your bulle is sleeping on the job."

Lune laughed and turned to Tresor. "And *you*—since when have you wanted to be a godmother?"

"My mother always wanted me to follow in her footsteps before . . ." Tresor's eyes flickered to Renée briefly. "I guess I am learning humans can be surprising." His lips curled. "So can fairies apparently."

Lune pointed to his mouth. "What's that I see on your face, cousin? Dare I say a smile? What is going on with you?"

"Don't go reading my aura, Lune," he warned. "For now, I'm just enjoying the moment. I never thought your mother would let me take godmother classes."

"Well, I have to say I'm delighted. You two wanting to join my ranks!" Nelley clapped. "More godmothers, who would have thought?"

"Sounds like your mother would be proud of your decision," Renée said gently.

Tresor, however, held on to his smile. "Yes, she would be."

"She was the finest godmother Faerie Province had ever seen," Nelley said, her voice wobbling.

Tresor grasped Lune's hand. "She was. But it's time we look forward. She would want that for all of us."

"She would," Lune said.

Suddenly, there was a tinkling sound and Nelley paused, holding her wand up in a show of silence. "I must go. I'm receiving a call." Nelley looked at Renée. "You did good today, child." With a wave of her wand, she was gone.

"I should take my leave as well," Lune said. "I was in the middle of a session with my bulle when the teacup hailstorm started."

Renée bit her cheek. "I should probably go clean up, check on Ms. Sneezewood."

"Don't bother," said Lune, and held up her wand. "All taken care of." She glanced from Renée to Tresor. "You two enjoy your victory."

And then it was just her and Tresor standing in the queen's office. Renée suddenly felt very aware of how close together they were standing.

"Well . . ." she said formally. "Congratulations."

He smiled. "To you as well."

The sun formed a spotlight on Tresor, its beams strong now that the clouds had shifted. Renée turned to gaze out the large windows in the office. With the rain gone, she could see a beautiful garden with paths that seemed to lead in several directions. Flowers and vines climbed over brick walls, making it hard to tell where the flora ended and the château began.

"So . . . should we celebrate?" he asked her, his hands now laced behind his back. He'd removed his green robe, and she could see he was wearing a white shirt over his tan breeches.

"Together?" she asked, her skin tingling again. "Or do you mean later when Lune is done?"

"The fée never need an excuse to fête. Haven't you learned that by now?" He opened a latch on one of the windows. "Come on. I saw you looking at my aunt's garden. Why don't I take you to see it?"

The tingling sensation in Renée's fingers grew stronger, traveling through her body. "Are we allowed?"

Tresor climbed through the window and offered Renée his hand. "These gardens were originally mine. Or should I say, my parents'. We can go any-where we please."

Renée looked down at his hand, hesitating half a second before taking it. His fingers were warmer than she'd expected. He helped her over the window ledge, and she dropped down outside. The air was cool after the storm, the ground still damp. Blades of wet grass tickled her feet as she stepped onto the stone pathway, following behind him. "You lived here?"

"When I was younger," he told her, brushing ivy out of the way so they could get through the path, "my mother was queen, and my father was a bot-anist. He loved creating new arrangements to delight her. He was always out here working on new paths they could stroll." He smirked at Renée. "Rumor is he's the one who asked Maman to put a portal in her office so she wouldn't have to spend more time away from us than needed.

Renée touched a yellow tulip filled to the brim with rain and tipped it, letting the water drain through her fingers. "Does she still let fairies use the one in her office?"

"No. She doesn't even use it herself anymore." His face clouded over slightly as he pushed through another boa of hanging ivy. "She didn't want to give me or Lune any ideas about crossing over. In fact, she didn't want *anyone* leaving Faerie Province. She closed most of the portals in the realm and banned any sort of travel for a year."

"A year?" Renée wondered how long that would have been in the mortal realm. Several years without fairy visits? More?

"She called time for mourning the queen and all the fée we lost when my mother . . ." He let the thought peter out. "My mother was entranced by humans, which is why she insisted on becoming a godmother, in addition to her royal duties. But I think my aunt has always been slightly frightened of them. She has always preferred to stay in our world, to view from afar. Perfect for her vocation as a seer. Ah. Here we are." He motioned to the end of the path, and Renée found herself staring at a small waterfall nestled into a rock bed where flowers sprung from the cracks. "My papa created this the day I learned to fly." He took a seat on one of the rocks and stared at the water.

Renée did the same, the falls spraying her legs. "It's lovely."

They sat silently for a few moments, and she watched Tresor, wondering what he was thinking. She could feel his sadness.

"May I ask what happened to your parents?" She noticed the muscles in his back tighten through his shirt. "We don't have to talk about it," she said quickly. "I just . . . I know what it's like to . . . I lost mine when I was a child."

"Today is my mother's birthday," Tresor said abruptly, turning to face her so that their knees touched. His voice was strained. "It's also the day she, my father, and several other godmothers were killed."

Renée instinctively placed a hand on Tresor's leg without thinking better of it. She'd felt adrift for years after Maman's and Papa's deaths, only finding her footing when she'd had Raymond and Celine to take care of. "I'm sorry."

"Jules was one of my mother's charges," he said, his voice tense. "Godmothers aren't supposed to get too attached, but my mother adored him. And that bothered my aunt. Margarite was a seer, and she had an uneasy feeling about him."

"Did she see something in her bulle?"

"There was something about Jules that struck her as odd—a thirst that couldn't be quenched. He kept demanding more and more of my mother's time, more visits. He called on her constantly and my aunt felt something was amiss, but my mother wouldn't listen. She adored Jules. When he fell ill, I wasn't surprised to learn she granted his wish to make him the first part-fairy our province ever had."

"Ah. And he took advantage of her kindness? He tried to overtake it?"

"Not exactly. At first, he was beloved by all. He even somewhat won my aunt over—although she still quietly expressed her fears to others. He grew to be good friends with my father, spending his free time out here in the gardens with him. Jules was a hard worker, and eventually he became a fairy scout for my mother, helping her find charges."

"Weren't they worried about him prematurely aging?" she wondered.

"No one knew part-fairies had such limitations then. As I said, he was our first, and all his scouting missions were short. Back then, the fée came and went between worlds as they pleased without checking in. In fact, Maman and Jules bent the rules, embarking on missions together." He gave her a look. "She was a bit rebellious that way."

"She sounds wonderful," Renée said wistfully.

"She was. That's why my mother didn't question when Jules said he'd met a young human king he thought would make the perfect charge. He told her the man had a rather aggressive master general, who was encouraging him to do away with most of the kingdom's creative endeavors—theatres, art studios, literary salons—to focus on military expansion. There was even a proposal to clear much of the natural land to create more training sites."

"How horrible," Renée said, angry at a king she'd never met.

"Jules said the only way they could help him better rule would be to prove to him that magic was real, that wondrous things like nature and art were worth saving. He begged my mother and my father and several others to join him on a mission, and they agreed. They planned to appear to this human king and perform spells that might make an impression."

The pain was so visible on Tresor's face she could almost feel it.

"I remember my aunt refused to go," he continued. "She thought his plan was reckless. She couldn't see the outcome and that worried her greatly. Before my maman and papa left, they had a huge row. She begged them to stay. My aunt feared my mother was walking into a trap." He looked at her. "She was right."

"What happened?" she whispered.

"In a bid for wealth, Jules had made a deal with the king to provide a unique day of entertainment for his court. Fairy entertainment." Tresor's long lashes fluttered closed. "When the group appeared at the human castle, they were promptly captured and put on display."

Renée was horrified. "He kept the fairies captive?"

"Like birds in a cage." Tresor's jaw clenched.

"Couldn't Margarite find them? Being a seer?"

"She tried. When they failed to return, Aunt Margarite sent scouts, but even the bulles couldn't locate them. She shut down the portals, keeping anyone from getting in or out of our world without permission. Faerie Province had lost its queen. We were heartbroken, but my aunt kept searching, taking over my mother's duties in the meantime." He was breathing hard now. "Aunt Margarite found them much later with help from a young human . . . but it was too late."

"Too late?" Renée whispered, aghast. "How so?"

"Fairies rely on the magic of our world," he explained. "It's what gives us life. Rejuvenates us. After visiting the human realm, we return home to replenish our magic. When Maman, Papa, and the others couldn't return, they were slowly drained of their magic." His voice was bitter. "The only saving grace was that Jules didn't escape the same fate. According to the human who helped my aunt, while Jules wasn't locked up with the others, staying in the human world aged him quickly. He didn't survive a week."

Renée found herself placing a hand over the spot where her heart once beat. This explained why Margarite was so cold. Why so many fairies feared her presence. A part-fairy had taken everything from them . . . and here was a new one asking to change the rules again. She reached for Tresor's hand and held on tight. "No wonder you have such complicated feelings about my realm."

He looked down at their joined hands. "My aunt paused the godmother division for a while," he said. "She made the fée promise to never grant another human a wish to become one of us again. But as heartbroken as she was to lose her sister, and to be forced to take her throne and parent her only child, Aunt Margarite later found she couldn't get rid of the program forever."

"Why?" Renée felt every muscle in her body tense as she looked at their hands.

His gold eyes held hers. "She realized what I did: The truth is that humans and fairies need each other. It is the connection between our worlds that keeps them both running. If it were lost, if the spark of belief from the mortals didn't hold fast, magic would be extinguished as well. For a long time, I had no desire to visit the other side, but now . . ." A smile played on his lips. "I've seen a bit of the world my mother loved and understand why she was always eager to return to it."

Renée felt a lump form in her own throat when she thought of her past life. "It is beautiful, isn't it?"

Tresor brushed a tendril of hair away from her face. "It is. There is beauty in humans, and humanity, even if it is flawed. Some mortals," he said, with a far-off look in his eyes, "are quite delightful."

His gaze was so bright, Renée felt her cheeks begin to flush. She had no choice but to look away. "I hope you know I'm not Jules. I love this world, too."

"I know you do." His voice was gruff.

"Yes, there are humans I miss, and I know it won't be an easy path." She thought achingly of the children. "But I truly think I can do more."

"I do, too," he said, trying to get her to look at him again. They'd both leaned in now, their upper bodies so close, she could reach out and hug him. He lifted his chin so that his eyes were in line with hers. "Go with me to the Summer Solstice Ball," he said suddenly.

She stiffened. "What? Go with you to . . . Why?"

He started to laugh. "What better way is there to celebrate our new god-mother studies than in triumph there?"

She suddenly felt woozy. "There must be dozens of fairies who would love to go with you."

He took her other hand. "And they'd spend all night parading around, making sure everyone saw us and having nothing interesting to say." He pursed his lips. "If I go with you, at least I'll know you can hold a conversation."

"What a ringing endorsement," Renée said dryly.

"It was meant to be a compliment." Tresor looked directly at her. "What do you say, Dubois? Will you attend the ball with me? I'm expected to go, and having a friendly face there would make it infinitely better."

Renée felt the tingling start at her head and drop down to her toes then back again. Her pulse was racing. "What would your aunt think?"

He continued to stare at her as a smile started to dance on his lips again. "I don't care what my aunt thinks, Dubois. I thought you knew that by now."

"Right. Well. Then." Why couldn't she form a sentence all of a sudden? It was just a dance. Correction: a ball. Tresor wasn't feeling amorous. He simply wanted a friend, a date to commiserate with at the festivities.

The flowers on her gown seemed to gaze up at her and wait for a response. Her face was so warm, she thought she might burst into flames. *Say yes*, every bone in her body screamed. *Say yes!*

"All right, I will go to the ball with you," she finally said, the words rushing out of her.

"Good answer," Tresor said, that smile still twitching at the corner of his lips.

TWENTY

When Renée had told Nelley and Lune not only was she attending Summer Solstice Ball, but she was going with Tresor, they created a cloud of fairy dust that exploded in Daffodil Hall, and it took two days to disperse. She'd had a fortnight till the ball and there had been much to do, but more importantly, she had new courses to focus on. Renée threw herself into her new godmother studies.

There was so much to remember, hundreds of godmother lessons written up by the fairy storytelling department. Most of them were made up of rules or exceptions to rules. One stuck out clearly: *Godmothers are to be heard, not seen. And if they* must *appear, they should gently guide! Encourage! Be compassionate! Yet strong.*

Godmothers also needed wands, which of course Renée did not yet have, but at least she'd found her magic words, which were making spelling slightly more manageable. She learned how to problem solve for specific situations. If your charge needs a horse, a horse could be conjured if only for a brief time. A boat? No problem. But make sure the journey is a short one. Same went for tailoring. A godmother could make clothing like no other, but it was only for that one outing.

Remember, the handbook stressed, *magic is a temporary solution, not a permanent one.*

Magic, like everything else in life, was fleeting. In the end, its power was said to feel almost like a dream—there one moment, gone the next, and the details would be rather hazy. Kind of like how she felt about that night she'd met her own godmother. She could still hear her soft voice. *It's going to be all right, child,* but the details of her face were as foggy as the rest of her memory now.

There should be no record of your visit! the handbook warned. *The gift is but a distant miracle for the charge to think back on. How sad*, Renée had thought. She wanted to keep memorizing godmother details, but the ball was nearing.

"I can't believe I'm going to say this, but you have to stop studying and get ready for the ball," Lune said, flying into their room, with Nelley close behind. "You haven't put that book down in days!"

Renée hugged it to her chest. "I can't help it. This is even more fascinating than *Fairies among Us*. Plus, there is so much to learn . . . and retaining it has been especially challenging."

"You'll get there," Nelley assured her. She reached down and started eating from the vegetable display Renée had been testing out in a corner of the room. "These radishes are so succulent!"

Renée paused, her mind flying in a hundred directions at once. What was it about the radishes she was supposed to remember? She had no idea. "But I don't have a lot of time to prove to Margarite that I should finish the program, let alone that I should become an actual godmother at the end of it. What if she tests me?"

That had been a reoccurring nightmare—Margarite making her spew godmother facts.

"Pishposh! Margarite wouldn't be testing you tonight," Nelley said. "Just enjoy your first official ball! With Tresor, no less! What a match."

"Indeed," Lune agreed, smirking at Renée. "And I revealed nothing, even if a teeny, tiny piece of me sensed this very thing happening."

"You consulted your bulle about this?" Renée asked, eyes wide.

"I *might* have checked in on your path in Faerie Province after Mother agreed to let you take more classes," Lune said defensively. "But I wasn't looking for anything about your love life, especially with my cousin."

Renée colored and the flowers on her now periwinkle robe (a fairy godmother training robe) turned bright red. "This has nothing to do with love. He asked me to keep him company. That's all."

Nelley and Lune side-eyed each other.

"Yes, yes. You're just acquaintances," Nelley tutted, and took another bite of her radish. Renée started to protest. "Even *acquaintances* need something to wear to Summer Solstice Ball. You haven't focused on this at all and now there will be no time to find you a dress. But no matter. I can help. Here."

Nelley waved her wand high above her head and gave it a quick counterclockwise swirl. "This is the dress I wore to my first ball almost four hundred years ago. It would look lovely on you!"

Poof! A coral-pink gown that looked more like a flour sack than a dress appeared on her frame. Renée started to cough from all the dust. Two moths flew out of the hemline, which was past Renée's ankles. On her head was a bonnet. Renée glanced in the mirror and gaped.

"What do you think?" Nelley asked, and took another radish. "A classic, is it not?"

Nelley had been nothing but kindness itself, and the last thing Renée wanted to do was insult her. She glanced warily at Lune. "Yes! It's beautiful! But I couldn't wear your prized gown. . . . What if I got something on it and ruined it? You should wear it tonight."

"That's a splendid idea!" Lune agreed quickly.

Nelley's eyes lit up. "You think so? I never wear anything but my godmother robe these days." She thumbed the material on Renée. "Are you sure you don't want it?"

"I insist," Renée said solemnly. "I'm sure Lune has something I could borrow."

"Actually, first I must give you the gift my cousin sent over." Lune flew to her bed and brought back a small satin box.

"Ooh! A present! I told you the boy is smitten," Nelley insisted.

Renée felt her fingers tingle. She stared at the word scrawled on the crisp piece of parchment on top of the box: *Dubois.* "But I didn't get him a gift."

"He said you had to accept it," Lune told her. "He said when you saw them, you'd know they were meant for you."

"They?" Renée questioned, but as she lifted the lid, she understood. Inside the box was a pair of canary-yellow satin slippers.

They had long silk ribbon straps that would wind up her ankles and tie around her calves, reminding her of the shoes dancers wore in Paris. She lifted one slipper with trembling hands and looked at the craftsmanship—such precise stitching. Such beautiful fabric. Had Tresor made these with magic?

"Oh," Nelley said, her voice barely hiding her disappointment. "Why would Tresor give you footwear? Fairies don't wear shoes."

"When I was a human, I used to think . . . something about the slippers . . ." Her voice caught in her throat. "Oh, I forget . . ."

Lune put a hand on her shoulder. "Take your time."

Renée closed her eyes and thought of Raymond laughing, Celine twirling. The thimble of milk and the pieces of cheese she'd left in . . . slippers. As fairy offerings. "I used to leave fairies slippers," she said, relieved to remember. "That's why Tresor gave me these."

Lune shook her head. "That is so out of character for my cousin."

There was a tinkling sound and Nelley frowned. "Odd. I saw my charge yesterday. But . . ." The tinkling sound of bells grew louder. "I'd better go. I'll see you tonight, my dears. Save a dance for me!" With a wave of her wand, she disappeared.

"That's strange," Lune said. "Nelley is the third godmother I've seen since this morning get called away. I wonder what's going on in the human world. I didn't see anything in the bulle earlier."

Renée felt tingling up her arms. "You would know if something was wrong, wouldn't you?"

"I would think so," Lune said, biting her lip. "Maybe I'll check again in a moment. First, we should get dressed so we're not late."

Lune was attending the ball with a group of fairies, which included Peony, who had been talking all week in fairy ring class about her seafoam-green gown. Renée suspected Peony wanted to be sure no one else was wearing that particular shade of green.

Lune waved her wand and *poof!* She appeared in front of Renée in a long, sheer lilac dress that had several skirt layers and multiple ribbons tied in neat bows along Lune's back. When her wings fluttered, the ribbons rippled.

"Oh, Lune, you look divine!" Renée told her, and the flowers on her robe started to curl toward her again, the vines growing happily. She'd gotten adept at her wand technique, using her "Renée supervising time" to practice her own spell work.

"I rather like it, too," Lune said, and stared down at the slipper in Renée's hands. "And I think you would look perfect in a gown to match your slippers."

She waved her wand again and in an instant, Renée was wearing a dress that was the color of freshly churned butter. The bodice was corset-style, though far more comfortable than a human corset, and flowers like the ones Renée wore on her robe cascaded down the skirt in ripples. The skirt length was to her calves, which meant the slippers would be on full display for Tresor and the rest of the province. It was a dress that looked perfect for lounging in a field of grass or spinning across clouds. Renée couldn't imagine wearing anything more perfect. She spun, watching the gown twirl out around her and for the first time in her life, she felt like she belonged. "This dress is . . ." She couldn't find the words without choking up. "More than I ever dreamed of."

"Good." Lune smiled as she fluttered up and down before her. "That means you're ready and . . ." A loud bell chimed, which startled both of them. It kept chiming. Lune frowned. "That's the alarm for seers. Something must be happening."

Renée felt the tingling start at the back of her neck. "Should I join you?"

"No, no. It's all right. If I need you, I'll let you know. Finish getting ready and I'll meet you at the ball." Lune waved her wand and pointed to the slippers. "And don't forget your shoes!" Then she was gone.

Renée tried not to worry. Glancing out her window, she could see fairies in other halls in bright open windows preparing for the ball while still more fairies—ones in blue robes—darted back and forth, calling out frantic directions to one another as they flew. What was going on?

Moving quickly, Renée laced up her slippers, finding they fit like a dream. While walking barefoot had given her the freedom she'd always longed for, she'd forgotten how nice a pair of soft slippers could feel against her skin.

For a moment, she was reminded of her old life. Her sitting by a small candle, sewing with Raymond, teaching him each stitch and each cut to create a shoe that would fit the wearer just right. She stared at the slippers in the mirror, admiring them from all angles, and saw a flash of light reflected in the glass.

"Hello, Renée."

Margarite was dressed in a gown that resembled a glowing sunset, a vibrant orange at the top that faded into the darkest of blues. Her crown of flowers had been replaced by an actual crown, this one made of clear crystals. Her butterfly companions flew around her like fairy dust.

"Your Majesty," Renée said, dipping low into a curtsy and feeling the flowers on her skirt start to curl tightly. "I'm sorry, but Nelley and Lune are not here."

"It is you I came to see," Margarite said, her gold eyes widening as she took in the slippers on Renée's feet.

"Oh." Renée paused.

"Tresor told me you're attending the ball together this evening," the queen said.

"We are." Renée tried not to sound nervous. "Though I hope he doesn't mind standing near the dessert table all night."

Margarite's smile was thin. "I think it goes without saying how much my nephew means to me. And how much my sister meant." She stepped forward and touched the tip of Renée's chin. "And while you might be excited about attending your first ball, wearing a dress my daughter created for you and slippers my nephew gave you, from where fae only knows . . . I came here because I need to tell you this: He is meant for great things. But there are many directions one's life can take. I just ask . . . Please do not hold him back from his brightest future."

Hold him back? Renée tried not to react, even though she felt like pinpricks were digging into her skin. She continued to stare at the queen as waves of meaning kept crashing over her. She refused to cry. "I promise."

"Good. You should get going," Margarite said, already starting to fade away. "You don't want to keep Tresor waiting."

TWENTY-ONE

RENÉE TRIED NOT TO BE RATTLED BY MARGARITE'S VISIT AS SHE RUSHED TO meet Tresor at the fields by the Grand Verre. Not wanting to ruin her slippers, she carried them in her hand, running through the courtyard and the fields till she reached the base of the mountains. That's where she found a giant fairy ring, glitter flying in large bursts of color as hundreds of fairies danced around it. The typical mushrooms had been replaced by flowers illuminated by floating lanterns. A large orchestra of fairies played as other fairies sat at oversized dandelions that served as tables under arches of ivy and canopies of flowers. The falls of the Grand Verre reflected images of fairy balls past in its waters.

As Renée rushed down the path to the festivities, the music stopped and it felt like all of Faerie Province turned to look at her. Or maybe it was her slippers. She slipped them on. Ignoring the stares, she stood on tiptoe trying to find Tresor, but there was no need. It only took moments before he landed beside her in a jacket made of yellow thread with matching breeches that made his aureate more visible.

He flashed her a smile as he offered his arm, which she looped her own through. "Hello, Dubois."

"Tresor," she said, feeling flush already and unsure if it was because he smelled and looked so good, or the fact she was holding his arm, or that the fée were looking at the two of them. His aunt's warning rang in her mind. "Hello." She looked down. "Thank you for my present."

His face lit up. "Do you like them?"

"I love them," she gushed before trying to rein herself back in. She cleared her throat. "How did you find shoes in Faerie Province?"

"I can't reveal all my secrets just yet." The strains of a violin began again as he lifted her into the air using the power of his wings, prompting her to put her free arm around his waist as he flew them over to the party.

They touched down right outside the fairy ring, where dozens of fairies were already dancing, some sneaking glances at them. As if she didn't feel awkward enough standing beside a fairy who smelled like pine needles and soap and who was the most handsome being she'd ever seen. Not that she would tell him that. It wasn't like he was courting her. She snuck a glance at him again and found him staring.

"Your dress is lovely," he noted. "Lune's work, I assume?"

"How do you know I didn't whip this up myself?" she asked lightly.

He looked amused. "Did you?"

"No," she admitted. "But I can summon a glass of water while I'm still lying in bed," she said hopefully. "And if I misplace one of my books, I can call for it. And then there is my work with vegetables—enlarging them, as you know, and transforming them into household objects." She concentrated hard to see if she was missing anything. "Of course, many spells have been a bit of a mystery."

"I like mysteries," he said as a new song began to play. "They remind me of peeling onions. Something new in every layer."

"Or a bruised apple," she offered. "Sometimes the fruit underneath is unexpectedly crisp."

"Unexpected is a lovely surprise," he said softly, and she thought he might have inched closer, which made her stomach drop. He motioned to the fairy ring. "Shall we give the fée something to talk about, other than your shoes?"

"Yes, but I should warn you, I haven't danced in a long time."

Tresor placed his hands around her waist. She gamely placed her hands on his shoulders. They were standing close now, their chests touching, and she suddenly felt unsure where to look. At that moment, the violins picked up, prompting them to jump in the circle. The music was fast, forcing her to move quickly to keep up, but at least keeping count kept her from thinking about how close she was to Tresor.

"No balls like this in the human world?" Tresor shouted, lifting her into the air on a spin.

"I'm afraid not," she said as they started to move faster. "At least none that I knew of." She could feel fairies watching, so she focused on Tresor's neck, which didn't help her nerves. She caught a whiff of him, reminding her of the night they met.

"I find it hard to believe you wouldn't be invited to many parties, Dubois."

"I'd only recently come of age, and instead of entering society, my aunt was ready to marry me off." She was keenly aware of his fingers on her waist.

He scowled. "At such a young age? If a fairy decides to make a commitment like that, they do not do so until they're at least a hundred."

"That sounds wise." She fell silent, feeling a bit strange for bringing up marriage. Instead, they continued spinning, fairies leaping and jumping in the air as if their routine was synchronized. Tresor was a good partner. He knew the steps and helped her keep in time to the music by whispering what move came next. She found herself starting to enjoy the dance just in time for it to end. The second song, however, was much slower, and fairies in pairs glided closer, swaying as they stared into each other's eyes.

Tresor studied Renée's face. "Up for another?"

"I'm thirsty. Are you thirsty?" she asked nervously. "You *look* parched. I think some punch would be good. Would you like some punch? I haven't eaten." She looked around. "There is food here, isn't there?"

He chuckled. "Yes. Why don't you get us some punch and I'll get us a plate and meet you at that free dandelion over there?"

"Good idea." When she let go of him, she felt slightly off-kilter.

What was happening to her?

Didn't she find Tresor arrogant and rude?

Yes, she understood him better now, but that didn't mean she liked Tresor in a *romantic* way, did it?

She thought of Margarite's plea in her room again. It was for the best if she didn't fall for the queen's nephew. She had just gotten her to agree to more lessons, had just started to carve out a life here. She had enough to contend with. Renée focused on the task at hand—go to the punch bowl! When she made it there, she poured two glasses with unsteady hands as a group of fairies hovered around gossiping.

"My roommate has been gone for hours. They said it was all wings on deck," said a male fairy in midnight-blue breeches.

"How can that be? I thought the portal can only stay open so long. And only a few godmothers are allowed to jump at a time. Why would they need so many?" asked the fairy next to him. She had short white hair and was wearing a gown made entirely out of butterflies.

"A battle maybe?" asked a fairy floating above the punch table.

"Can't be. We would know about a human war," said the male fairy again. "This was sudden. My friend is a seer and she said she didn't predict anything of note happening today. They never let us schedule a ball when there is the potential for human strife."

"I heard it's a natural disaster," whispered a fairy close to the punch bowl.

"Wouldn't the seers be able to predict that?" Renée asked.

The one wearing the butterfly dress side-eyed her, as if the answer were obvious. "Nature is powerful. Not even seers know everything." Several of her butterflies fluttered away.

"Does anyone know what kind of disaster it is?" Renée asked the others.

"I don't know. But my friend said the situation is dire. Hundreds of humans will die. All the godmothers left to check on their charges."

Renée felt a prickling sensation at the back of her neck. "Did you say hundreds? Where is this taking place?"

The fairy just looked at her. "Aurelais, of course."

Renée dropped her punch, splattering pink juice all over her dress. The other fairies gaped as she rushed away to find Tresor, pushing her way through the crowds of fairies to find him at the daffodil eating vegetable quiche. "Tresor!"

He saw her face and stood up, grasping her by her shoulders. "What's wrong?"

She had trouble keeping her thoughts straight. "Something's happened in the human world. In Aurelais. I just overheard. That's why Lune and all the seers and godmothers haven't arrived yet." Her skin started to tingle. "I'm worried."

He frowned. "Are you sure? The seers would have said—"

"I know." Renée felt ill. "But something's changed. I need to find Lune or a godmother. I can't sit here and do nothing. What if Celine and Raymond need me?"

"We'd know." His voice was sure.

She trusted Tresor, but what if he was wrong? "We should still find out more. Can someone tell us what's going on?"

He stopped a fairy rushing by him. "Hyacinth. What are you hearing about this situation with the godmothers?"

Her expression was grim. "My friend left hours ago, and I don't think she's getting to this ball anytime soon." She looked around to make sure no one was listening. "Apparently it's a storm that changed course. They predict it will wash away half of Aurelais."

Renée felt her stomach start to sway.

"You're certain?" Tresor said sharply.

"Yes. It came on suddenly." Hyacinth looked fearful. "They say it's going to be like nothing the human realm has ever seen."

Would Uncle Gaspian be traveling? Were Raymond and Celine safe? How old were they now? Where were they living? Renée didn't even know how to find them if she could get through a portal.

"My friend's bulle said a charge is going to lose her father," said a fairy, flying up to them. "My friend and the godmother are in a panic because the godmother doesn't know what to say to her charge to get her out of the valley and leave everything in time. She can't let her drown, too." She clutched the flowers around her neck. "This is terrible."

"They've only got so much time before the flooding," Hyacinth continued. "I guess they'll have to save the humans who are most important."

Renée bristled. "Every life is important!" She closed her eyes for a moment, reliving the moments she spent spinning, churning through dark cold waters, fighting to keep her head above. "Why are we just standing here?" she asked. "We need to go help!"

"No one is allowed in the academy," the fairy told her. "They're busy and we need to stay out of the way."

"But—" Renée started to argue.

"We aren't godmothers or seers," Hyacinth reminded her. "All we can do is wait for word." She turned back to Tresor. "Let me know if you want a dance later." Then she flew off.

Good riddance! Renée fumed.

"It will be all right." Tresor put an arm around Renée, seeming to sense her unease as the other fairy flew away.

Renée's skin started to pulse, the tingling growing so intense she could hardly hear herself think. "Lune said she could see Raymond and Celine had a godmother, but what if she's wrong?"

"Lune saw your cousins with a fairy?" Tresor asked. "When?"

"I don't know, but what if they aren't deemed 'important' enough to save? I can't let anything happen to them. I need to try to get through a portal."

He turned her to face him. "Dubois, listen to me: If you do anything rash, it could jeopardize your chances in the godmother program. Both our chances. Let's just think this through."

"That matters not!" she protested. "I can't lose them." Her voice cracked.

"You won't. I promise." Tresor pulled her close, holding the back of her head, and she let him, listening to the sound of their breath syncing. For a moment she felt a brief second of calm, but then the tingling in her arms and legs returned. That's when she heard a voice calling to her.

Renée!

Help! Please!

Renée pulled away and looked at Tresor in alarm. "I just heard someone calling to me in my head. Like a message."

"A voice?" He looked confused. "Whose voice?"

"I don't know." It made her nervous. "That's never happened before. What if it was the children?"

"It can't be," he said, stroking her hair. "You're worried and I understand why, but we'll make sure they're okay."

"How?" she asked, her voice rising. Fairies turned to stare.

"I'll find Lune in the academy. They won't be pleased with the interruption, but it would make sense for me to look for Lune since she's family. I'll see what she knows. If the children are in trouble, we will find a way to send help to them at once. But promise to stay here till I do that." Tresor stared at her intently. "Can you do that? Can you trust me?"

She hesitated. Did she trust anyone to care about Celine and Raymond the way she did? The tingling in her arms returned.

Renée! Come find me!

Was it all in her head? She looked at Tresor again. "I trust you," she said, not quite answering him.

"I'll come back with answers." Then he took off, leaving her there to watch the rest of the ball go on as if nothing important was happening in a world so close to their own. And that's when she heard the voice again.

Renée! I need you!

Follow my voice!

Find me, Renée! Find me!

She couldn't ignore it. The voice was louder now. More insistent. Someone needed her and it could be the children. What choice did she have? A storm was a fickle thing and time wasn't on their side. Renée decided she didn't have a choice.

She took off her slippers and started to sprint toward the academy.

It wasn't until she was too far gone that she realized she'd lost one along the way.

TWENTY-TWO

THE MAIN ENTRANCES TO THE ACADEMY MIGHT HAVE BEEN GUARDED WITH magic, but Renée knew there had to be a way inside. As she hurried to the large castle, she looked up at the highest tower and the windows. Every pane of glass seemed to have a slight haze. Renée frowned.

Hurry, Renée! the voice in her head seemed to say again.

I'm trying! She kept looking around for an entrance. Something about the right side of the academy was calling to her, the prickling sensation in her arms growing stronger. That's when she spotted the wooden doors.

No one in Faerie Province entered by door when they could fly through a window, which meant maybe Margarite wouldn't have thought to charm them. Renée rushed to the main doors and pulled on them. Locked. She hurried to another set. Those wouldn't budge either.

"Now you use a door?" she yelled at the brick walls. "Key . . . Key . . . I need to find a key," she said to the rose bushes by the entrance, hoping they'd help. Instead, they barely moved their vines when she came to look through their leaves.

Roses could be so prickly when they wanted to be.

Something sharp cut into her arm. "Ouch!" She saw blood trickling down her limb. "I'm trying to help. Thanks a lot."

Tweet. Tweet. Tweet.

A blue jay sitting on a vine appeared to be staring at her. She didn't know all her birdcalls yet, but she could try. "What is it?" she cooed. "Do you know a way inside?"

The little blue bird flew off the branch and disappeared behind the rose bush. Carefully, Renée inched around and found the bird hopping near a small window—one that was neither glowing nor surrounded by fairy dust! It probably led to the level where her fairy rings studies class was held.

"Nicely done! Thank you," she said, brushing the vines away and pushing the window open. With a quick glance to be sure only the obstinate roses were watching, Renée yanked up the hem of her dress and stuffed her remaining slipper in the top of her gown. Then she dove through and hit the ground with a loud thud.

Hurry! Hurry!

Renée ignored her sore head and bleeding arm and peered at the shelves overflowing with papers, some open, revealing numerous files inside. This was not the fairy ring studies room. Mr. Agaricus kept his mushrooms study area spotless. He also didn't have many books. Renée peered at the open books, scrolls, numerous artifacts, and map of what looked like Aurelais. Renée made her way around the stacks of books on the ground.

Help! Help me! Hurry, Renée!

The voice in her head was louder and more persistent now that she was in the academy. In fact, it almost felt as if it was right here in this room.

"Renée!"

Was the voice outside her head now? Either that or the vase of decaying tulips on the desk was talking to her. "Hello? Is anyone there?" Renée looked around.

"I'm in here!"

In a flash, she recognized the voice. "Nelley?"

"Yes, child! Hurry!"

"Where are you?" Renée felt the books on the shelves, wondering if there was a secret doorway.

"Behind this wall! We're running out of time!"

"But how do I get in?" Renée spun around. Then a flash caught her eye—a mirror. She ran toward it and moved the frame aside and saw a small trace of light.

Aha, she thought, following the beam, pushing more debris aside and finally spotting a small doorway in the wall. She shoved it open and found herself face-to-face with something otherworldly.

It was a portal.

It couldn't be anything else—a wall of light, circling round and round like a vortex, each beam so warm and radiant, Renée felt like she was staring at the sun. She couldn't look at the beams straight on either or say exactly what color they were—like stardust? The portal's colors kept changing, the light brighter and dimmer each second as it swirled around in front of the wall, pulling everything in its path.

Moving slowly, she could hear voices; people talking, flashes of images appearing across the white light. She wanted to be near them. The closer she stepped, the more the air in the room felt like it was being sucked out of it. When she was a foot or two away, the light started to pulse, the voices growing louder, the flowers and the ivy surrounding the bookcase beside the door curling away.

Renée, she thought she heard the portal call out. *Renée.* Whispers were calling to her as she neared the wall of magic. She reached out a hand to touch the light.

"Renée!"

She spun around at the shout and spotted a figure in a pale blue robe slumped on the ground. "Nelley!" Renée rushed to her side and tried to lift the older fairy up to a sitting position. How could she have gotten so distracted? "What happened?"

"Radishes . . . in your room . . . I think they were tainted," she sputtered.

"Radishes?" Renée frowned, trying to understand. Suddenly, she gasped. "The *radishes*." Of course. "The ones in my room were from the discard pile," she recalled, the information flooding back to her. "I was working on mutating them into flowers. They were not fit to eat, were they?"

"No." Nelley started to cough. "No sooner did I get to the academy than I felt this wave of nausea." Nelley's pale face was clammy, her hands cold. Beads of sweat mixed with the white curls in her hair. She was shivering head to toe. Leave it to Renée to give an ancient, powerful fairy food poisoning.

Renée cringed. "Oh, Nelley, I feel dreadful. I'm so sorry. I can't believe I forgot something so important and didn't warn you! How am I ever going to be a godmother?"

"You have no choice—I need you to be one now."

"Excuse me?" Renée wasn't sure she was hearing her correctly.

"I'll be right as rain by tomorrow, but I need your help now—you have to go for me." Nelley started gagging.

Renée looked around for a bucket. "Go? Where?"

"To the human realm!" she said, choking out the words.

Renée paled. "What do you mean?"

"My sickness will pass, but my charge can't survive this storm without me. That's why I called you." Nelley closed her eyes. "I can't believe it worked. I haven't used telepathy in over fifty years, but if anyone could hear me, I knew you could."

"Me? Why me?" Renée didn't understand. She hadn't learned telepathy, had she?

"Questions later. I don't know how much longer this portal will stay open," she said, motioning to the swirling vortex of light so casually one would think Nelley was pointing out a trail of ants. "Margarite is only letting a few godmothers through at a time. This much back-and-forth from the human world makes her nervous, but we didn't have a choice. So many charges crucial to the future of Faerie Province are in mortal danger."

Renée looked around. "Where are the other godmothers? Is this where they keep the portal? In the basement?"

"No, no. This is one of the hidden ones the godmothers keep in case of an emergency and—there's no time to explain. I need you to listen to me."

Renée grabbed a handkerchief near Nelley and used it to blot her sweaty brow. "I know all about the storm. It's supposed to be terrible and it's affecting Aurelais. I'm worried about Celine and Raymond."

Nelley attempted to pat Renée's hand. "They're going to be fine."

"How do you know?" Renée asked desperately. "If something happens to them—"

"Renée Dubois, focus!" Nelley's blue eyes bored into Renée's head, and she gripped her tightly. "They have protection, but my charge only has me and I can't get to her like this. You are my replacement."

"But I'm not allowed. Margarite would have my head. She'd surely banish me if I disobeyed. I'll find a godmother." Renée moved to get up, and Nelley held on tighter. For an older fairy with an upset stomach, she was strong.

"It has to be you, Renée," she said, her voice almost a whisper. "You're the only one I trust to make sure she survives this. You can understand her fear."

"But, Nelley, I don't know how to be a godmother yet." She felt a rising sense of panic. "I've barely started training. Or finished reading the handbook! I'm not even allowed to leave Faerie Province. Plus, you and Lune said when I jump, my forgetfulness and aging could be a problem and—"

"This is an emergency! It's your first jump and you won't be gone long, so you'll be fine." Nelley took her hand and firmly placed her wand inside it.

Renée gasped. Nelley's wand was a tarnished silver wonder—up close she could see it had small birds and the letter N engraved on it. The weight of it in her hand made her somehow feel stronger. Renée shook her head. "I can't take this! It will only work for you and besides which, I don't know how to use it."

"I told it all about you. The wand will listen, it will guide you." Renée started to protest. "But you must leave now." Nelley was breathing harder now, shaking so badly, Renée wished she had a blanket to drape over her. "If you don't, she will be lost. Lune consulted the bulle, and there's a possibility our future could very well depend on her line. I told Margarite, but she wouldn't listen, which is why I came here and . . . please, Renée." Nelley was begging now. "I wouldn't ask you to do this if I didn't think you could manage."

The portal started to crackle, the wind whipping up around them, blowing papers everywhere. Renée knew from the handbook that the appearance of a wand told it a fairy was ready to make the leap. If Renée didn't move soon, it would close and Nelley's charge would be lost. She could feel her skin tingling, her stomach swishing, a million thoughts rushing through her mind.

"I'll do it," Renée said, leaning over fast to hug the woman who had given her so much already and was now gifting her the chance to prove herself once more. Renée rose and faced the portal.

"Thank you, child! Now, go! While you still can," Nelley told her.

Renée clung to the wand as she approached the portal again, her legs shaking. She covered her eyes with her hand, trying to peer through the light. She wished she could see through to the other side, but all she could make out were flashes of images appearing and disappearing. Were these the ones Nelley was supposed to see? Or were they meant for her? They moved too fast to decipher. It all looked like one giant jumble, voices crying out at the same time—some laughing, others sounding like they were begging for help.

She blinked hard and looked again. An image of a fairy ring flew by her. Next, she saw a river. Then a downed tree. Was this her past she was seeing? Or was someone calling to her now? She didn't even understand how a portal worked. Could she communicate with it? Tentatively, she took another step forward, inches from stepping right through.

"Hello? Can you hear me? Is anyone there?" Her voice echoed and the portal seemed to brighten. There was a flash. She closed her eyes tight, the light too bright to keep staring at even if she wanted to.

"Jump!" Nelley shouted. "It's closing!"

Renée prepared to leap and suddenly heard a child's laughter. It sounded familiar. Her eyes flew open again. "Raymond?" she shouted. "Celine? Is that you?"

The portal swirled faster now, images jumbled so tight she couldn't see heads from tails, but then she heard a voice as clear as day.

"Renée! We need you!"

"Raymond!" Renée shouted, thrusting her hand out and watching as it pushed through. It didn't hurt. It just felt like grains of dirt slipping through her fingers like in fairy rings corps. She wanted to keep going if it meant seeing the children. "Raymond, I'm here!"

"Renée!" came Nelley's strangled cry. It sounded far away.

Her whole body started to tingle, a force she couldn't control pulling her forward. It was as if the portal wanted her to go to Celine and Raymond, but when she looked down at Nelley's wand in her hand again, she remembered. Her job was to help Nelley. It was *Nelley's* charge she was being asked to protect.

What if her godmother had left her that night in the fire? Or she'd been left on the riverbank to die? True godmother or not yet, she had an oath to uphold.

Looking down at the wand in her hand, she grasped it tightly, feeling a new resolve. *Save the girl.* She glanced back once more, though her vision was blocked by the swirling beams. "What is her name?" she cried, holding both her arms out now, letting them slide through the light.

"Genevieve!" Nelley shouted. "Find Genevieve!"

Renée took a deep break and looked at the wand again. "Take me to Genevieve in Aurelais," she told it, praying it knew who it was meant to find. Then she leapt.

Renée felt herself being pulled through, the voices growing louder, the world swirling in front of her like the churning water of the river in which she'd almost drowned. Suddenly, everything in front of her brightened to a glow she couldn't look at a moment longer. There was a flash and sparkles and a loud boom.

Next thing she knew, she was gone.

TWENTY-THREE

RENÉE FELT HERSELF TRAVELING AT AN UNUSUALLY FAST SPEED, BEING stretched and pulled like soft white nougat, the kind Anne made her and the children. The sensation was new. She didn't remember crossing with Lune and Tresor, because she had been unconscious, but this time she tried to remember every sight and sound she experienced in those few seconds. It was impossible, of course. Things were flying by so quickly, words jumbled, voices amplifying and hushing. She held tight to the wand. It seemed to be pulling her as she flew through time and space.

And then she was crashing into a vat of mud. Thunder boomed overhead and sheets of rain fell so hard and fast, it was impossible to get her bearings. Was this the human realm? Was she in the right place? Renée leaned forward and felt her body sinking deeper, her dress weighing her down. The sensation reminded her of drowning, and she started to panic.

"Bibbidi-bobbidi-boo!" she sang to the wand. Suddenly, she found herself on dry land, looking out at a river in Aurelais where a river had never been before. The road into the village had been completely wiped out, and now, she realized in horror that trees, houses, and splintered furniture were flying by like a tower of blocks. The wind howled so hard she couldn't hear herself think. The sky was black as coal, only illuminated by the occasional flash of lightning. How would she ever find . . .

Find . . .

She felt a rising sense of fear as she struggled to remember the name Nelley had just given her. *Genevieve!* A sense of release washed over her.

Genevieve. Genevieve. Genevieve. Keep saying the name, Renée. And don't forget the . . . time!

She looked down at her hands to see if they appeared different, but the rain was falling so hard, she couldn't see anything. Did she feel different? Maybe a little woozy. As she took a step forward, it felt as if her whole body was moving slower.

Was she imagining things?

A spark flashed again, and Renée pushed her wet hair out of her eyes. She spied a familiar small village, dense with homes nestled on top of each other, a castle rising high above them. The sight reminded her of the night Uncle Gaspian had brought her back to his manor. They'd traveled through this very village on the way to the countryside. For a moment, her mind failed her. *Genevieve. Genevieve!* she reminded herself. *Uncle Gaspian!* And then the memory was there again.

Look, dear Renée! he'd pointed out. *That is where the king and queen live.* Even as a small child, she knew he was trying to engage her because she was so distraught from the night's events. She remembered thinking, *Why bother looking at fine things like castles? I'm an orphan.* She'd just stared sullenly ahead, sneaking glances at the white castle when Uncle Gaspian wasn't watching. She remembered the palace's multiple towers, one higher than the next, seeming like they could touch the stars.

How strange, she thought, *to live in a tower twice the height of this one now.*

She inhaled, taking in gulps of mortal air, expecting it to feel strange. The only difference was the rapid beating in her chest, so loud it almost drowned out the thunder. It was as if her heart had awoken again, beating like a ticking clock. She couldn't stay long . . . could she? No. Nelley said no. Why was that again?

Remember the time. Remember Genevieve! Renée thought, praying these two important details would stay in her head. She hadn't even bothered to ask Nelley how old Genevieve was, what she looked like. "Help me find her," she begged the wand, holding it out like a sword. "Wand? How do I find Genevieve?" she tried again. There was no reaction.

A lightning bolt cracked, zipping down to earth and splitting a tree in two in front of her. Renée ran for cover. Her body felt slower somehow, heavier, each movement harder than she'd remembered when she was human.

Suddenly, she heard a bray. She looked up from her hiding spot. A horse and a carriage had been feet from where the tree came down. The terrified animal started to buck, and Renée was sure the carriage would careen out of control.

"Whoa! Whoa!" she heard the driver shout. Next to him sat a woman, fear written on her face as she tried to hold on.

Was this Nelley's charge? Renée wondered. *Her name would be . . . Her name would be . . . Genevieve!* Renée's heart beat faster. Time was moving. How long had she been here now?

The horse and the carriage came to a stop right in front of the felled tree. Renée watched through the driving rain as the man jumped down and tried to push the tree out of the way. But he was just a man and there was no way to move such a large object. He made his way back to the wagon, fighting the wind to get back to the seat. He was saying something to the woman, but Renée couldn't hear him.

Renée looked at the wand. "Take me to them, but don't let them see me," she said. The next thing she knew, she could feel herself beside the wagon.

"There is no other way around," the man was saying. "We have to go through."

"But, Gabriel, we have no idea how high the water is!" the woman cried. They stared at the river that had formed where the road once was. "You saw what happened to that other carriage."

"We don't have a choice, my love," he said, placing a hand on top of the woman's. "We can't survive out here much longer. We need to find cover before the storm grows worse. For Genevieve's sake as well as our own."

GenevieveGenevieveGenevieve.

Renée's ears perked up.

The woman nodded. "I know, but if something were to happen to the carriage . . ." Her next few words were drowned out by the rain. "She can't swim."

"She will be safer in the carriage than out here with us."

"All right," the woman said. "But let me tell her."

The woman crawled into the back of the carriage, which was covered with a fabric that was pulled taut in the wind. Renée could see some slashes in it already, probably from fallen trees.

"Take me closer," Renée begged the wand, and suddenly the wand shot forward and so did her . . . energy? Spirit? Essence? She wasn't sure what to call it. The next thing she knew, she was inside the carriage, where a small girl was huddled in the corner. She wore a simple white gown that reminded Renée of a nightdress.

Her heart started to beat faster. She pressed a hand to her chest to hear it again and wondered why she was so mindful of the beating.

Renée focused on the little girl.

She looked about ten, with auburn hair that fell in waves to her shoulders, a hint of freckles dotting her nose, which was pink. She clutched a rag doll tightly.

"Genevieve, darling?" the woman said, crawling inside the wagon.

The girl looked up. She had bright blue eyes like Nelley's. "Are we there? Are we safe, Maman?"

"Not yet. Soon," the woman said. "But I need you to be brave for a little while longer. Your papa has to take the wagon through the water and then we will find shelter. There is a village in Aurelais up ahead."

The girl smiled. "We've made it to Aurelais?"

"Yes." Her mother nodded.

"Is it beautiful?" the girl asked, her voice whisper thin over the sound of the rain pounding the tarp, making it ripple like waves.

Her mother laughed lightly. "I suspect it will be, once the sun comes out." She grasped her daughter's hand. "You hold on tight. When it's okay to come out, I will come for you."

The girl's eyes were round as saucers. "Promise, Maman?"

Renée felt her stomach lurch, and her heart skipped faster. *That's a very nice idea, but I'm never going to leave you, Raymond* she heard herself say.

"I promise," her mother said, kissing her hand and returning to the front of the carriage.

Only Renée could see the look of terror on the woman's face.

Genevieve waited till she was gone before she pressed the doll to her chest again. "Be brave. Be brave," she heard the girl tell herself. "I can be brave. Right, Godmother?"

Renée paused. Did Genevieve know about Nelley? Nelley hadn't mentioned that part. Did that mean Renée could show herself? She decided to wait, holding tight to the wand as the thunder continued to roll as loud as a thousand men marching past the château during the war. But how long could she stay? She looked down at her hands in the carriage—they still looked like her hands. Maybe she hadn't aged? Her back was a bit achy though. She'd never had that feeling before.

The carriage gave a lurch and Renée wondered what she should do—stay where she was or see if the father was steering well enough to get them through to the other side. She thought again of Nelley. What had she wanted her to do with Genevieve?

Watch over her?

Keep her safe?

The ticking of her heart seemed to mock her. How could she save a child who wasn't in danger yet?

The man started shouting to the horse, then the woman. She heard a sob and looked over at Genevieve again.

"Please, Godmother. Help Papa. Guide us through the storm," Genevieve said, holding the doll tight. "I wish you were here with me."

Wish.

Renée racked her brain trying to remember the rule she'd read about wishes. Her brain was starting to feel foggy. *Not now.* Her knees started to ache.

A crack of lightning flashed, and the handbook's passage came back to her in a whoosh. *Life-changing, big moment wishes, the kind that required the charge to say "I wish . . . ," can only be given once. Be sure this is the right moment, because you won't have an opportunity to change the course of your charge's life again.*

Was Nelley expecting her to grant one of those wishes to Genevieve tonight?

Renée's stomach twisted. She'd said to save the girl. She didn't mention wishes. Did the wand know? Would it tell her?

Renée's panic started to rise as the carriage lurched left then right. The ticking in her chest grew louder. They flew forward and Renée heard a scream. She wasn't sure if it was her own or Genevieve's. Before she could raise her wand, the carriage righted itself again.

"Hold on, Genevieve!" her mother called to her. "The water is moving fast. Loop your fingers into the rope in the tarp, darling."

"Maman!" Genevieve cried. "I'm scared! I want to be with you!"

"Stay there, darling. Please! It's safer," her mother begged.

Renée felt her panic churning like the waters outside the carriage. Water started to slosh into the back, spilling across the wooden floor. René could feel her skin tingling, and she closed her eyes tight thinking of herself tumbling forward and back in the cold, dark water.

Her breath came fast, and she clutched the wand tighter.

Why would Nelley want her to be the godmother for a mission such as this? One involving her worst memories come to life again?

Maybe because she had no choice, a voice in her head said. *And because she had faith you would know what to do.*

Genevieve let out a sob and held tightly to the doll. "Please help us, Godmother! Please help us fly away."

An image of a carriage flying through the air came to mind, but Renée shook it away. She had no idea if the wand, or she, had the strength to do such a thing. The wand warmed in her hand, and she suspected the answer was no.

As the little girl cried harder, Renée felt a familiar ache in her chest. She couldn't let the girl feel so alone. She could do *something*. Even if it was against the rules.

"Wand, let the girl see me," she told the instrument, and suddenly fairy dust gathered in the air, falling like the rain outside the wagon.

Genevieve looked up, her eyes widening as Renée materialized in front of her. "Godmother?"

"No, child," Renée said kindly. "But I am a friend of your godmother's."

Genevieve's face scrunched up as she stared at Renée's soiled dress. "Who is my godmother? I've never met her before."

"Oh. Well, your true godmother is an incredible fairy named . . ." Renée paused, all words suddenly out of reach. "No, no, no. I was just with her, I . . . NELLEY!" she shouted the word flying into her head. Genevieve smiled as Renée covered her mouth. "Whew!"

"Nelley." Genevieve seemed to consider this as she scooched closer. "And why did she send you instead of coming herself?"

"She's a bit under the weather, funnily enough," Renée said as another thunderclap sent Genevieve scurrying backward. She buried her head in the doll again. "But don't worry. She's much older and wiser and told me how to help you." *In a way.*

"Older than Maman?" Genevieve scooched closer now. "Because *you* look like a maman."

"Me?" Renée immediately placed a hand on her face. "No, I'm not old enough to be . . ." She trailed off. She had no clue how old she was to Genevieve. If she had already aged, maybe she looked much older. But how old? She felt a wave of nausea wash over her and placed a hand on the floor of the wagon to steady herself.

"Are you all right?" Genevieve asked.

"Yes. Yes. Fine. Thank you."

The carriage started to turn sideways, and the pair looked at each other. She could hear the father shouting to the horse, the woman screaming about the rising waters. Genevieve glanced behind her.

As her heart continued to remind her of the time, Renée had an idea. She knelt down by the girl, squeezing her hands. "You know, whenever there was a storm like this in the home I grew up in, we'd sing a little song to calm our nerves. Would you like me to teach it to you?"

"All right . . ." Genevieve said warily, lowering the doll from her face.

Renée racked her brain to access the memory. *Please let me remember. Please!* The tune came first, the lyrics following on its heels. *"Rain may fall, thunder may boom. Take shelter, my heart has room,"* she sang shakily. The silliness felt both ridiculous and perfectly at home in the treacherous circumstances. This, more than anything, summed up living in this realm—terrifying, beautiful, tragic, hopeful.

Genevieve smiled. *"Rain may fall . . ."*

"Thunder may boom," Renée encouraged her.

Genevieve inched forward with her doll. *"Take shelter . . ."*

Renée helped her with the rest: *"My heart has room."* They smiled at each other.

Suddenly, there was a loud clap and the next thing she knew, the carriage was rolling, water flooding the wagon . . . and sucking Genevieve out with it.

TWENTY-FOUR

In seconds, the tarp was ripped off the wagon and all of Genevieve's earthly possessions were tossed into the storm. Renée squinted hard, trying to get her bearings, but the rain was hitting hard as thorns.

Where was she?

Renée heard another scream, this one clearly Genevieve's. She tried to call out to the girl but swallowed so much water she found herself gasping for air, struggling to keep her head up. She clutched the wand, terrified to lose her only hold on magic. Was Renée's fate to drown after all?

Suddenly, the child came tumbling past, her auburn hair bobbing up and down as she frantically tried to stay afloat. Renée spun, watching the wagon drift farther away, hearing shouting and calls of "Genevieve!" but unable to see where they were coming from. The sense of déjà vu was almost too much to bear. A piece of wood drifted by and she reached out to grab it. Then she shot the wand in the air.

"Bibbidi-bobbidi-boo!" she shouted. Like the rain song, the words felt both absurd and at-home here. The wand produced a stream of light that came close to hitting the girl but missed.

"Help!" Genevieve cried, her breath ragged as she floundered and went under again. "I can't swim!"

Say, I wish! Renée desperately thought.

Then again, *could* Renée give the girl a wish with Nelley's wand? *Nelley, what am I supposed to do? Is there something I'm forgetting?!* Renée grunted in exasperation and held tight to the wand, trying to think. Wish or no wish, she was saving that girl.

"Genevieve! Hang on!" Renée cried. *I won't leave you.*

First things first: She had to get the child onto something that would float. Treading water, she looked around at the floating pieces of driftwood, broken chairs. She didn't know how to use any of those. Then she spotted the flash of orange floating in the darkness. A bag of carrots, presumably for the horse.

Vegetables she could work with. *Make them grow,* she thought and waved the wand again. *"Bibbidi-bobbidi-boo!"* she sang. Renée tried to stay above water as the carrots blew up to the size of a mule, shimmering and bright like the lightning dotting the sky. Another absurd parallel—a bit of whimsy within disaster.

"Genevieve!" Renée shouted, trying hard to push herself toward the girl. "Grab on!" she said as she took hold of one of the spelled roots herself, hanging tightly with one hand as she clung to the wand with the other.

Genevieve lunged and held on to the leafy green top.

Renée let out a cheer that bordered on a sob. The girl was afloat. Now she just needed to reach her.

The ridiculous mutant carrots were rushing downstream, past trees and other things that shouldn't be floating in the middle of a street. Renée kicked hard, her feet cutting against something sharp as she pushed herself forward. She was close enough now to grab Genevieve. She took a deep breath and briefly let go of her floatation device to grab hold of the girl. "I've got you!" she shouted.

"Maman! Papa!" Genevieve cried. "Where are they?"

Renée felt herself being pulled into the dark recesses of her mind. She saw her younger self, yelling for her own parents outside her house and somehow knowing they were gone. But Genevieve was not her. Her parents could be looking for her. Renée just had to get the girl to safety.

"We'll find them," she said.

"How?" Genevieve cried just as they hit something hard.

It was a tree and the jolt loosened Genevieve's grasp. In seconds, her small body went underwater.

Renée had to decide what to let go of: the girl or the wand.

She didn't hesitate: Her fingers released the wand.

"I've got you," she said as the girl cried in her arms. "I've got you."

More lightning lit up the sky, and Renée saw what appeared to be the remnants of their wagon along the side of the rushing water. If they could hit it, maybe she could have Genevieve climb up and get her onto the dry ground. The ticking sound in her ears grew louder.

"Genevieve! Listen to me, we're going to hit something hard again in a moment and when we do, I want you to grab on to whatever you can. All right?"

The little girl was crying so hard, Renée wasn't sure if she heard, but then she saw her nod.

"Here it comes!" Renée shouted, her fingers tingling. *Get ready*, she thought as the water splashed over them again, making it hard for Renée to breathe. "Now!"

The carrot hit the wagon sideways, cutting into Renée's arm, but she tried to anchor herself against the wood and push Genevieve up so that the child could climb.

"Go! Faster now!" she said.

"I'm trying!" The little girl kept slipping.

If only I had the wand, she thought desperately, and then she realized: She didn't need it. She could use the levitation spell!

"Bibbidi-bobbidi-boo!" she sang, thinking of the children and Nelley and Lune and herself as a girl and dry land.

Suddenly, the little girl was lifting into the air and up and out of the water.

But it wasn't just Genevieve.

Renée was suddenly rising, too, and so was a small blue item, sparkling in the lightning strikes.

The wand!

All three hit the ground at the same time.

She went running for Genevieve and lifted the child up. This time

Genevieve was laughing and crying at the same time. "You saved me!" the girl said, throwing her arms around her. "You saved us both!"

"Yes," Renée said, pushing the child's wet hair out of her eyes and holding her tight. "We saved each other," she told her, as her heart sped to an alarming rate.

Genevieve gulped down tears. "You never told me your name," she said, her teeth chattering.

"It's . . ." For a moment, she hesitated. Could she possibly forget her own name? The ticking sound was reaching a fever pitch. "It's—it's Renée."

"Renée," Genevieve repeated.

She felt another wave of nausea wash over her and suddenly her knees went weak.

"Are you all right?" Genevieve asked, alarmed.

Her heartbeat was so loud now it was hard for Renée to hear. Her legs felt like jelly. Her back seared in pain. "Fine . . ." Renée forced herself to say, but suddenly she was very cold.

"Genevieve! Genevieve, where are you?"

Renée turned shakily and saw the girl's parents rushing down the embankment toward her. "Your maman and papa are all right, too!" Farther behind them, she saw the horse had survived even if the carriage had not. "You should go to them."

You have to go, Renée! she heard in her head as the beating sound was out of control. *Go!*

Genevieve hugged Renée again and looked up at her. The storm was starting to pull away, the rain beginning to let up, but the lightning still allowed her to see Genevieve's face. "Will I ever see you again?"

"I don't know," Renée admitted, her teeth chattering. "But I won't forget you. That is a promise." She touched the girl's chin.

The child smiled. "Nor I." Her expression faltered. "Oh!"

"What is it?" Renée managed to whisper.

"Your face . . . It keeps changing," Genevieve said, alarmed.

"I'm fine. You should go now," Renée insisted. *You should go.* The girl nodded once, then took off running toward her parents. The ticking sound was so alarming, Renée had to cover her ears, but she watched, letting out a sob of gratefulness.

Now she needed something to get back herself. What was it?

She felt herself starting to lose consciousness as the drumming sound increased. Her breathing started to slow, the tingling in her cold hands returned.

And she remembered: the wand.

She stumbled forward through the grass and mud, falling twice as she half-walked, half-crawled. Her legs felt so heavy she wasn't sure she could go another step. "No, no, no!" she cried, feeling around in the mud, searching, wondering now if the wand had already been washed away after all. The drumming in her head was going to drive her mad. She pictured herself aging out of this life, stuck here, gone in a week without the wand. *No, please no.* And then, she saw a glimmer sticking out of the mud. She threw herself forward and her hand closed around it.

You did well, the wand seemed to say. *It's time to go. You just have to ask.*

I'm ready. Renée expected to be sadder to leave the human world once more. But she was ready to go back. "Take care, Genevieve," Renée said softly. "Thank you for allowing me to be your temporary godmother."

The wand started to shine.

Wand, she thought as she started to see stars. *Bring me home.*

The air around her shimmered. One minute she was there, looking at Genevieve's retreating frame, and the next, she was gone.

TWENTY-FIVE

Something was wrong.

As the wand pulled Renée through the portal, she could feel resistance. Her body was being yanked in two directions, as if the human realm didn't want to let her go. She could still hear her beating heart, the heaviness in her legs and nausea that wouldn't subside a small price to pay for not being pulled apart at the seams.

I stayed too long, Renée thought, holding tight to the wand. *Bring me back to Faerie Province*, she begged.

Trying, the wand seemed to say as it struggled, moving as if in mud.

For a second she felt frozen, neither in one realm nor the other, her body in a state of suspension. Any second she could snap in two. She felt a rising sense of panic at the thought.

A portal can only stay open so long, she remembered reading. What would happen if she was stuck here between worlds?

I need help, Renée thought, but her lips wouldn't move. *Bibbidi-bobbidi-boo! Bring me back to the fée!* And that's when she felt the change in the air. Nelley's blue wand started to glow, the sensation warming her hand to the point she wanted to let go because it was starting to burn, but she knew she couldn't. There was a crackling sound, a huge gust of wind, and—

Boom!

Renée fell through the portal.

"Renée!" Lune rushed toward her. "Thank the fée you're all right! Nelley, she's all right!"

"Of course she is!" Nelley tutted.

Renée looked up. She wasn't in a small, cramped basement filled with books. She was somehow back in Daffodil Hall in her room, and Nelley was sitting up in a chair, surrounded by flowers, holding a cup of tea. Color had returned to her face, and she looked well.

"Didn't I tell you everything would be— Oh my!" Nelley dropped her teacup (a flower swooped in to catch it). She jumped up, helping Lune support Renée under one arm. "She's stuck!"

"Stuck?" Lune replied, pushing the hair off Renée's forehead. "What do you . . . Oh . . . Oh my . . . She's . . . aged almost ten human years! She's supposed to revert back to her fée form when she comes back through the portal, right? Why isn't she?"

What is happening? Renée wanted to ask but she had no strength. The room was spinning. "I . . ."

"Shh . . . it's the reentry," Nelley explained, smoothing Renée's hair. "It's not easy for her." She uttered her magic words, and a blue potion bottle appeared in her hands. "Drink this. Quickly now. Quickly."

Renée wasn't even sure she could lift the bottle to her lips. Her breathing was rapid. The wand wouldn't release from her shaking hand. Nelley put the potion to her lips. Immediately, she felt a warmth start to spread from her face to her neck through her torso down to her toes. Lune and Nelley were standing over her, watching. The next thing she knew, her eyes were closing.

When she awoke, she could feel the difference immediately. Her body felt so light, she was sure if she let go of the chair, she would float.

"There she is!" Lune said, still hovering over her, her wings fluttering fast. "You look much better."

"Most definitely!" Nelley agreed. "Thirty human years looks good on you."

Renée let go of the chair. "I've aged here, too?"

Nelley started to laugh and Lune gave her a stern look. "I'm sorry, child. I couldn't resist. No, no, your human body doesn't heal as quickly as ours does, but not to worry. You're back to your old fairy self now." She came in close and squeezed her hand. "And yet you've aged in wisdom, haven't you? I want to hear about how you saved Genevieve."

"How do you know I saved her?" Renée wondered, her voice returned to her.

Nelley beamed. "The bulle showed Lune and me everything. I knew you could do it."

"I did," Renée said, feeling an immense feeling of pride. "And her family is safe as well. They're all fine."

"How wonderful!" Nelley hugged her fiercely.

Lune inhaled. "Next time you go, you'll be prepared."

Renée's eyes brightened. "You mean they'll be a next time?"

Nelley laughed. "I should hope so! Look how well you did today!"

Renée cleared her throat. "There's still one problem." She held up her right hand and showed them the blue stick in her hand. "Your wand won't let go of me."

Nelley and Lune gave each other a look.

"What is it?" Renée worried, sensing the tension. The flowers around her all turned to look as well.

"We will deal with that later," Nelley insisted. "First, tell us about Genevieve."

"No," Lune said. "First, we have to tell Renée what to do if she gets called to the human world again. If she can't release your wand, she must be prepared. We have to give her tools to help transition as a part-fairy or she won't survive another jump."

"You've got a point," Nelley said, a deep line forming on her forehead. "We need to make sure you have an easier time of things. You can't lose track of time! That's of the utmost importance!"

"I know, but how? My heart was beating loudly . . . like a clock," Renée told them.

"That's good," Lune said. "We can work with that."

"Yes," Nelley agreed. "But for now, there are a few things we can do to keep you safe when crossing realms. Next time, you need to chew on pepper-mint leaves as soon as you return. Ginger can also help your hands and feet so they don't get cold. A bit of rosemary in a cup of tea could have cleared your head. Here's the potion we just used. Zinnia, zinnia!"

A small potion bottle with a bright blue liquid appeared in front of her, bobbing in the air.

"This is the perfect antidote for you as we already know it helps you readjust to the fairy realm."

"Perfect." Renée stretched out her hand. "This means I can come and go whenever I please?"

Nelley spelled it out of reach. "I'm afraid not. While you were resting, Lune and I did some calculations." She glanced Lune's way.

"Yes." Lune cleared her throat and her wings fluttered faster. "Aging about eight years when you were barely gone an hour feels . . . especially fast." The wrinkles in Lune's own brow deepened. "If your human side ages that much with each jump . . ."

"That only leaves you with ten jumps total—if you're *very* lucky," Nelley supplied. "Now we don't know how long your life will be, of course, but the last thing we want is to have you cross over and be unable to get back. I'll tinker with the potion a bit. Judging by how well it's worked so far, I may be able to get you to a dozen."

"A dozen?" Renée repeated. "How often do godmothers normally cross over?"

Lune and Nelley shifted.

"To get to know their mortal, observe their patterns and behaviors over

240

time, we usually go . . . oh . . . about twenty times, maybe twenty-five per charge," Nelley said meekly.

"Twenty-five?" Renée cried.

"Now, now, let's stay calm," Nelley said. "We will help as much as we can. I'm afraid this is a side effect of being part-human that we can't take lightly."

"To make sure you don't forget, I made this." Lune handed her a silver charm hanging on a necklace. It appeared to be glowing with a sparkling numeral *one*. "The number of jumps will change when you cross through a portal. It will help you keep track."

"And next time, take this vial with you," Nelley said, sending the little potion bobbing in front of Renée's face. "Then drink half before you make the leap, and half afterward. Understood?"

"Keep track of my jumps and drink the potion. I can do that. Is there anything else I can do or— Oh no." Renée's right hand, the one still holding the wand, flew out in front of her, forcing her to rise from her chair. "What's happening? What is the wand doing?" She tried to wave her arm to release the wand, but it wouldn't budge. "Why can't I let go?"

Nelley cursed under her breath. "She knows."

"Who knows? Knows what?" Renée asked, still shaking her hand. The wand started to pull her forward toward the window and Renée shrieked. Was it going to send her to her death? "Bibbidi-bobbidi-boo!" She started to levitate. That was one problem solved, but now she was sailing out the window. "Where am I going?"

Lune rushed over, her expression grim. "To see Mother."

TWENTY-SIX

THE WAND ZIPPED ACROSS THE COURTYARD, PULLING RENÉE STRAIGHT TO THE academy and directly to the fairy godmother balcony. She landed beside dozens of fairies already waiting. As soon as they saw her, they flew into a tizzy.

"You?" One with a pink aura pointed a finger in her face. "You're not a godmother! What are you doing here?"

"Hello," Renée said meekly. "I am in the godmother training program and—"

There was a gasp from a fairy with a blue sheen. "She has Nelley's wand. Did you use it to make an illegal crossing during the storm?" They started to move in a pack toward her.

"No, I didn't," Renée said hurriedly, walking backward, mindful of the edge of the balcony a few feet away. "Well, I wouldn't exactly call it illegal."

"She did! She's lying," said a pink fairy.

"No!" Renée cried, looking back to see how close the balcony ledge was now. "I was helping Nelley! She asked me to go because—"

"You give that wand back," said a pesky yellow fairy, trying to swipe it from her.

Renée moved her hand away. "I can't. Please. If you would just let me explain—"

There was a large crackling sound and a rumbling beneath Renée's feet. Fairies scurried out of the way as a portal opened up right behind Renée at the edge of the balcony. Tresor appeared, a wand in his hand. He saw the crowd and looked like he was about to turn around and cross over again, but the portal closed before he could.

His eyes widened as he spotted Renée. "Dubois? What are you doing here?"

"I could ask you the same," she exclaimed.

"Tresor?" interrupted the yellow fairy, her demeanor softening as the fairies started to approach again. "Hi! I didn't know you were in the godmother program."

"He must be," cooed the pink fairy, giving him a small wave. "He opened a portal with his wand."

Nelley and Lune flew in the window. "Tresor? You don't have your own wand yet," Lune said accusingly.

Renée glanced at the wand in his hand, which was glowing like hers. She'd learned from all her readings that every wand was unique to the fairy who earned it. This one was pale blue with stars etched around the base.

"He must have had a good reason," the pink fairy piped up, and Lune glared at her.

"Sorry. This is a family matter. Fae! Faerie! Be!" Lune said, and a bubble formed around her, Nelley, Tresor, and Renée. "There. Now we can discuss this privately."

Tresor ran a hand over his dark hair. "What are you doing here? I thought we were meeting back at the ball. And—" His eyes widened. "Is that Nelley's wand?"

Renée stared. "I believe we should start with the one who just unceremoniously appeared from a portal. Talk about discreet."

He threw his hands up in exasperation. "You weren't supposed to know! No one was!" He looked at Renée again. "Where did *you* go?"

"You tell me where you went first!" Renée used Nelley's wand to point to the leftover fairy dust still floating in the air. His gold breeches were soaked, and there was a gash quickly healing itself above his right knee. His jacket was gone, but his white shirt was drenched and see-through, giving her a view of his chiseled midsection. She might have blushed if she wasn't so angry.

"For the love of the fée, why are humans so stubborn?" Tresor asked.

"Humans?" Renée railed. "Why are the fée?"

"I think you both should calm down," Nelley suggested, motioning to the crowd. "They can't hear us, but they can see you."

"What is going on?" Tresor complained. "This isn't where I was supposed to return. I wasn't even ready to leave! And why . . . can't . . . I . . . get . . . this . . . wand . . . out . . . of . . . my hand?" Tresor said, trying in vain to let go.

Nelley cleared her throat. "If you've been using a wand that isn't your own to cross over to the human world, it seems to have alerted the queen, who will probably be arriving here any moment." She touched Renée's hand. "I will explain everything for you, dear."

"So will I," Lune said.

Tresor's eyes flashed and he stared at Renée. "So you did cross over. You're not supposed to leave Faerie Province!" he said, which only made her angrier.

"And you told me not to butt in because I would put our godmother training at risk!" Renée reminded him. "But I suppose *you* could?"

Tresor growled. "It's not what you think!"

Lune flew between them. "You two—we have bigger problems. If you still have those wands when Mother gets here, she'll—"

Their bubble popped.

"Be furious," Margarite finished. Iris was at her side. Her orange and navy gown, which Renée had found so unusual, was fiery like the queen herself. She looked from Renée's hand to Tresor's. "I heard there were illegal crossings. But I didn't think either of you would be so reckless after I just granted you the ability to take more classes. Tresor, how could you?"

"Auntie, I—" Tresor started, but she cut him off and looked at Renée. "And how dare you take another fairy's wand for your own personal use!"

"My queen? I gave Renée the wand." Nelley flew in front of Renée. "It was an emergency. My charge was in danger, and she could be the key to the future of Faerie Province, so I asked Renée to—"

"She is not a godmother!" Margarite thundered, and looked at Tresor again. "And you are not either. Now, neither of you will ever be!"

Renée felt like the floor was going to drop out from under her. She and Tresor started talking at the same time. "No. You don't understand!"

"That isn't fair, I—" Tresor started to say.

"I don't want to hear either of your excuses. Do you understand what could have happened to you there?" The queen's hands were shaking as she looked at her nephew.

"Nothing would have happened, because I go there often!" Tresor thundered.

Margarite stood in stunned silence. Renée looked at Lune and Nelley, who seemed as shocked as she was.

"You have my sister's wand," Margarite realized, speaking softly as she looked at him again. "That's how you've been able to access the portal. . . . The moving objects on my desk. You've been using my office."

His voice was strained: "My mother left the wand for me. She told me what I had to do if I ever needed it."

"But why did you need it? Where did you go?" Margarite asked, her voice sad rather than angry now. "What could be so important in the human world?"

Tresor's expression was anguished. "Her family!" he said, looking pained. "The children she left behind."

Renée was almost too shocked to speak. "You went to Celine and Raymond?"

"Yes," Tresor admitted. "I've been watching over them since . . . shortly after you arrived."

"Why would you do that?" Margarite asked.

Renée didn't understand. "Yes, why? I thought you said you didn't care about human life, because it was so short. That humans weren't worth caring for, because they were so selfish. And after what Jules did to your mother—"

246

He cut her off. "I was wrong." He looked from her to his aunt, then back to her. "I was curious what would make you want to go back, to risk your new life. I had to see the children for myself. And when I did, well, I understood," he said, his voice hoarse. "Though it's been years in that realm, what you've taught them has remained. They both continue to leave presents for the fée, in your honor. Your uncle allowed them to keep your silly books about the fée, which they still read."

Renée choked out a sob, and Nelley put her arm around her to hold her steady.

He looked at his aunt. "From what I've witnessed, these mortals continue to be respectful of nature and are kind to the animals. When the storm hit, their first thought was to move all the neighboring horses to higher ground to keep them safe. Celine refused to leave them, riding out the storm in the barn, which is where I was, too, to keep an eye on her." He looked at Renée. "And when the storm ramped up, and everyone grew fearful, it was Raymond who sang to them—a song I suspect he learned from you—to keep them calm. And it did."

"They're all right?" Renée asked, holding her chest.

Tresor smiled. "They're fine. They're all fine."

Renée started to sob now. Her babies. Celine and Raymond. They weren't just all right—they remembered everything.

"They have grown to have full lives, but you are never far from their minds," Tresor added with a smile, reading her thoughts. "They are an infuriating mixture of everything you are, Dubois."

Even Nelley and Lune were tearing up now. If she wasn't mistaken, Iris was dabbing her eyes. The queen looked on stoically.

Renée felt such a wave of emotion she wasn't sure where to place it. There were so many things she wanted to ask. *You did all this for me?* Her skin prickled as she remembered something. "My slippers," she said suddenly. "Where did you get them?"

But before Tresor could respond, Margarite spoke up. "I think it's time Renée and I speak in private." She turned to the crowd. "You all may go. And you, my nephew, I will continue this discussion with you later."

"Yes, Auntie," Tresor said, and squeezed Renée's shoulder. "Ask me again next we meet," he whispered to Renée, and she watched him fly out of the room.

"Renée?" Margarite offered her arm.

Renée's stomach started to churn again. She glanced at Nelley and Lune, who were both nodding as if to say, *You'll be fine.*

She couldn't help but think about the last conversation they'd had alone. And worry: What would the queen bar her from this time?

TWENTY-SEVEN

Renée reached out her free hand and Margarite clasped it. Seconds later, Renée was surprised to find they weren't in the queen's office.

They were in the vegetable patch behind Daffodil Hall, the one Renée had been using for her spell work. She bit her lower lip. She didn't think anyone other than Nelley and Lune knew about it.

To the naked eye, the patch was unruly: long vegetable limbs crisscrossing plants and comingling, climbing up the brick wall next to the patch like ivy. The patch had gone from just growing radishes and carrots to include cucumbers, tomatoes, pumpkins, and green beans. Renée was sure the patch was big enough to hold them all, but she hadn't counted on her fertilizer being such a hit.

Her secret: the spoiled vegetables.

She wasn't sure if it was the spell work or the produce itself, but it turned out if she buried the used veggies in the ground, they helped new ones grow.

Nelley's wand suddenly flew from her hand into Margarite's.

"I'll take that, thank you," Margarite said, stepping over a vine that had left the patch and was trailing along the grass. "I'm told this vegetable patch is your handiwork."

Renée straightened her shoulders, trying to appear more confident than she felt. "That's correct. I found practicing spells on vegetables in the safety of the outdoors, where I couldn't hurt anyone, was helpful," she said, thinking of the oversized pear and of Nelley's spelled radish poisoning. "But I hated wasting the ones I ruined, so I turned them into fertilizer and now the patch seems to have exploded." The leaves on the plants turned in her direction. "I was thinking of seeing if we could use some of these in the kitchen."

Margarite nodded, her gold eyes sparkling. "I'm also told your insistence on taking other coursework has inspired other fée to do the same. Did you know Peony came to me this week?"

"No, I didn't." Renée felt her brow perspiring.

"She came to me to express an interest in tailoring. She made an impassioned plea."

Renée tried to contain her excitement. "Peony would make a wonderful tailor! She has a gift for design and colors."

"She may be right, which means the Grand Verre was wrong, or"—Margarite turned to look at her curiously—"that fée are more complex than one discipline." She motioned to a large pumpkin. "Like this vegetable patch, they can grow and change in ways we didn't expect."

"That's a good thing, right?" Renée asked, standing on her tippy-toes.

Margarite sighed. "Honestly? I'm not sure. Unlike humans, the fée are not meant to be so emotional. Godmother work is hard. It can be cruel. And then there is the matter that when Tresor is with you, he acts so much like my sister it worries me." The butterflies in her crown stopped flapping their wings. "She never guarded her heart. She admired her charges feverishly. She doted on them. It's how she grew so attached to Jules."

"But you knew she shouldn't," Renée guessed.

"Yes." The queen looked out at the mountains beyond the province, some snowcapped at the tips, others still lush and green. "His pull to the human world was too strong for us to manage. He wanted to use us to get further ahead there. She trusted Jules's word over my own. She would not listen to my warnings, and after a while I stopped giving them. For that I will never forgive myself." A single tear fell down her shimmery cheeks. "It's why I can't let anything happen to Tresor. When he's near you, I see he feels too much—he acts before he thinks. For fairy's sake, he's been secretly crossing me to watch over two humans who were never assigned godmothers!"

"Maybe that makes him braver than all of us," Renée suggested, and she stood up straighter. "Your Majesty, what happened with your sister is tragic, but so is locking your heart away so you can no longer love another. Love can bring heartbreak, but it also can spark joy. It can inspire hope—it can heal. Yes, it was painful to lose the ones I've loved in my human life. But I'm who I am because of them."

Margarite sighed deeply. "You always have been too smart for your own good, child. Since the day you were born."

Renée looked up as the words registered.

The queen locked eyes with her. "Crying in your bassinet for your parents,

251

but quiet the second I held you in my arms. You understood love even then."

Renée heard a whooshing sound in her ears. Her skin prickled and she heard soft voices in her head, playing like a melody. *Don't be afraid.* She could see a young fairy leading her out of the manor's flames and suddenly it started to come into focus. "You are my godmother," she realized. "It was you who saved me the night of the fire. Wasn't it?"

Margarite's butterflies, like Renée, seemed to hold their breath, waiting for the queen's answer. "Technically, I stepped in as your *father's* godmother when my sister and the others died," she explained. "Though I have always been a seer, as queen, I took over their charges for a while, so no one else would have to cross over. He was one of those mortals." She closed her eyes, and Renée saw her lips quiver slightly. "And it was his dying wish that I save you that night. That I look out for *you*."

"Papa gave his wish for me?" Tears spilled down her cheeks.

The queen gave a small nod. "Maybe if I'd come sooner, I could have saved you all the heartache. But I'd missed his call when I'd stepped away from the bulle for some ridiculous ball. I didn't see the fire start." Her voice cracked. "By the time I found him, both your parents were beyond healing, but I would have tried. He was impossible not to be charmed by."

Renée couldn't breathe. Papa. Dear Papa with his sweets, reading by the fire, teaching her how to care for a garden and help the vegetables grow. She could see his smile, feel his warm embrace. "I know."

The queen swallowed hard. "He adored you. And he was insistent until the end. He wanted me to become your godmother. It was unheard of, but it was part of his dying wish. How could I deny him?" Renée thought she saw Margarite's eyes brim with tears. "Though the other godmothers had taken up their previous duties by then, I honored your father and watched you grow. I saw you struggle with your aunt Olivia, how you tried to give the children love where their maman could not. I saw who she wanted to marry you off to. A man who would never make you happy. I tried to stay out of your affairs. I didn't show myself."

Renée clutched her stomach, unsure if she was going to double over or cry out. Papa had given his life to make sure hers was saved. Her skin felt like it was on fire it was prickling so much, her whole body tingling in a way that made her shiver. Her tears continued to fall.

Margarite was her godmother.

This explained why she'd been so hesitant to let Renée in. "So you stepped in that night at the river and made sure Tresor and Lune found me even though I'd already been granted a wish."

Margarite's cheeks turned pink. "Well, sometimes as queen, you must bend the rules." She played with the folds of her dress, plucking a bloom from her skirt. "You had so much of your father in you—not thinking twice about saving someone else. I couldn't stand by and watch you perish. So when I saw in the bulle what was to happen, I sent Lune with Tresor on his first botany assignment, making sure the fairy ring they visited was on your property at the exact time you needed aid."

"You knew Lune would see me and not be able to keep from stepping in," Renée realized. "And you knew that technically I had my wish left since the first time you stepped in it was my father's wish that was granted."

"I thought she'd save you before you went over the falls. I didn't know she'd make you a fairy," Margarite said miserably. "I thought I was ensuring your human life would continue, but when you turned up here . . ." She faltered, placing her face in her hands. "I was so angry. I felt as if I'd failed your father all over again."

"No," Renée cried, rushing for Margarite and hugging her. The queen let her. "He'd be so proud to know you looked out for me. You gave me a second chance and then a third. It was you this whole time!"

"I was trying to spare you pain after all you'd lost in your short life." Margarite held Renée close. "But when you arrived and I saw how determined you were, what Lune saw in you, and what Tresor was drawn to, I tried to deny the truth."

Renée looked at the queen quizzically.

Margarite sighed. "You have walked two worlds, and while that worries me, when I consulted the bulle to see what each godmother did tonight during the storm, I was most impressed by you."

"You were?" Renée felt a rush of pride.

"Up against a clock and thrown into a situation with someone else's wand to care for a child you never met—in a situation so eerily reminiscent of your own tragedy—you didn't buckle. You soared," the queen said. "It would have been easy to grant the child a wish and save her life, but you fought to get her through the storm so that she lived to see another day and *still* had the wish you'll someday grant her. When the time is right." She cupped Renée's face with her hands. "Seeing as how you managed all that, how can I keep you from godmother work?"

Renée felt a swell of joy rise in her chest and the flowers on her robe burst into full bloom. "Really? I can stay?"

"You may." Margarite smiled softly and looked at the sky. "Nelley? Lune? You can come out now."

254

Nelley and Lune arrived in a cloud of fairy dust, the two grinning fever-ishly when they saw her. In Nelley's hand was a robin's-egg-blue robe.

"This, child, is for you," Nelley said, holding it out for her. "You are offi-cially Genevieve's godmother now."

"But you are her godmother," Renée said, not daring to believe what she was hearing.

"Dear, the child needs *you*." Nelley clucked, wiping her eyes with a handkerchief that hovered in the air in front of her face. "I only visited her twice before this, and she never saw me." Renée started to protest. "Now I've already popped in to check on her and she asked for you. You clearly made an impression. She even sang some song about thunder and lightning."

"We see her working well with you," Lune added. "The bulle hinted you should be in her future. You're meant to be her godmother."

Renée pursed her lips. "But what if she needs me longer than I . . . have?"

"Do not worry about that," Nelley told her. "We told you we'll help you try to slow the aging during the jumps and during reentry."

"And we're going to also predict just how many jumps you'll need so that you can see your assignment with Genevieve all the way through," Lune said with a smile.

"I don't know what to say." Tears spilled down Renée's cheeks.

"Then say nothing for a change and try on your robe," Margarite told her.

Renée looked down at the smooth fabric in her hands, staring at it for a moment before sliding on the blue sleeves. The material was softer than her training robes, made of silk and luxurious with its two layers of fabric. The robe's interior was the same pale pink as the hydrangeas that bloomed in her and Lune's room and the closure was a long, thick piece of satin ribbon in a shade a few colors darker—almost magenta but not fuchsia. With shaking hands, Renée tied the robe closed.

"Beautiful," Margarite said with a sigh. "And now for the finishing touch of godmother work, you need a wand." She pulled Nelley's wand out of a fold in her dress and presented it to her.

"But that's Nelley's wand," Renée said in surprise.

"Pishposh. I'll get a new one," Nelley insisted. "And someday you may, too. But you two bonded when you saved Genevieve together. You gave up your greatest tool to save a life and the wand respects that. While you are working with Genevieve, we agree this wand knows what you need best."

Renée hugged Nelley, who laughed, and then she hugged Lune as well. She turned around to embrace Margarite again, but then thought better of it. She was still the queen, and now they had company, godmother or not. She dropped into a curtsy. "Thank you for this gift."

"You're welcome." Margarite smiled. "But remember one important thing: Every situation you encounter with your charge will be different."

"You are not there to grant their every desire, nor make their every worry disappear," Nelley added. "You are their advisor. Their spiritual guide, so to speak. You're there to watch over them and decide when they need a nudge. Your charges will always have requests and obstacles, but you cannot act on all of them."

Renée nodded, trying to remember their advice. "But how do you know when the right time comes to grant the wish your charge needs the most? And how can you be sure it's the right wish to grant?"

Margarite smiled. "Child, that's what we're here to help you learn."

TWENTY-EIGHT

"I know you're there, Godmother."

Genevieve sat in the sitting room of her family's modest château, now a young woman, almost the very age Renée had been when she became a fairy. Her hair was long, worn in ribbons of curls that fell down her back as she sat hunched over the piano bench and played a melody without sheet music.

How quickly time passed in the human world compared to the slow march in Faerie Province. Renée still hadn't gotten used to it. With Lune's help, she'd watched Genevieve settle into Aurelais from the fairy realm via the bulle. Genevieve's father was a farmer, who spent long days in the field working, while Genevieve spent all her time with her mother, caring for their small home and the animals they raised. Like Renée, Genevieve favored song when she was doing her chores, creating little ditties to pass the time. (*"Mr. Rooster, why so loud?"* was Renée's favorite.) She'd never met someone who loved music as much as Genevieve did. Whenever she dropped in on the girl, she was always at the piano, or wandering around the farm humming melodies to herself.

As much as Renée wanted to be there in person, she was mindful that her time in the human world remained short. She had been saving her visits for when they thought she was most needed.

Finally, that day had come. Lune seemed to think something important could happen if Genevieve ventured into town that day. So Renée had rehearsed all the spells she'd thought she might need, had put on her special necklace, had sipped half of her potion. She hadn't shown herself yet, but she'd been watching for a few minutes now. And somehow Genevieve sensed her presence.

"It would be lovely if you would show yourself," Genevieve said, tinkering at the piano with a song Renée hadn't heard before. "I dream about you all the time. But it has been too long since I've seen your face. I've even started talking about you to the nightingale who visits my window each morning. They sing all day, you know."

Renée touched her skin, wondering how much she'd aged already. (Hours? Days?) Several mice stuck their pink noses out of the cracks in the château's interior walls and watched Genevieve play.

"I even made up a song about nightingales. Listen . . ."

Renée listened closely, a smile on her lips as Genevieve sang a song about the sweet nightingales with very few words. And yet, it was lovely: The way she played the melody with the words, her octave range going higher and lower in such a melodic fashion, it was infectious.

Genevieve stopped playing. "Did you like my song, Godmother? I hope so. I have been writing music for you my whole life. It was the only way I could think to thank you for that night we came to Aurelais."

You don't have to thank me, Renée thought. *Getting to be here, watching you, is gift enough.*

Especially being there today, for a moment when Genevieve could begin a new chapter, a new step in her journey if Lune's bulle was to be believed. Lune wouldn't say too much or look too far ahead. All she would tell Renée was that Genevieve would be met with an important crossroads. Renée could not wait to assist in any way she could.

"Bibbidi-bobbidi-boo," she sang quietly.

Genevieve jumped up from the piano just in time to see the fairy dust pop through the air.

"Hello, dear," Renée said, hearing a slightly lower timbre to her voice. She looked down at her hands and saw they had aged slightly. Her necklace lit up with the jump count: her second visit. She felt the folds of her robe to make sure the rest of the concoction Nelley had made was still on her and felt it in the pocket she'd sewed into the lining.

"Godmother!" Genevieve rushed toward her, hugging her like a child. "I knew you were nearby. I could feel it, like a song on the wind."

The birds and mice watched as Renée led Genevieve out to a small bench near the garden gate. "Let me get a good look at you. My, how you've grown!"

"And you, too. You're older," Genevieve said, her cheeks flushing. "I'm sorry. I don't mean to be rude."

"Hush now," Renée said. "It's true." She could feel it, too. Her body felt different, more lived in somehow, than it had on her first visit "I loved your song."

"Thank you, Godmother," Genevieve said, her smile making Renée beam.

"Your mother is busy feeding the animals, so I thought you and I could go walk into the village. Is that all right?" Renée asked, having practiced this question earlier on Nelley.

"All right, Godmother," Genevieve said.

Renée stepped back. "Let me see what you're wearing." She tsked seeing Genevieve's mud-soaked apron over her simple housedress. Once upon a time, this would have been Renée's uniform as well. But today called for some special fairy color. She waved her wand. *"Bibbidi-bobbidi-boo!"*

Genevieve's body started to glow and sparkle before a sensible dress appeared on her frame. It was yellow like the slippers now on her feet. Renée had paired the dress with a bright royal-blue apron and given her a matching ribbon to tie back her mangle of curls and make them manageable. The girl's skin was flawless, sun-kissed and gold, peppered with freckles.

A horse stuck his head out an open stable window to see for himself. Even the mice scurried closer, watching while the bird sat patiently.

Genevieve laughed and looked down at her dress. "This is beautiful, but too much for a walk, don't you think?"

"Not today," Renée said, trying to contain her excitement. She held out her hand, mindful of her beating heart, still at a steady pace. She had to watch the time. "Walk with me, dear." Genevieve took her hand. "Tell me everything."

For a while, it was just the two of them. Genevieve told her all about her music, how she'd fixed the piano when it broke, and all about life on the farm. As much as Genevieve liked farmwork, Renée could tell the girl was lonely. In the distance, she spotted the cropping of rooftops.

"I should probably hide myself now, dear," she said. "So that . . . so that . . . I . . ." Oh no. She was forgetting again. "I . . ." What were they doing in the village? She remembered the pausing technique she'd been working on with Nelley, to breathe deeply, to empty her mind. And it came back to her in waves—Lune's bulle, the importance of getting her charge to the village. "I'll give you time to talk to the folks there. Find ones who can help you grow and thrive in Aurelais."

"What do you mean?" Genevieve inquired.

Renée squeezed the girl's hand. "I know you long for more."

Genevieve looked away. "I am very grateful to have what I have. My parents, our farm . . ."

"I know you are, dear," Renée told her. "But I wonder if there could be something missing from your life? Something new? You have no idea what can happen when you open up your world."

Genevieve seemed to consider this, when a commotion sounded around the bend. Renée's heart was starting to tick faster. "I'm going to slip away now, but I'll still be here watching. You keep going into the village and . . ." She got a sudden burst of inspiration. "Sing. Loudly." It might help the girl's confidence.

"Sing?" Genevieve asked with a chuckle. "Sing what?"

"Anything. Just as long as it's loud." Renée felt herself start to slip away, but she kept her feet steady. She wanted to see what would happen.

"For you, anything, Godmother."

"Sing now!" Renée waved the wand high above her head and sang the phrase again: *"Bibbidi-bobbidi-boo!"*

Genevieve started to sing a sweet little song about summer winds, and suddenly the gusts picked up and blew through the path, sending several townsfolk her way. They were surprised at first, but once they heard Genevieve singing, they gravitated toward her. No wind necessary.

"What a beautiful voice you have, dear," said one.

"Thank you!" Genevieve said.

A woman and her child approached as a crowd grew. "Your father is the farmer, no? I've heard you play the piano. Do you give lessons?"

Genevieve paused. Renée made a small tinkling sound like bells to encourage her. "Yes. Yes, I do," she said as more people approached, asking the very same thing.

Renée could feel her heart beating faster now as the crowd gathered, brought by the wind that had carried Genevieve's song to them. The melody was so beautiful, Renée made sure it carried through the countryside, reaching even the king in his castle. Who was the girl who could sing like a songbird?

Renée's heart was beating very fast now. She reached in her pocket for peppermint leaves and began to chew to ward off the nausea. She drank the rest of the potion in a swift gulp. Her work was done. For now.

In a flurry of fairy dust, Renée disappeared.

Renée wouldn't return for two mortal years, when Genevieve married a man with kind eyes called Mattieu, the older brother of one of her beloved piano students.

Oh, to be young and in love, Renée thought wistfully, watching them picnic in the grass outside the small château they called home. Mattieu was a hard worker, traveling as a merchant like Uncle Gaspian. Between his work and Genevieve's music lessons, they were able to take over her family's manor.

Genevieve reminded Renée of Celine, perhaps the grown version she never knew—gentle and kind, a teacher whom the villagers sought out for her patience and uncanny ability to help even the most difficult students. It seemed as if everyone in Aurelais, even the king's men, knew about Genevieve's talent.

And so far, Renée could not see when Genevieve would need a wish. Yes, she made sure her piano was always in tune and that flyers promoting Genevieve's lessons always wound up wherever they were meant to be, swept through town by the wind. She made sure that people everywhere could hear her, including Mattieu when he was making his way back from a journey.

They are always so happy to see each other, Renée would think when they reunited. *Imagine someone looking at me the way Mattieu looks at Genevieve.*

Of course, that was when he was there. The heartache her charge felt when the days were long and she was alone in the manor with only her students' lessons to keep her busy was constant. On those days doubt crept in, and Renée thought it was better to be sans partner after all. Which wouldn't be a problem.

Ever since Margarite had shared her worries for Tresor, Renée tried hard to keep her distance from him. Her feelings felt too complicated, and she would not go against her godmother's wishes. She wanted to focus on her own charge anyway, the godmother role, while she still could.

Tresor seemed to sense this. He kept his distance, too. He was busy with his own charge—the young prince of Aurelais who would someday rule the kingdom. She had heard through Lune when Tresor earned his wand, when he'd gotten his first assignment, but he never came to share his good news himself. It made Renée wonder if she'd misread the signs and been a fool to think he cared for her. Maybe he'd truly only been seeking a friendship, their shared interests and unique path throwing them together.

She wondered if he still saw Celine and Raymond, but she didn't ask. Asking meant talking to him and she wasn't sure she could handle that feeling in her chest, the tingling in her arms, the smell of his neck when she neared him. She tried to push images of Tresor away. She couldn't break Margarite's heart again. Or her own.

There was no use wanting something she couldn't have.

One night, while creating new spells with Lune, Renée noticed Nelley's wand start to glow.

She looked at it curiously. "I've never seen it do that before."

"I think you're being summoned," Lune said, flying over to see the wand. "The wand must sense you're needed."

"But you said the bulle didn't show anything pivotal today," Renée told her, grabbing the wand and quickly searching in a drawer for one of Nelley's potions.

Lune shrugged. "Something changed. Either that or this moment happening is both nonimportant and very important at the same time."

My third jump, she thought, and knew her necklace charm would change the minute she leapt. "Then I need to get to a portal right away."

Lune offered her arm. "I'll fly you over to the academy."

Seconds later, they were off, soaring over the grounds, then floating through a window on the godmother level of the academy where Lune dropped Renée so she could begin her journey. As Renée approached, she could see the portal was already open, another fairy preparing to walk through first.

She inhaled sharply when she realized who it was, a low swoosh deep in her stomach.

"Hello, stranger," Tresor said, his shiny wand held at the ready.

"Hello," she said, feeling awkward.

Her wand jumped impatiently in her hands. *Tell him you miss him!* it seemed to yell.

"Are you—are you crossing over, too?" she asked.

He nodded. "Seems my young prince isn't being watched and has a habit of walking off on the castle grounds alone. Someone has to babysit." He looked at her fondly. "And you? Where are you off to?"

"To see my charge," Renée said, and held up Nelley's wand. "But as to why, I'm not sure. The wand seems to think I'm needed."

Tresor stepped aside. "Then you better go first. I was only heading out early to watch the little one have his supper." He chuckled. "It's amusing when he throws peas at his father."

Renée laughed. "Raymond used to—" She caught herself, feeling funny talking about her cousin to Tresor. If he was surprised, he said nothing. "Well, thank you. Have a good trip."

"You too," he said, his brow crinkling. "Don't stay too long."

She held up Nelley's potion and felt her fingers tingle. "I won't," she promised, and then with a running leap, she was gone.

Moments later, she felt her feet hit the ground outside the château. It was evening. Her necklace gleamed. The wind was light, the air cool, but not chilly, and two figures stood in the shadows: Mattieu and Genevieve.

"Good night, my love," she heard him say. "Are you sure you aren't ready to retire?"

"I want to see the new moon in all its glory first," Genevieve said, holding her husband close.

"All right, but don't be long." He pulled the shawl tight around her. "You'll catch your death."

Genevieve kissed him once more and headed into the gardens.

Renée marveled at the blooms, but then watched Genevieve's face fall. The young woman sunk onto a garden bench and dissolved into tears.

Genevieve looked up at the moon. "Godmother, if you can hear me, I could really use your guidance."

Renée's heartbeat slowed. "You were right," she whispered to the wand.

I know, the wand seemed to say.

Renée could feel the fairy dust appearing before she even willed herself into being. When she materialized, she was sitting on the bench with Genevieve's head in her lap.

"Godmother!" Genevieve cried. "You came!"

"Of course, child. What is wrong? Are you all right? Is it Mattieu?"

Genevieve dabbed at her eyes and looked at Renée anew. It made Renée wonder how old she looked. At least forty. She could feel it in her back when she sat down. "No, Mattieu is perfect," Genevieve said, and Renée tutted, which made her charge smile. "No one is perfect, but he's a good man."

"Good girl," Renée said, patting her head. "Then what is troubling you?"

Genevieve's face crumpled. "You know, we have have tried for so long and still not been blessed with the gift of a baby. I wish to be a mother more than anything in this world. And I know Mattieu would be a good father."

"He would," Renée had to agree.

"Oh, Godmother." Her voice was full of emotion. "I wish to be a mother more than anything else in this world."

I wish.

Renée felt her skin tingle. The wand seemed to speak for her.

This is the one, it seemed to shout.

Was it?

How did Renée know for certain that this was the wish to grant Genevieve? Her heart started to beat faster.

Truth be told, she still didn't see how Genevieve's life could affect all of Faerie Province the way the bulle had once told Lune it might. Renée adored the girl, but she wasn't a ruler, like Tresor's young prince would be. Would her life's path change with this wish? Or was this wish meant for another moment that could have a profound impact on both worlds?

As her heart started to tick faster again, Renée thought of leaving and consulting Nelley and Lune, but the way time worked, it could be years before she returned to Genevieve. She had to make this decision on her own.

This is what she truly wants, she thought. *I can feel it in my bones. This is the wish that is meant to be granted.*

Was there a downside to ushering in more love and kindness in the world?

You're ready, the wand told her. *You know what to do.*

I know what to do, she repeated to herself.

She breathed in and out. She pictured Genevieve with child. She focused on the gift of motherhood and thought of her wand work and then stood up to give herself some space.

"All right," she told Genevieve, pushing up the sleeve of her robe. "Let me just try to remember what I need to do."

Was it an herb she was supposed to call for?

Or a hare?

Something with a *T*.

Oh, this was always so frustrating!

Then she felt Nelley's potion jostle in her pocket, and she recalled what she needed: a tonic! With a *"Bibbidi-bobbidi-boo!"* and a wave of her wand, a drink appeared in her hand. It was in a small porcelain teacup that was reminiscent of the one she'd made levitate in Ms. Sneezewood's class. Steam rose out of the pale drink.

"Sip this," she told Genevieve, who took the cup gratefully. "Every night before bed, leave the cup in the garden on this bench and it will refill itself. Finish the tea, every night."

Genevieve took a sip and let the warmness seep into her. She looked up at Renée in earnest, her eyes tearful. "Then I'll become a mother?"

"Yes," Renée promised. *I promise*, she said in her head, thinking of Raymond again.

Nine months later, Genevieve gave birth to a beautiful baby girl.

Her name was Ella.

TWENTY-NINE
Lune

"What do you two have to say for yourself?"

Lune and Nelley glanced at each other as they fluttered in front of the queen's desk one sunny afternoon. Iris looked on lazily as she took notes in the corner, spelling a quill to write on its own.

Mother waited for them to speak. Knowing Mother, it could be about any number of things. Like . . .

The new breed of hybrid rose-begonias they'd created in Daffodil Hall, affectionately referred to as regonias.

The full moon party that went on way after the moon had set.

The kingdom's push for updates on all types of academy robes after the fée saw how Renée customized her own. (Lune had to agree with her friend on this count—why did uniforms have to be so dull? Everyone was adding blooms to their robes now, thanks to her, accessorizing them with pearls!

Vibrant stitching! Robes made of silk and satin! There were even whispers about slippers.)

But Lune could venture a guess what this was about. Without looking into the bulle, she knew this was about Renée. She'd been working as Genevieve's godmother for several years now (if one counted time in terms of human years) and was enjoying herself. But that didn't mean they didn't worry about her.

"She's excelling in all her upper levels of godmother training. She knows the handbook rules better than anyone at this point, including me," Nelley tried explaining.

Inwardly Lune winced. This was the wrong thing to say. Which was confirmed when Mother shouted so loud the butterflies in her crown took flight.

"I'm talking about the crossings! Renée is making too many! It's bad enough she's influenced the other godmothers to interact directly with their charges. But I've told her over *and over* again that she can't keep visiting the human world." She stared moodily at the two of them. "She's made nine jumps now. Nine! Didn't we agree she had ten at most, in her *lifetime*, if we were being cautious?"

"Yes," Nelley said. "But we've been slowing the aging magically. The tonics seem to be working. By my calculations she could have twelve, perhaps fifteen jumps available to her."

"*Could?*" Mother narrowed her eyes. "So now we're gambling with her life?"

"No, of course not," Nelley said quickly.

"We've tried talking to her about using them sparingly, of course," Lune added.

"Several times," Nelley added.

"But she's smitten with Ella," Lune explained. "And she's so proud of her wish, she doesn't want to miss a second of the girl's formative years."

"Can't say I blame her," Nelley tutted. "Ella was the sweetest baby."

Nelley had always had a softness for infants. Mother, however, had been more of a fan of her and Tresor when they could walk and talk on their own.

"I'm not even going to question whether *you've* visited someone else's charge, Nelley," Mother said pointedly, and Nelley looked green. "My point is, Ella is not Renée's charge! Genevieve is. Ella has a mother. And she doesn't need a playmate. These short visits are wasteful! Appearing in the human world to teach a child to garden and talk to animals—that's a fairy skill. And the silly songs they sing together."

Lune tried not to smirk. Clearly, Mother had been paying attention to Renée's travels, even if she claimed not to care.

Her mother's expression faltered. "You both know the toll these trips take on her. No matter how short, she won't survive many more visits. Doesn't she realize the price she will pay for this?"

Lune felt a tingling sensation. Her mother cared for Renée more than she'd ever admit. "She does," Lune said softly, even though she'd had the same argument with Renée herself.

"Then why?" The ache in Mother's voice was apparent as the butterflies slowly inched their way back to her crown. "With Jules, we didn't know how his mortal part would react. But now we do. Renée needs to keep her feet planted here." She drummed her fingers on the desk. "Doesn't she have any other interests in Faerie Province that we can persuade her to take up? When

271

I'd visit her in the human realm, she was always working on crafts, and we know she adores gardening."

"She does both those things with Ella," Nelley said miserably.

Lune shook her head. "Her dedication has always been to godmothering. You know how much she misses Celine and Raymond. Ella has filled that hole in her heart."

"I'd say it's ridiculous, but I know you're right." Mother sighed. "She's always cared too much. Even her aunt couldn't break her spirit." She looked out at the greenery. "Maybe if Renée made more connections here. I know she's close with the two of you, but perhaps if she met someone she fancied . . ."

Nelley coughed. Lune looked down at her toes.

Mother didn't say anything at first. Finally, she looked at her daughter. "Does he ask about her?"

"Often," Lune said quietly. "Though I sense he can tell she wants to keep her distance."

She had long suspected Renée was steering clear of Tresor because of something Mother had said. The similarities between Renée's and Jules's journeys were striking, but couldn't Mother see how Renée cared for her cousin? He obviously felt the same—he wouldn't have risked so much to check on Celine and Raymond if he didn't. But now that Renée was keeping her distance, he wouldn't put himself out there again. *Ugh*. Lune wished she could just put them both in formal wear at a fête. Or on a romantic boat ride. Or just in a closed room where they could talk about everything. Why did everyone have to be so stubborn?

"And does she . . . ask about him?" Mother asked, her voice pensive.

"No." Nelley frowned. "I think she keeps herself busy to avoid thinking about him. But if you're looking for a reason the girl crosses over so frequently, this could be it."

"So this is my fault?" Mother said in annoyance. "I was doing what was best for both of them! You know Renée. Somehow despite the losses she's had in her life, she still loves fiercely. And Tresor has lost so much, I can't bear to see him follow in his mother's footsteps." She looked forlorn and the flowers on her desk moved closer. "I don't want either of them to get hurt."

"I don't think Renée would ever hurt Tresor, Your Majesty," Nelley said gently.

Margarite turned to a stained glass window, staring at the mix of blues and greens. "Not intentionally. But she feels too deeply. When she faces loss again, I worry how she'll handle it."

Lune felt a tingling sensation. *She knows something.* "What is coming, Mother?"

The butterflies in Mother's crown stopped flapping again. "Never mind. Iris, when is my next appointment?"

Iris popped up from her corner. "Not for another two hours. When you got angry at the bulle earlier, you said to clear your schedule."

"What did you see?" Lune asked her now, wondering if she'd missed something with Renée.

Then it occurred to her: Maybe it wasn't Renée whose path was in jeopardy.

She felt a buzzing in her arms. "Is something going to happen to Ella?"

Her mother didn't say anything, but Iris's quill stopped writing.

Nelley started to fly up and down, pacing. "Oh no. Oh no."

Her mother waved her wand above her head, her expression grim. "You

273

might as well see for yourself. It would be only a matter of time anyhow, talented seer that you've become." She gave a wan smile and Lune's bulle appeared on the desk.

They looked at each other, sharing a rare moment of tenderness. Then her mother put her hands around hers as they cradled the luminescent orb, just as she had done when Lune was a girl, first learning to hone her discipline, the gift she had inherited. Lune cleared her mind, focused on Ella, on the château, as she had done so many times before. But then she started to pull at a thread, a somber gray path that seemed to throb. The object waffled slightly. An image started to swirl and take focus, the clouds of the globe pulling away.

Lune's wings fluttered at the sight of Renée sitting with Ella at the piano. Little Ella looked to be around seven or eight. Golden hair, a button nose, and eyes so blue they reminded Lune of the blue jay that always sat on their balcony. The animals at the manor seemed as besotted with the child as Renée was.

But Renée . . . Lune could see why Maman was worried. In the human world, she was now almost seventy years of age, her hair gray, her body going soft and round, her frame slightly hunched, making her look shorter than she did in the fairy world.

In the bulle, Lune could see Genevieve watching them in the background. From Renée, Lune knew Mattieu traveled much of the time, leaving Genevieve alone with Ella, and that worried Renée. Genevieve busied herself with giving lessons and caring for her daughter, but she was lonely. She enjoyed Renée's company, even if she seemed a bit surprised to see how much her godmother changed between visits. Renée and Ella were singing together at the piano.

"*Violet bees and making trees with la-da-dee design!*" Renée and Ella sang. Lune recognized the song. "*Spell together, mind the weather, all will be fine!*"

"Aww." Nelley sniffed. "How cute is that little voice of hers?"

Mother shot Nelley a look. Lune didn't understand what was so wrong with this scene. Everything looked just as it should. The three were content in each other's company.

"Wonderful, Ella!" Renée said. "You play as well as your maman."

"Thank you, Godmother," Ella said politely.

The queen grimaced. "She's not her godmother!"

"And I help Maman feed the animals, too. Even the mice," Ella added.

"Mice can make wonderful friends," Renée noted.

"They're friendly," Ella told her, standing up and sounding excited now. "Oh, did Maman tell you? Papa brought me back a horse from his last trip! I named him Major."

"A horse!" Renée exclaimed. "That is a wonderful gift because as you get older, you can learn to ride. Wouldn't that be nice? Getting to trot around Aurelais?"

"He's a bit older," Genevieve said, walking toward the piano.

Lune inhaled sharply. Up close, Genevieve looked pale, her brow sweaty, her body thinner than Lune remembered.

"And very tired. I'm not sure how much riding Ella and Major will do." Genevieve started to cough.

"Are *you* all right, dear?" Renée asked.

"Yes. Yes. Fine," Genevieve insisted, smiling faintly.

"We've been dusting the piano. Achoo!" Ella faked a sneeze and Renée laughed, but her expression was as concerned as Lune's was now.

Lune felt a tingling sensation as she looked at the young woman and took in her pallor. It wasn't obvious unless you knew to look for it—something was wrong. "Oh, Mother . . . is she?"

Mother's expression seemed to confirm her suspicions. "Wait," she said softly.

"Keeping house is a lot of work," Renée agreed. "It's good your mother has you to help her when Papa is traveling."

"We also have Bruno! He's a puppy!" Ella said, bouncing up and down on her toes, which were bare.

"When do I meet this pup?" Renée asked.

"He's in the kitchen." Ella began tugging on Renée's hand. "Can we see him, Mother? Can we?"

"Of cou—" The words got caught in Genevieve's throat. She started coughing so hard Ella and Renée both rushed to her side. But before they could reach her, Genevieve dropped like a stone in water, the basket in her hands tumbling.

"Genevieve!" Renée rushed to help her up.

"I'm fine. Just tired," Genevieve said. "I think it's the heat. Help me to my bed, will you?"

"Of course," Renée said, using Nelley's wand to gather the basket as she led Genevieve upstairs. The image in the bulle faded away.

"She's very ill," Mother said grimly.

"Renée cannot help?" Lune asked. "Medicines? A tonic?"

Mother shook her head. "Her body is failing her. Even if Genevieve still had her wish, I don't think anything could be done. Genevieve's life is coming to an end." She looked sadly at her daughter. "It's her time."

"But what of Ella?" Nelley worried. "She is so young. Who will care for her?"

"Her father . . ." Mother hesitated. "For now."

Lune felt her fingers tingle. Did that mean her father would leave this world soon, too? "Ella is not going to have an easy road ahead of her, is she?"

Mother looked sad. "No, she's not."

There was a commotion outside Mother's chambers and the next thing they knew, Renée was rushing through the door. "Something's wrong with Genevieve," she said, sounding out of breath. Fairy dust still fluttered around her from the reentry, and her voice was still a bit gravelly. Lune watched as Renée ate a fistful of peppermint leaves. "We have to help her. Mattieu is away. Ella is alone with her. I wanted to stay longer but . . ."

Lune waved her over to a chair. "Sit down. You're completely out of breath."

"These crossings in quick successions are hurting you," Mother admonished.

"Did you hear me?" Renée remained standing. "I think something is dreadfully wrong. Ella is too small to understand, but . . . maybe if we could do a spell to send a doctor, or medicine—" Renée took in their stunned silence, tears filling her eyes. "No, please." She sunk to her knees. "We're fairies! We must be able to do something!"

"I'm sorry, Renée," Mother said. "This is not something that magic can fix."

"But Ella is too young to lose her mother. And Mattieu won't be able to manage. Oh, why did I already grant Genevieve's wish?" Renée started to cry.

"You gave her the gift of motherhood," the queen reminded her. "This is what she wanted."

Lune felt tears spring to her own eyes. "She'll live on through Ella."

"It's not the same," Renée cried.

"Oh dear," Nelley held out her arms for Renée. "You've come to the hardest part of being a godmother—letting go."

"I can't do it," she said, crying in Nelley's generous embrace as Lune rubbed her friend's back. "I gave Genevieve my promise I'd be there for Ella. Is this what she meant? Does Genevieve know she's sick?"

Mother nodded. "She does."

Renée looked at her, realizing something. "What will happen?"

"We don't yet know," Mother admitted. "Though Ella hasn't been assigned a godmother."

This is it. Lune's skin started to tingle again, as she got a peculiar sense of déjà vu. Was this the moment she'd sensed the first second she'd laid eyes on Renée?

"Well, she needs one," Renée decided, wiping her eyes and letting go of Nelley. "If she loses her mother and then I disappear, too, it's cruel. I have to stay on to watch out for her."

"You've made too many crossings already. You don't have enough left to do the job," Mother insisted, looking at Nelley for backup. "Besides which, all godmother requests must be made in writing and then there is a quorum and paperwork. It's not like I can just wave my wand and give Ella a fairy godmother."

"Really?" Renée raised her right eyebrow. "You're the queen."

Lune tried not to smile despite herself. Margarite shot her a look. "This is not amusing. You've seen Renée's path—tell your friend the truth. Her body can't take much more of this. Her time in the human world is coming to an end." She stared stonily at Renée. "I won't risk your existence because you care too much for another to look out for yourself."

Renée looked at Lune for confirmation. Lune sobered, chastened. "Mother is right. You only have a handful of crossings left. If you're going back to check on Ella, it has to be infrequently. Even with the tonic and the tricks we've taught you, we fear one of these jumps . . . well, you won't make it back."

Iris's quill stopped writing for a moment, and everyone in the room seemed to hold their breath.

Renée was quiet, her face full of determination. "When my papa was dying, you promised him you'd look after me and you became my godmother even though I wasn't assigned one. Isn't allowing me to care for Ella when I'm losing Genevieve the same?" She motioned to Lune. "Lune's bulle once said Genevieve could be the one to save the fée. If her time is up, then it stands to reason that possibility will be passed to Ella."

"That is true," Margarite said warily.

"So Ella needs protecting," Renée insisted. "I won't visit as often, but I can't just stop. You wouldn't either."

Lune and Nelley glanced at each other. Lune felt her skin glow. Technically, Renée was right, and Mother knew it.

The queen hesitated. "I want to say yes, Renée, but this is so dangerous. Your health . . ."

"I will be careful," Renée vowed. "I understand her pain just as you understood mine. Please. Give me the chance to grant her a wish. Someday."

Mother sighed. "Very well. *Someday*. But you will wait a while before your next jump. You can observe with Lune from here in the meantime."

Lune felt a prickling sensation at the back of her neck. She squeezed Nelley's hand.

Renée smiled sadly. "Thank you."

"Don't thank me. This is going to be difficult. You haven't even lost Genevieve yet. Losing a charge is never what one expects," Mother said softly, and Lune wondered if she was thinking about Renée's father, about a charge she'd never expected to inherit, let alone care for.

"I'm stronger than I look, Godmother," Renée promised.

Mother hugged her as Lune, Nelley, and Iris watched the pair. "That, child, I know for certain."

THIRTY
Renée

GENEVIEVE DIED ON A TUESDAY.

Renée was there, making her tenth jump, unable to leave little Ella's side as she mourned her maman. She wanted the child to feel her warmth as she cried in the gardens, reminded of her own well of grief at Uncle Gaspian's. Their château was as silent as a tomb, the sadness hanging like a low cloud. Even the animals—Major, Bruno, the mice, and farm friends—seemed to sense the loss. Genevieve had been a beautiful soul, a song of a life. And now her journey was over.

Lune finally had to fetch Renée, and the long day spent in the human world took a heavy toll on her body. "I'd guess she has three crossings left at most before we lose her completely. Even the tonics aren't working as well anymore," she heard Lune whispering to Nelley one night.

Renée didn't want to think about it. Instead, she slept, the flowers nestling around her, letting her tears fall on their petals and vines. Lune was quiet as a mouse, making sure Renée ate and drank, nourishing her fée body. "You need your strength," she'd say, and spoon-feed her fruit and broths.

But grief held Renée hostage, drowning her in its depths. She stayed in bed, preferring the cocoon of sleep. When she awoke one afternoon, she was surprised to hear Margarite's voice.

"Have you checked on Ella?" Margarite asked.

"Daily," Lune said. "And I've given Renée updates even though she hasn't asked. Ella's father remarried and took a new wife. Lady Tremaine came with two daughters he had hoped would be fine companions for Ella."

"But they're not?" Margarite inquired.

"They're terrible," Nelley interjected bluntly, unable to hide her ire. "As they grow, they're more jealous of Ella's nature and beauty. They keep it at bay when her father is around, though I can sense those days are coming to an end. I know Renée is having a hard time, but a shift is coming, Your Majesty, and Ella will need her, even if she can only visit a few more times."

"She will come around for Ella," Margarite said.

But despite Margarite's assurances, Renée didn't feel ready to rejoin either world. She couldn't get past the loss of Genevieve, replaying their moments together—their songs, their friendship, Ella's birth, and finally the last, most heart-wrenching day, where she was ripped from the world. Her head knew she had to get up and keep going for Ella's sake, but her heart wasn't ready. Losing her parents, Celine and Raymond, and now Genevieve. It was too much. *Maybe there is someone better suited to be Ella's godmother.*

"Stop that right now, Renée," Nelley said, somehow hearing her thoughts.

"Ella is asking for *you*," Lune said. "We know you're heartbroken, but time doesn't stop marching on, especially in the human world. Ella is practically a young woman now. You should see her in the bulle. Despite losing her father and her stepmother's cruel treatment, she's the most hopeful girl you'll ever meet. You've rubbed off on her."

Stepmother, Renée closed her eyes again thinking of Aunt Olivia. The children were what had kept her going and now to think Ella wasn't even a child anymore. Renée had already let Ella down. What would change coming to her now when she was almost fully grown?

Maybe that's why Lune and Nelley stopped trying to push her to work on her spells and vegetable transformations. Nothing could get her out of bed.

Or so she thought.

"Sleeping the day away, Dubois?"

Renée's eyes fluttered open. Tresor hovered beside her bed.

"What are you doing here?" Renée asked, her own voice sounding strange after so many days of silence. She threw her covers over her head to avoid looking at him, but it was too late. His appearance burned in her mind. Green was a good color on him; it reminded her of the pine trees he always smelled like. But no. She couldn't go down that road. And neither would he. If anything, she could only assume he'd had the same lecture.

"I figured since you hadn't visited me in ages, maybe it was time I came to see you," Tresor said, fluttering beside her. "Mourning or not, you have to get out of bed. You're making us new godmother recruits look bad, Dubois. Don't you have work to do?"

Renée felt her skin prickle. "Worry about your own charges."

"Yes, about my charges. *Technically*, I only have one. A young prince in

Aurelais, sad and lonely in his big castle, unable to find love despite all the young subjects pining for him. Sound familiar?"

He could be so arrogant, she wanted to throttle him, but his voice was so teasing, she found herself smiling.

"It seems his father is tired of waiting for him to pick a spouse so he's going to put every eligible Aurelain in one room so the prince has no choice but to find one to his liking. He's throwing a ball."

"Good for the prince." Renée kept her head under her covers. "Maybe you can go and be his captain of the gourd."

"Clever. Though need I remind you, *you're* the one with the talent for such transformations. Besides, I've had my fill with balls. Especially after that last one when my date rudely ran out on me."

Renée threw back her covers and two butterflies flew out and almost smacked Tresor in the face. "I did not," she glowered. "I got called away by Nelley to help save her charge, who became my charge, who—" She faltered, taking in the smirk on his shimmering face, his eyes, still a fiery gold. "What are you doing here?" she asked again, her resolve weakening.

He took a seat on the edge of her bed and looked at her. "My aunt said you missed me."

Renée's fingers tingled. "I never said any such thing," she blustered, and looked away, but she felt her chest rise and fall faster now. Had her god-mother changed her mind about them? Why would she send Tresor here?

"She also said *I* missed *you* and she was tired of all the moping, so I might as well come here and . . ." He trailed off.

She held her breath. "And?"

He hesitated. "And remind you that you have a duty to uphold."

Her stomach fell. The flowers at her side slinked away. "Oh."

"Am I wrong?" he asked sharply. "Ella is your charge now, and you've abandoned her."

Why was she bothered by his answer? She'd clearly waited too long to tell him how she felt, which was . . . she wasn't sure. How did she feel? "I have not abandoned her."

"I know you need to limit visits, but have you even checked in with Lune and her bulle? The girl lost her mother and her father, and from what Lune tells me, her surrogate family isn't warm and cuddly. Now I know how I'd handle things if I were Ella. Fairy be, it's how I handled things when my parents died. I'd cut the human world off and vow never to help another self-serving soul again. Her stepmother and stepsisters are foul. But Ella, despite all odds, keeps going. She tries to rise above their ugly words."

Renée couldn't help but smile.

"From what I've learned about you, your paths are similar. When you lost your whole world, you didn't hide, you threw yourself into caring for two children in need of love and guidance. Which is why I'm confused at your behavior now, Dubois. Are you really going to disappear when another girl needs you?"

A sob caught in her throat, and she held it there. Her flowers sensed it, curling around her bed again, a regonia resting on her chest. "She's almost fully grown," Renée said, trying to act as if she didn't care. "She doesn't need me anymore."

"Is that so?" Tresor scratched his head. "Funny. I had Lune check the bulle right before I came here and it sounds like everyone in the Tremaine house—that's Ella's house, or it was before they started treating her like a scullery maid—is readying themselves for a ball at the request of a certain prince I happen to know. Lady Tremaine is seeing to it that her two girls have the finest threads to impress the prince, but Ella doesn't have much time on her hands to make something. I hope she can manage. Would be great if she knew someone who could sew."

Renée didn't say anything.

"She seems to want to go," he said lightly. "Which is more than I can say for my prince. He isn't thrilled about this party. I understand. Balls can be a chore, but this one is for him and he's losing hope he'll find a partner, someone who will love him for him, and who he'll love in return. I've assured him he's wrong."

She turned and looked at Tresor. "You told him that?"

Tresor held her gaze. "I told him the right person is out there for him. And maybe Ella's future happiness is linked to this ball, too. Fate has a strange way of connecting people, don't you think?" He smirked. "But what do I know? She's your charge. If you don't want to help her, don't. Just stay here in bed and continue to feel sorry for yourself."

Renée thought for a moment. "Maybe she's already forgotten me."

Tresor looked at her steadily. "How could anyone forget you, Dubois?"

So much loss. She thought of Celine and Raymond and then Genevieve and little Ella, and crumbled. She'd avoided asking him this ever since she learned he'd been visiting the children. "Do they remember me?" There was no need to say who she was referring to.

Tresor held out his hand. "Why don't you see for yourself?"

Renée started to tremble. "You mean?"

"They won't see you and you can't stay long, of course, but I've cleared it with Nelley and Lune," he said kindly. "And I think it's time. Don't you?"

Tears spilled down her cheeks. "Yes." She took his hand.

For a second, she thought about pulling away. When they crossed over together, he'd see her human side, which was decades older than her fée body. What would he think of her then?

But the pull to see Celine and Raymond was too great. She held tight to his hand as Tresor waved his wand with his other. "Marion! Mason! Meant to be!" he said, and Renée recognized Tresor's mother's and father's name in his magic words. Then they were flying fast out of Daffodil Hall and to the academy and the portal, which was open and waiting when they arrived.

Go. Go. Go, her wand told her, but as they neared the portal, it flew from her hand, refusing to join her.

"Wait!" Renée cried, watching in horror as the wand sailed off the balcony to destinations unknown. "Nelley's wand just left me," she said to Tresor in surprise. "Where is it going?"

He smiled. "If I had to guess—back to Nelley. Maybe it finally feels you're ready for a wand of your own. Like I was. I passed my exam." He held up an emerald-green wand with a leafy pattern etched into the shaft. He handed her Nelley's small blue potion, which she pocketed, then raised his wand. "Ready?"

She felt a lump form in her throat. *I promise*, she could hear herself say. "Ready."

They leapt, disappearing onto the other side.

287

THIRTY-ONE

MOMENTS LATER, RENÉE FOUND HERSELF IN A SMALL VILLAGE. IN *HER* VILLAGE. Hers and Genevieve's and Ella's. She peered at the castle in the distance where she knew the king and the prince were waiting. "Celine and Raymond still live here?"

"Aurelais is where they felt closest to you." Tresor held out his wand, and the two fairies seemed to shoot forward like balls of glitter in the sky, not stopping till they reached a small manor on the outskirts of town.

Renée spotted a woman sitting in the meadow with two small children on a blanket. The woman's dress was not one of nobility, but it was still beautifully made, and simple, like it was intended to be worn outdoors and be lived in. There was a trace of dirt along the hemline—like Renée's dresses always had—and her feet were bare. So were both children's.

She knew immediately who she was looking at.

"Celine," she whispered, her voice catching on the wind. And for a second, the young woman seemed to look up. Almost as if she had heard her name.

The little girl danced around her mother and younger sister in a circle, carrying a basket of small trinkets. *"What do we say to a whisper? A whisper? A whisper?"* the girl sang. *"What do we say to a whisper on the wind?"*

Renée squeezed Tresor's hand. "One of my old songs!"

"Wisp! Wisp! Shush! Shush! Listen, hush. Wisp-shush-whisper!" The girl kissed the toddler's head. "I'm sorry, Clotilde."

"Good girl, Renée," Celine said. "Clotilde forgives you. Maman does, too."

Her heart seemed to stop. "Did she say Renée?"

"She named her first child after you," Tresor told her.

Renée's eyes brimmed with tears. "Celine . . . my darling Celine. A mother? With two children of her own?" she said, feeling her spirit move closer to her cousin. She wished she could reach out and touch her. Her lips trembled. "How is she?"

"Happy. Married to a fine man six years ago. A farmer. A love match, you'll be pleased to hear. Your aunt was not. You're always on Celine's mind, and she shares stories about you with her husband and the girls often. She'll have two more—a boy and another girl. It seems they will be comfortable and well, all the things you'd hope for her."

Renée wasn't sure what to say, but she had the overwhelming urge to throw her arms around him. She restrained herself.

Celine held the little girl in her arms up to the sun, making the toddler squeal. "Maybe you could let her help you leave the fée their gifts?"

"All right," said little Renée, reaching into the basket and giving her younger sister a thimble and a button, which made Renée chuckle. Next, she pulled out something familiar. "Can I use this slipper, Maman?"

"Yes, chouchou, place it by the tree like I told you so the fairies can find it."

"I've got a collection of the silly things now," Tresor complained, but the amusement behind his eyes betrayed him.

"She still does this? And she makes the slippers the way I taught her?" Renée exclaimed, the emotion coming over her in waves. She was surprised to find she wasn't sad about the passage of time. She was happy to see Celine so content. She could feel the joy radiating off her, and this pleased Renée more than she could ever imagine.

"Actually, no," Tresor said. "Celine buys her slippers from the resident cobbler. As does everyone in Aurelais. His slippers are lovely, very unique."

She looked up at Tresor and felt her skin tingle. "Who is the cobbler?"

Tresor gazed at her fondly. "Come see for yourself."

Little Renée's giggles gave her pause. She wasn't sure she was ready to say goodbye yet.

Tresor squeezed her hand, and Renée sighed, gazing once more at the happy scene before her. She had wanted to see that the children were okay, and clearly Celine was thriving. She would cherish this memory forever.

She nodded once to Tresor, and he tapped his new wand confidently. Then she felt them whisk through the village once more. As they flew, she reached for some peppermint leaves she always kept in her pockets, chewing on some to keep the nausea at bay. They whizzed through the streets till they landed at a cobbler's shop, a wooden-shoe shingle swaying above the door. Renée felt them pulled inside, where there were two bright, warm rooms with multiple cases filled with colorful shoes. She could hear someone humming in the other room.

Raymond.

She moved to see him but stopped short at the sight of the slippers, marveling at the gorgeously arranged display. She could feel herself growing misty.

These were her slippers. The ones she'd make with Celine and Raymond, but with much more care and skill. These slippers were made in a range of colors and fabrics, some with laces that could wind their way around a delicate calf, others just meant to slip on, with a tiny bow for adornment. There were red slippers, bright blue ones with a floral accent, and pale pink pairs with a sheer overlay. One particularly handsome golden pair sat on a tufted purple pillow. MADE TO ORDER read the tiny handwritten sign below the shoe. She felt an overwhelming sense of pride for her boy.

"He's doing well," Tresor said, as if hearing her thoughts. "And if he can keep up his order rate, there is talk of him being asked to be the official royal cobbler."

"Working for the king?" Renée couldn't be prouder.

"It hasn't happened yet, but I suspect it will. With the ball coming, more and more customers have paid his shop a visit."

Renée spied the yellow slippers on display and looked at Tresor curiously. "Is this where you got *my* slippers?"

He nodded. "It was one of his first pairs. He left them in the forest." She watched Tresor's throat bob. "I was going to tell you that night but . . ."

The beauty of such a gift wasn't lost on her. "We had our fight and then I pulled away."

They just looked at each other, in between time and realms, and Renée hesitated, wanting to tell him how she felt. But the moment was interrupted by three women shouting, each one pushing her way to be first to get in the door.

"I want to pick first!" whined one with long red curls. She held tight to the folds of the fine lace gown she was wearing.

"No! Mother, I want to pick first! She always gets first pick, Mother!" said a dark-haired girl. She shoved the redhead out of the way. "It's my turn!"

Renée cringed.

"Girls. Girls," said an older woman with a severe bun in her streaked gray-and-white hair. She spoke quietly, but her tone was commanding nonetheless. "I won't have you upsetting yourselves." She turned to the young cobbler, who had walked into the room. "Monsieur Damery."

"Oh, Raymond!" Renée exclaimed. He was tall. She knew he'd be tall! And so handsome in a tailored white shirt and brown breeches on his slim frame. Around his neck was a measuring tape, and several pins stuck out of the collar of his shirt. His hair had darkened, but he still had that boyish look around his blue eyes.

"Lady Tremaine," he said politely. "How may I help you today?"

Renée felt herself circle around him, marveling at how the boy she'd saved had grown, turning into a man who was clearly finding his way in Aurelais. She paused. "Did he say Tremaine? Is this Ella's stepmother?"

"I'm afraid so." Tresor scowled.

Poor Ella, Renée thought. These three made Aunt Olivia seem like a kitten. *She must be miserable.* She felt a wave of guilt for staying away so long.

"Our excitement that the castle is hosting a ball has us all a bit overwhelmed," said Lady Tremaine. "I have two daughters in my household, and I want them to look their best for the prince."

"Doesn't she mean three?" Renée demanded.

Tresor shrugged, though she suspected he had more to say on the subject. "I told you. To the Tremaines, Ella is nothing more than a servant."

Renée felt her blood begin to boil.

"We'd be grateful to purchase two pairs of the golden slippers we've heard about," Lady Tremaine said, opening her purse to begin taking out coins.

"I'm sorry, there will not be enough time for me to craft two more pairs of those before the ball," Raymond told her, not sounding very disappointed to share this news.

Lady Tremaine's mouth formed a fine line. "I see. Is there nothing we can do? Perhaps if we pay more?"

The girls batted their eyes hopefully at Raymond. Their smiles felt phony, making each girl appear uglier than she was. Maybe that was just the heart-lessness Renée sensed in each of them.

Raymond cleared his throat. "I'm sorry. I only have what is in the main display to sell. May I suggest the green ones?"

Renée beamed. That was her boy, not letting money push him around. "Look at the way his eyebrows furrow when he hears them speak. I wish Ella could wear some of his slippers. I wonder which pair she would like."

"*If* they even let her go." Tresor wouldn't look at her.

Renée fumed. "But you said every eligible Aurelain is invited."

"Yes, but she has to finish her chores first and even then, she will still need means of transport and something to wear . . ." Tresor said in an innocent voice.

Renée needed to get away from this awful woman and her bickering daughters. She willed her spirit to move to the back room in the store, where Raymond had his workshop.

The musky smell of wood and glue hit her straightaway. The room wasn't tidy; tables were topped with sewing tools and measuring sticks and parchments covered in sketched designs. She could picture Raymond sitting atop one of the stools, using the magnifying glass to eye the details of his latest creation.

A beam of light caught her eye as it flickered across a half-finished black satin shoe. She followed the light and spied a tiny window above a cabinet, which seemed to shimmer.

Sucking in a breath, Renée drew closer.

Sitting on a tufted purple pillow, elevated above other silky slippers, were shoes of glass, so clear they reminded Renée of water. They shined, too, like they might glow in the right light. The heel was just high enough but not too high to be uncomfortable. Renée could see how on the right person, a shoe like that could create a feeling of wonder.

Inside the special slippers was a small assortment of trinkets—thimbles, buttons, little scraps of silk ribbon—all gifts one would give a fairy. She felt her skin tingle again.

"I haven't touched those," Tresor said in a low voice behind her. "It seemed they were meant for someone in particular."

Tears pricked Renée's eyes. Both children remembered. All of it. All of her. More than she ever could have imagined.

She'd touched their lives and they'd been imprinted on hers, and not time, not space, nor different worlds could do anything to change that.

She could feel Tresor beside her, and she reached for his hand. There was so much she wanted to say to him, for giving her this gift, this chance to see Raymond and Celine one more time. To know what she'd meant to them both. But once again, time was not on her side. What she had to say would have to wait. "Let's go," Renée told him instead. "I have much work to do."

THIRTY-TWO

"Do you have everything? Potion? Peppermint leaves? Ginger?" Nelley asked, watching as the portal started to glow.

"Remember, you can't stay long. Listen to the sound of your beating heart and pay extra attention to its speed," Lune told her as Nelley kept fussing over Renée's blue godmother robe.

They'd agreed, for the occasion, it should be simplified. Just a pink ribbon tying it at the neck. No flowers. Nothing that could get in the way of the task at hand. This would be her twelfth jump. Most likely her last. While none of them knew *precisely* how much time she had left in the human world, it was clear from the advanced age her human body appeared to be in that realm to the recovery time after her trip with Tresor that Renée was getting dangerously close to the end of her human days.

"And if you start to feel unwell, return here immediately," Margarite insisted.

"Yes, Godmother. I know. But you're making me nervous," Renée said, looking around the room. "You all are."

Every godmother had come to see Renée off at the academy. This would be the second—and, again, most likely last—wish she'd grant, but it would be the first with the new wand that Margarite had just bestowed on her. ("Read the inscription later," she'd insisted.)

Renée hadn't been certain another wand would fit her hand the way Nelley's had, though she was wrong. This one was silver and had etchings in the shaft. It had been made by the wandmaker with her essence in mind and she could already feel its playful nature, it whispering, *Let's go! Let's go!*

"Be mindful of your forgetfulness," Margarite added. "When you get confused, pause, and let the answer come to you. Remember the practices we've been working on."

"Yes, Godmother," Renée said, nearing the portal. "I'll remember to . . . remember."

Margarite frowned. "Maybe one of us should go with you."

"Yes. Yes," said Nelley, nodding vigorously. "Just to make sure nothing goes wrong."

"We don't want you to get too overwhelmed," Margarite added.

Renée barked out a laugh. "I promise you! I'm fine! I'm ready! And I appreciate everyone being here to send me off. It means a lot." She sounded more confident than she felt. But if this was the last time she'd visit Ella and her old realm, she wanted to do it alone.

She searched the crowd for him, but she knew if he had been there, she would have noticed right away. They hadn't spoken since their crossing. The last few weeks had been a flurry of healing and then preparations for her to get to Ella tonight, and there hadn't been time to tell Tresor how she felt.

But she needed to. Soon.

Let's go! Let's go! said the wand.

Lune flew beside her. "He wanted to be here." She had read her mind. "But he's in the human world already. The prince needed some nudging before the ball. He said to wish you luck."

She tried not to seem disappointed. "Of course." There was still so much she knew she had to say to him. She only hoped her words didn't come too late.

Lune squeezed her hand, then hugged her. "I always knew you would be great."

Renée felt a lump form in her throat. "Thank you, Lune. For everything," She hugged her back as the portal began to pulse.

"It's time, Renée! Hurry now," Margarite said.

With one final look at the beautiful fairies around her, Renée turned and leapt through the portal, landing exactly where she was supposed to—outside Ella's château.

Immediately, she tuned in to her charge, could feel the girl's emotions radiating through the garden—her heartbreak, her uncertainty, her loneliness. Most potently, Renée felt the girl's hopelessness.

She tried to focus. Tonight was a big night—for both of them. Her body moved slower at this human age (she had to be approaching eighty-five now), but she moved purposefully, ignoring the throbbing pain in her right knee.

A ball was, perhaps, a frivolous thing, yes, but Renée understood the power they held, too. The wonder of it all. The magic in stolen glances and in dances and the reminder that anything could happen. That was what she wanted Ella to experience.

The garden was quiet. As Renée floated along invisibly, she could see all the animals—as small as mice and as big as Major—watching something. It took Renée a moment to realize Ella was leaning on her mother's garden bench, crying. Her mother's pink gown was tattered, the aftermath of cruelty.

"I can't believe. Not anymore," she heard Ella say.

Oh, fairy be. What would Genevieve have said in this moment? What would she have wanted for her daughter?

Renée drifted toward her charge, reminded of all the times she'd watched Genevieve play with the girl in this very garden. She could have sat and thought of Genevieve all evening, but the moon was high, the ball was starting, and oh, she had so much to do! She couldn't get distracted. It was too easy to get distracted here.

Show yourself, the wand reminded her. Renée thought hard, and sparkles began to glow around the garden before she materialized on the bench, Ella crying in her lap.

"There's nothing left to believe in," Ella continued. "Nothing."

Renée patted her head. "Nothing, my dear? Now you don't really mean that."

Ella didn't even blink at the intrusion, though it had been so many years since she'd seen Renée. Of course, magic and wonder had always come easily to the girl.

"Oh, but I do."

"Nonsense, child," Renée said as Ella sat up. "If you'd lost all your faith, I couldn't be here. And here I am."

Renée took in the young woman, her callused hands, her tired eyes, her tearstained cheeks. Despite all this, she was as lovely as the day she was born.

"Godmother!" Ella gave a start, as though remembering, however faintly, the part of her childhood that had been dusted with fairy magic.

It was time to do what she'd come here to do.

Now where was her new wand? She just had it, didn't she? *I'm here!* the wand said. That's right. She'd kept it in her robe for safekeeping. *Focus, Renée!*

Renée got to work, some of her best work yet, if she was to be so bold. She silently let the animals know what to expect, how they should enjoy their evening out, and transformed Bruno and Major into a veritable footman and coachman. The tattered dress became a ball gown like a cloud. And when she saw the giant pumpkin in the garden, she grinned, magicking it into a plush, filigreed carriage.

Renée hesitated for a moment. Her mind became momentarily hazy, her joints ached, and she felt her wand arm tremble. The effects of the human world were hitting her harder than they ever had before. Perhaps the enormity of the spells she'd just performed had sped up the aging. Whatever the case, she could not recall the last bit of enchantment she'd wanted to bestow on dear Ella.

She took a breath, glancing at the moon, at its beams illuminating this beautiful garden. It was a night much like this one that had started her journey.

And then she remembered.

"Bibbidi-bobbidi-boo!" Renée called forth the glass slippers from Raymond's workshop, magically emptying their contents into her robe

pockets on their way to Ella's feet. She knew he'd left them for a fairy, but she suspected he wouldn't mind her regifting them.

Ella gasped, taking it all in. She twirled in her new gown, lifting one sparkling foot. "Glass slippers! It's like a dream. A wonderful dream come true."

"Yes, my child. But like all dreams, well, I'm afraid this can't last forever. You'll have only till midnight and then—"

Ella's posture straightened, her smile widened. "Midnight? Oh, thank you."

Renée shook her head, trying to convey the urgency she suddenly felt, to make sure she got this out before she forgot. Time—there was never enough of it. "Now, now, now, just a minute. You *must* understand this, my dear. On the stroke of twelve the spell will be broken. And everything will be as it was before."

"Oh, I understand," Ella said, grasping her hands. "But it's more than I ever hoped for."

Renée's eyes sparkled with tears. What a remarkable child.

After a few more hurried exchanges, she sent the girl on her way, knowing that whatever happened, Ella could handle herself. She'd get home before midnight. Just as she'd carve a beautiful new life when all was said and done.

Renée's excitement was pulsing. The wand was cheering *You did it! You did it!* as the carriage turned the corner and disappeared into the night. She coughed, straightening herself.

And then he was there.

She felt a tightness in her stomach and the tingling in her fingers.

Instead of heading back to Faerie Province to rejoice in his own job done, he'd come to check on her.

Tresor had been waiting for her all along.

Now it was her turn to believe in a new path. It was her turn to change her fate. She had to make a grand gesture. Even if she didn't have all the words she needed at the moment to convey how she felt.

All she knew was she was running out of time.

With a whoosh, the portal appeared again, and Renée took Tresor's hand, took small, shaking steps toward the light. Together, they leapt, and with the last bit of her strength, she pulled him to a stop in that vortex of light, their bodies half in one world, half in another. As her fairy self began to materialize where a kindly old godmother once stood, Renée knew she had to tell him.

Before the clock struck midnight.

Before they returned and learned just how much healing she would need, how long it would take, and what her next step would be.

"What are you doing, Dubois?" he said, the smile on his lips telling her he already knew before she even stood on tippy-toes in her bare feet.

"Something I should have done a long time ago," she said, and then she kissed him the way she'd thought of doing a thousand times before.

Tresor leaned into her, his soft lips firmly planted on her own as the light pulsed around them, their wands glowing.

She clasped his face in her hands. "If this life—both lives—have taught me anything it's that you should never wait to tell someone how much you love them."

"Love?" He looked amused as he held her tight, neither one wanting the portal to whisk them to one world or the other.

"Yes. For so many infuriating reasons, one of which being that I'm pretty certain you love me as well."

"I do," he said, his voice hoarse. "Dubois, you are a hard Fairy not to love."

"So are you, Tresor." Renée buried her head in his chest. The portal seemed to grow tired of waiting. It knew the importance of getting her back to the fairy realm. It started to pull her through so they could await midnight and what came next together.

As they let themselves get pulled back to Faerie Province, her lips found his again, the two kissing with such force, she felt glitter sparkle around them. His lips, warm yet soft, on hers felt like the most natural thing in the world, and a small part of her—or maybe it was the wand—seemed to sigh with contentment and say, *What took you two so long?*

THIRTY-THREE

One last time.

One last crossing.

Of course, she knew she was pushing it. But she had to see this through. And after this visit, she knew she would be leaving her charge in good hands with Tresor. The bulle hinted at extraordinary events moving forward, and whatever happened, she was ready. She had fulfilling work at the academy beside Nelley and Lune teaching human-fée relations courses. Even Margarite begrudgingly agreed that Renée's empathy was an asset to godmother training. Who knew the more godmothers tapped into their feelings, the stronger their magic became? Now she started her day working with godmother trainees asking, "How do you feel?"

If they asked her how she felt today she would say "Glorious."

And perhaps if today's visit went well, Margarite would agree to allowing more in the future.

In any case, she wouldn't miss this moment for anything in either world.

"My love," Tresor said, extending his hand to take hers as they approached the portal together. "Shall we?"

She smiled up at him. Then she looked at the others. Hundreds of fairies assembled outside. They were dressed in their formal robes. (That's what they called the outfits she'd come up with—adorned with flowers and gems and trinkets. Ooh! That gave her an idea. Maybe they could give out awards, too, and they could be added like badges of honor. She'd have to remember to mention this to Nelley later.)

"We'll be back in minutes," she told the queen and the others. "And when we arrive, I think it would be nice if you all cheered. Not shouted, mind you, but a cheer would probably delight her. Just not too loud. She is still a child. We don't want to scare her."

"We won't scare her," Margarite said. "We're welcoming her with open wings."

Renée frowned. "I didn't ask her mother about flying. Of course, there will be some flying, but I don't want to make her any more nervous than she already is, letting her child cross worlds when she's never been here herself."

"She was easier to convince than him," Tresor reminded her.

Renée shrugged. "She can be pretty persuasive. Wonder where she learned that?"

Nelley cleared her throat.

"Yes, good point. It's time." Renée squeezed his hand. "Allons-y!"

Then, wands at the ready, they jumped together, landing in the castle, where the stones were cool and hard beneath her feet.

The king and queen stood at the sight of the two fairies materializing in the throne room. The queen, splendid in a peach gown, her blond hair loose and curly beneath the crown that now sat on her head, saw Renée and smiled, forgetting decorum and rushing to hug her.

"Godmother! It's so good to see you."

"You too, my child," Renée said, hearing the deep gravel in her voice, the wrinkles in her skin, badges from some of her best work.

"My king," said Tresor, nodding.

"Tresor," said the king, smiling but still standing near his throne. It was only then she heard the giggle coming from behind him. "Someone has been waiting for you two."

A girl, around the age Ella was when they'd first sat at the piano together in Genevieve's château, peered around her father's legs. She looked much like Ella, but with her father's dark hair and deep-set eyes.

Tresor put a hand above his eyes and pretended to search the room. "Where could Maeve be? Is she here?" he asked playfully.

Renée loved seeing this side of him. "I don't know. I don't see a small babe anywhere. Do you, Tresor?"

"I do not," Tresor agreed as Maeve's parents watched, both clearly delighted.

"Hello, Godmothers!" Maeve said, jumping out and bouncing on her toes. "I'm ready for my visit!" She was dressed in blue.

"Are you, now? Are you sure?" Renée asked. "It will feel short, but to Maman and Papa it could be as long as a week."

"I'm sure," Maeve said. "Maman said I must be a very special little girl to get to go to Faerie Province."

Renée touched her head. "That you are, chouchou." If she weren't, Margarite wouldn't have allowed a human—the very first human—to visit Faerie Province.

It was an idea Renée had come up with. She'd been roaming the academy, moving slowly as she'd recovered from her last jump. As she'd stared at the doorways and stairs and ladders, she'd realized this place must have been built with non-fée visitors in mind . . . at least at one point. And when the human prince and new princess had their precious firstborn, a girl with her mother and grandmother's fondness for nature and wonder, and her father's loving heart, Renée had started planning.

Lune had foretold this. Maeve could be the key to uniting Aurelais and Faerie Province in a way they never had been before. A child who could walk both worlds and help them grow together, a rarity not seen in centuries.

They couldn't deny Maeve this moment.

It was all meant to be, Renée thought. "Kiss your maman and papa and tell them you'll see them soon."

Maeve did as she was told, then rushed to Renée's side, taking her and Tresor's free hands.

"Does she look all right?" Ella asked. "I had a new blue dress made for the occasion and Monsieur Damery whipped up a pair of slippers for her. I didn't know if that was appropriate."

Renée looked down and smiled at the child's pink slippers. Her Raymond, the kingdom's official cobbler. "They're perfect."

"We will take good care of her," Tresor promised the king and queen.

"I know you will," said Ella, smiling at Renée and her firstborn.

"Ready?" Renée asked, looking down at Maeve with a smile. The child nodded.

Then with a wave of her wand, Renée sang the three magic words that would allow Maeve through to Faerie Province: *"Bibbidi-bobbidi-boo!"*

And in a flash of light, the trio were gone, leaving a trail of fairy dust behind them.

ACKNOWLEDGMENTS

Getting to explore Fairy Godmother's origin story and dream up ideas for the magic makers of Disney tales for the Enchanters series feels like a pinch-me moment I may never recover from. I'm eternally grateful to my brilliant editor, Brittany Rubiano, who is always up for an adventure in the Disney world and the best collaborator an author could ever ask for.

Huge thanks also goes to Team Disney for all they've done to spread the word about *Fairy Godmother*. Special thanks to Kieran Scott Viola, Dina Sherman, Crystal McCoy, Lisa McClatchy, Kaia Hilson, Holly Nagel, Augusta Harris, Holly Rice, Cassidy Leyendecker, Andrea Rosen, Vicki Korlishin, Monique Diman, Sara Liebling, Guy Cunningham, Jody Corbett, Sylvia Davis, and Martin Karlow. And to illustrator Chris Koehler, letterer and border-illustrator Dinara Mirtalipova, and designer Marci Senders, I feel like someone just handed me a glass slipper with this stunning cover. Thank you for such a gorgeous book.

To my agent, Dan Mandel, thanks for always guiding me and championing every new idea I dream up. If I waved my magic wand, I couldn't ask for a better agent. I'm also so grateful to my writer friends, especially the ones I talk all things Disney with. Thank you goes to my wonderful Twisted Tale family—Liz Braswell, Elizabeth Lim, Mari Mancusi, and Farrah Rochon—for all the love and encouragement.

Finally, to my Disney-loving family—my husband Mike and two boys, Tyler and Dylan—thank you for putting up with me when I'm watching Disney movies on a loop, singing Disney tunes in the car, and explaining why another trip to the Parks is crucial for "research." If I had all the wishes in the world, I'd still wish for a life with you three every time.